Praise for *T*

"*The Last Thing I Told You*
ise and captivating characters. Emily Arsenault weaves a thrilling, layered story that connects past and present, truth and memory. An original, unpredictable tale of psychological suspense."

—Megan Miranda, *New York Times* bestselling author of *The Perfect Stranger*

"A rich, finely observed, character-driven psychological thriller that creeps up on you, surprising as it unfolds, inevitable in retrospect."

—Hallie Ephron, *New York Times* bestselling author of *You'll Never Know, Dear*

"Ensnared in an intricate web, Arsenault's vivid characters seamlessly narrate a suspenseful tale in voices that resonate truth. But is that what they're telling? If you like a twist-filled page-turner, you'll love *The Last Thing I Told You.*"

—Wendy Corsi Staub, *New York Times* bestselling author

"*The Last Thing I Told You* is an expertly woven tale of dark obsession and bloody secrets. With her sharp eye and clear prose, Arsenault gives us a finely dissected portrait of a disturbed young woman as well as a tense thriller that defies categorization. Compulsively readable, and highly recommended."

—Francie Lin, Edgar Award–winning author of *The Foreigner*

And the Works of Emily Arsenault

"Emily Arsenault's mysteries are so much fun. . . ."

—*New York Times Book Review*

"Introspective, eccentric, charming contemporary mystery."

—*Wall Street Journal* on *What Strange Creatures*

"Arsenualt's gift for letting readers feel the characters' anguish from the inside while showing their irrational strangeness from the outside makes for terror that sticks."

—*Publishers Weekly* (starred review) on *The Evening Spider*

"From the opening pages, it's clear that this will be a haunting novel. . . . An engrossing, suspenseful mix of historical fiction and contemporary thriller, with some unexpected twists and wisdom: 'We have to learn to live with our ghosts.'"

—*Booklist* on *The Evening Spider*

"Arsenault never strays from the task at hand, which is to keep you up all night with a light burning until you reach the surprising end."

—Melanie Benjamin, *New York Times* bestselling author of *The Aviator's Wife*

THE LAST THING I TOLD YOU

Also by Emily Arsenault

The Evening Spider

What Strange Creatures

Miss Me When I'm Gone

In Search of the Rose Notes

The Broken Teaglass

The Leaf Reader

THE LAST THING I TOLD YOU

EMILY ARSENAULT

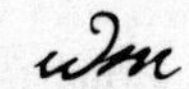

WILLIAM MORROW
An Imprint of HarperCollins*Publishers*

This is a work of fiction. Names, characters, places, and incidents are products of the author's imagination or are used fictitiously and are not to be construed as real. Any resemblance to actual events, locales, organizations, or persons, living or dead, is entirely coincidental.

HarperCollins books may be purchased for educational, business, or sales promotional use. For information, please email the Special Markets Department at SPsales@harpercollins.com.

FIRST EDITION

Designed by Diahann Sturge

Library of Congress Cataloging-in-Publication Data has been applied for.

ISBN 978-0-06-256736-9

18 19 20 21 22 LSC 10 9 8 7 6 5 4 3 2 1

To Cari and Leigh Anne

THE LAST THING I TOLD YOU

PROLOGUE

IT WAS TOO easy. It was supposed to hurt, and it didn't hurt at all.

Because the flesh wasn't mine. The blood wasn't mine. The scream wasn't mine.

The arm in front of me was bigger and hairier than mine—and bloodier than anything I'd ever seen outside of a TV screen. The hole in it was like a mouth stretched open too wide, drooling red.

I let go of the box cutter. When I heard the light clatter of its plastic handle hitting the floor, my heartbeat slowed down to meet the shock of this new reality.

This is you. This is real. This is what you've done. This will always be what you've done.

DECEMBER 16, 2015

HENRY

I HAD JUST SAT down at my desk when the call came in a little after nine thirty A.M.

A probable homicide on Clement Avenue, in one of the office buildings. Just two minutes down the road. I drove there quickly, but in a state of half disbelief. Campion hadn't had a homicide in years. Not since Brookhaven.

By the time I arrived, my old partner Greg had sealed off a whole office block and its parking lot. There were a few senior citizens and stay-at-home-mom types standing anxiously outside the yellow tape, wondering if they were going to have to reschedule their dental or chiropractic appointments.

Greg was chatting with these folks, telling them that there was an emergency in office 2C and that no one could go inside block 2 this morning—maybe all day.

When he saw me, Greg led me to 2C and briefed me outside the door. A male in his sixties. A psychotherapist, according to the diploma on his wall and the patient who had found him. *Dr. Mark Fabian.*

His patient had found him on the floor of his office, called 911, and asked them to send paramedics. The paramedics had quickly ascertained that this Dr. Fabian was dead—probably for many hours. He had the rig, and there was a deep wound on the side of his skull and bruises on his face.

"The patient—her name is Caroline Rouse—is still in the waiting room," Greg whispered to me.

"Get her out of the waiting room, Greg." I slipped on my shoe covers. "It's part of the crime scene, technically. See if she'll wait in your car. I'll get a statement from her as soon as I can."

"Right," Greg said. "Amy's on her way and—"

"Where are the paramedics?"

"Outside. Waiting to talk to you."

I put on my rubber gloves and pushed open the door to the dead therapist's office.

My wife had been telling me for years that I should see a shrink.

Well, now I would.

NADINE

I NEVER EXPECTED TO touch you, and I think the feeling was mutual.

But before I can leave your office, I have to make sure you're really dead. So I put my fingers to your arm. And—yes. Oh, God. Yes. I don't need to bother with your pulse.

But then, since you're dead, I have to close your eyes. I can't stand to leave you here like this on the soft gray carpet—open-eyed, coffee-stained, blood on your face and in your beautiful fluffy hair.

Regular blood—dark red.

Surprising, somehow. Maybe I thought a shrink's blood would run clear—or a luminous green or blue. Like antifreeze.

I'm not sure why I close the door behind me. All I know is that after that, I run. Out of the office, out of the suite, out of the building.

The lady in the parking lot—the skinny one with the black hair with white streaks—says hello and I say hello back and stare at her as she goes into your office building. It is so early in the morning still. Is she an Angel of Death? Did that just happen? Or did I imagine her? Either way, I unlock my car and fall into my seat and drive away. There is coffee down the side of my blue down coat. I can feel its wetness, but since we passed each other quickly, I doubt the Angel of Death saw it. Unless she is all-seeing, all-knowing. As I assume Angels of Death generally are?

Somehow I am already a mile or two down East Main Street.

And I hear myself whispering *Not again. Not again.*

The highway ramp is only a half mile away on the right. I don't know much else, but I know I'll be taking it.

Away from Campion.

Campion. Emerald-green jewel of Connecticut—shining suburban beacon in the state's very center, white congregational steeple poking up as pointy-sharp as Sleeping Beauty's spindle. "A bedroom community" they call it, and they really mean it.

Why did I ever come back here?

Not again.

HENRY

THE FIRST THING I saw of Dr. Fabian was his sensible brown loafers. Then my gaze jumped up to his ample gray-white hair, caked with blood on one side.

Mouth open, eyes closed. Caramel brown all over the bottom of his khaki pants. I wondered what kind of bodily fluid that could be until I saw an empty cardboard coffee cup on the floor by the couch.

The couch. Where all the patients sat when they told him about their problems. There was a Kleenex box next to it. I stared at the box's floral pattern for a moment and took a deep breath before looking at the guy again—at the lines on his face and the creases around his eye. The eye that wasn't covered in blood.

There were signs of struggle. Some books were tipped over from an upright position on the shelf behind the leather chair. A few were on the floor. I gazed at the bookshelf for a moment. Practically a full wall of books. All tidy except on that one eye-level shelf. Half in disarray, but on the opposite end, the remaining books were propped upward with a wedge of petrified wood.

And there was also the coffee—spilled all over the doctor and the carpet.

I went to the desk near the door. Pretty sparse. A lamp. An At-a-Glance calendar. And right in the middle, one of those thin exam booklets we used to use in high school and college. It was open to a page with *January 8, 1997,* scribbled across the top in messy—almost childish—handwriting. At the bottom of the page was a crude, faded pencil drawing of a couple of cartoon animals.

Nineteen ninety-seven? Written that year, or more recently? An account of something remembered? From the faded appearance of the booklet and the drawings, I'd guess it was written that year. At what point did papers from the year I graduated high school start looking like historical documents?

I picked up the At-a-Glance calendar and flipped to yesterday's page. Tuesday.

9 A.M.—Kate D.

10 A.M.—Bob

11 A.M.

12 P.M.—Eric & Sarah

1 P.M.

2 P.M.

3 P.M.—Mason

4 P.M.—Tricia

5 P.M.—Liam

6 P.M.—Connor

"Shit," I muttered. Just first names.

"Poor guy," Greg said from the doorway. He was picking at his mustache again.

"Call State Major Crimes," I said. "I'll go bang out the warrant."

NADINE

NOW THAT IT has stopped beating, why can't I finally stop trying to capture your heart? (And surely you must know that half of your clients only ever wanted that from you? To capture your heart? Maybe not because of anything specific about you, but because—with all due respect, Bouffant, and PhD notwithstanding—that's how people *are*?)

Listen to me—addressing you in my head as if you were still alive to care. Like I'm a teenager again. Back when I first named you Bouffant in my thoughts.

Back in those olden days, you had on your head not so much a hairdo as a triumph over gravity. It was the nineties, but I sensed from your general age and style that you were having trouble letting go of 1985. That big hair. Didn't you ever wonder if it distracted your patients? And how much time did you spend blowing it dry every morning? I'd wonder if you had a wife (you had a wedding band, I knew that much) who would help you or at least compliment you on it. Let's be real here. Yes. I *pictured* you blowing it dry. And I pictured you with a quivering golf ball–sized orb of mousse in your hand the moment before you squished it into your awesome head of subtly graying dark brown hair.

As a good and proper therapy patient, one tries, most of the time, not to go to these places in one's head. But you *do.* Your brain wants to do it, just because it knows it's not supposed to. Like when you're in Sunday school class as a kid, and the old lady teaching the class says that God sees and knows everything, even what's in your head, and then your head just keeps thinking *I hate Jesus I hate Jesus I HATE JESUS!* Not because you really hate Jesus (because what is there to hate about long hair and love and crucifixion?) but because God is listening and your brain just wants to screw you over for some reason that you will never—even decades later—ever understand.

My first appointment with you was in November of 1995, when I was sixteen. That was—let's see. *Twenty* years ago? Oh my God, Bouffant. I'm old and you're ancient.

I had to remind you of these specifics a few days ago, when I showed up in your office again after all these years. But I didn't need to remind you *why* I'd been your patient. *That* was memorable, even after all this time. There had been a terrible incident. And that incident made it quite necessary for my mother and stepfather to get me onto a therapist's couch—and *fast.*

They rather stumbled upon you, Bouffant. They got four or five therapist recommendations from their doctors and friends. (And since my stepfather was in healthcare finance, he just so happened to have a couple of doctor friends.) As I recall, you didn't specialize in teenagers particularly, but you were the only one with sufficient openings to see me multiple times per week, effective immediately.

My mother drove me to see you on the day before Thanksgiving, and I talked to you while she went to the grocery store for forgotten pearl onions.

"Let's talk about why you're here," you said. "Can you tell me a little bit about why you're here?"

"Umm . . . like specifically or generally?"

"Whichever you'd like to talk about."

"Because specifically would mean what I did to my social studies teacher. Did you want me to talk about that?"

"Do *you* want to talk about that?"

"Not really." I shrugged. "I talked a lot about it at the hospital. I mean, I know I'm supposed to keep talking about the thing with Mr. Brewster, but I'm sure my mom or my stepdad already explained it to you, so maybe we don't need to go into it. Right now, anyway. Even though that's, you know, *technically* why I'm here. Right?"

"Well . . ." You paused for a moment. "Yes."

"But if you're willing to start with *generally* why I'm here, maybe that would be better for a while?" I said it with a question in my voice, because I truly didn't know how all of this was supposed to work. You seemed more casual about it all than the hospital folks had been.

You put both of your arms on the rich chocolate leather of your deep chair, sat back a bit, bounced your pointy knees a couple of times, and considered my answer. Your hair billowed gently with your movement. There was something comically unstylish about it, but also something comforting—like the ripples in a pond after you tossed a stone in.

Your hesitation gave me a chance to look you up and down. The hair was perhaps styled to distract from your long face and bulb nose. Your dress style was decidedly cozy, professorial. A gray cardigan vest—knitted so loosely it reminded me of a fishnet—over a white Oxford shirt with the sleeves rolled up gently. (Let's get to inner *work*!)

And then you said, "Okay."

I got the feeling you were tired. You'd squeezed me in just before dinnertime, after all. You were probably eager to get home and have a gin cocktail while you watched your wife peel potatoes for tomorrow. I don't recall what your next question was—it must've been something easy to answer. An icebreaker or something I wouldn't or couldn't overanalyze. And I came out thinking not that I liked you, but that I appreciated the honesty of your fatigue, and I could tolerate you for a few months, if that was what was required of me.

That Friday, as I watched TV and ate cold pumpkin pie and tea for breakfast, I found myself wondering if you, too, had eaten pumpkin pie on the previous evening. It seemed to me that odds were you probably *did,* because most people did. And then I wondered what else I could figure out about you, using only observances and odds. Because surely I wasn't supposed to ever ask you anything about yourself directly. It unsettled me that I was even having these thoughts, mild as they were, about a man roughly twice my age—maybe a little more.

That was actually about how old Mr. Brewster was.

And then I couldn't finish my pumpkin pie. Because

I realized in that moment—barefooted in my Earth Day nightshirt that smelled like sweat and maple syrup—that I would probably start wondering what you ate for breakfast, and what your favorite movies were, and whether or not you wore pajamas, and whether you'd ever broken a limb, and if you had, had you screamed or cried when it happened? And could *I* ever make you scream or cry? And I wondered if you'd ever jogged shirtless and overly tanned on a beach, since you were a young man in the early eighties, and people did that sort of thing back then. And if you had, if you'd had a gold chain dangling in your sweaty chest hair. And I wondered—*if* you'd done all of that—if you'd been at all sexy by relatively objective standards, or if you just *thought* you were.

My stomach ached at these questions, because I knew I would be wondering these things for a very long time—possibly forever. And I knew what this meant: Whatever was wrong with me was incurable.

CONNECTICUT LIVE
March 7, 2010
10:32 A.M. EST

INITIAL REPORTS OF 9 DEAD, 7 INJURED IN CAMPION RETIREMENT HOME SHOOTING

The shooting at Brookhaven Manor Retirement Community began at about 7:15 A.M. Local news station WSCN reports that Connecticut State Police have confirmed nine dead.

CNN news reports that police have identified the shooter, who is a male in his 30s. He is reportedly alive, though injured from multiple gunshots when he exchanged fire with local police at the scene. He is currently being treated at St. Michael's Hospital, as are some of the injured victims. Other victims are being treated at Barnes Memorial Hospital.

HENRY

WHILE THE LAB guys were photographing, I got a preliminary statement from the patient.

She had a face that probably would be excessively pleasant on any other day—a day she hadn't found her shrink dead and stiffening next to his subdued paisley print couch. She was about fifty, her cheeks round and dimpled, her hair a dome of perky golden curls.

For now, though, her mouth was twisted into a fixed look of horror, her nose wrinkled upward—as if her face hadn't moved since she'd made the grim discovery.

"I waited about thirty minutes past my appointment time," she explained. "I was waiting for him to come out to the waiting room and invite me in, like he normally does. It didn't seem appropriate to knock, but I finally did because . . . time was running out. So I did, and there was no answer. And then I opened the door."

I nodded. "Okay. And then?"

"I saw him." Caroline sucked in a breath. "I stepped closer to him and I saw . . . well, that he didn't look conscious."

I considered asking her if she'd noticed the smell, but decided against it.

"Did you just look from the door, or did you go over and touch him or anything?"

"I didn't touch him, no," Caroline said quickly. "It didn't seem . . . appropriate. I just took out my cell and called 911."

It seemed to me this lady was a little overly concerned about *appropriate,* given the circumstances.

"Did you notice all the blood?" I asked.

"Yes . . . I . . . well, I was trying not to look. I just kept saying his name . . . Mark . . . Mark . . . hoping he'd . . . wake up. I started to panic, thinking I should go over to him and *do* something . . . but I couldn't do it . . . I just went back to the waiting room. And luckily the ambulance arrived in a matter of minutes, so . . ." Caroline's gaze shifted from the floor to me. "Oh!" she said.

"What? Are you okay?"

"You're that cop. That—" She put her hand to her cheek and then slid it over to her mouth. She looked like she was considering whether she'd said something *inappropriate.*

"Yeah," I admitted. At least she didn't use the *H* word. "I'm that cop."

"I'm sorry," she said. "You must get that a lot."

"Don't be sorry. I'm used to it."

"Such a tragedy."

"Yes, ma'am."

The *sir* and *ma'am* kicked in hard when people recognized me. *Was just doing my job, ma'am.* The Boy Scout routine sickened me a little. But people seemed to become unsettled when I responded any other way.

"Now, this was a regular appointment for you? You came every week?"

"Yes."

"So you hadn't seen Mark for a week before this?"

"Right."

"Did you notice anything out of the ordinary this morning, around the office, as you were coming in? Anyone hanging around outside, any sign of struggle, anything different from other weeks you've come here?"

Caroline seemed to really think about this, then shook her head.

"Caroline, to your knowledge, did Mark have a secretary of any kind? Anyone else who might know who his patients were?"

"No . . . well . . . oh. You know what? He would bill me through this company in New Haven called Caduceus Billing. They billed the insurance and then billed me for the rest. I don't think all of his patients would have been billed through them, though."

"Why's that?"

"Last year, I came more often than usual and met my insurance limit for this kind of treatment. At that point I was paying out of pocket directly to him at each appointment. I think he just used that Caduceus place to help him deal with insurance companies. I'll bet he had lots of patients who were paying out of pocket, period."

"Okay. That's helpful, though, Caroline. Thank you."

I took down *Caduceus Billing* and Caroline's information, then asked her to wait with one of the other officers for a little while longer.

When I returned to the office, I noticed the photographer was shooting the inside corner of the couch.

"What's that you're photographing?" I asked.

"I think it's your murder weapon," she said. "It was behind the throw pillow."

There on the couch, next to a streak of red, was another grapefruit-sized wedge of petrified wood.

"Looks like someone tried to wipe the blood off," I said.

The photographer nodded and moved on to the bookshelf behind the leather chair.

Detective Amy Ahearn came up behind me.

"It looks like there was an attempt at clean-up," she said. "Not a good attempt. A panicked one."

I nodded and I stared down at the petrified wood—the flat part mostly wiped clean on the fabric of the couch, but with a little blood still on the rougher edge. I thought of Dr. Fabian buying those bookends at a Brookstone or a Williams-Sonoma, considering what they would cost him only in dollars. Never for a moment considering how much it would hurt to have one fly at his head.

NADINE

SO BEGAN MY appointments with you—and my life as a teenage recluse.

I wasn't allowed to go the public high school anymore, but my mother didn't want me to be home alone too much, cooking up new little insanities. So she would drop me off at the town library on her way to work in the morning. My tutor would meet me there midmorning, and then I'd walk home for lunch. Three times a week—and then down to two, after a couple of months without incident—I would go see you at one o'clock. But I'd always be inside by 2:30 when all the kids I used to know got out of school.

I watched *Donahue, Oprah,* old *Star Trek,* and *Days of Our Lives* and ate a lot of ramen noodles and microwave popcorn. I particularly liked *Days of Our Lives,* because there was this one loveably gruff and handsome character who had been a rapist in a previous plotline years before. And in my tiny and TV-centric teenage brain, I figured that if this guy could redeem himself so seamlessly and so winningly, couldn't I, too, eventually?

With three hours a week on your couch, to start, we had a lot of time on our hands. So of course it wasn't long before you asked about my dead father.

The first time you asked, I started with something neutral—with a memory of a specific day from a summer when I was eight or so. There were two other little girls playing with me in my yard. My father watched us from the kitchen window while he strummed his guitar. Julie declared that she needed to use my bathroom. She went in and used it, and then so did the other girl, Amanda, and then I decided to as well. As I walked out of the bathroom, through the kitchen to the door, I heard the lyrics my father was mumbling along to his cheerful strumming:

"You think you're a tiger/but you piss in a tiny box/You think you're a lion/in that smooth way you walks . . . and then you go and you poop in a box."

It was a song he'd written spontaneously the night before, which he had titled "Cat Piss Blues."

I remembered sighing and turning to stare him down, noticing he smelled like cooked onions and wondering if both Julie and Amanda had heard earlier rounds of the song. It was maybe the exact moment I realized why my mother sometimes found his guitar-playing annoying rather than uproariously funny.

"You're weird," I declared.

He nodded and kept playing. I ran outside to be with my friends.

"AFTER THAT, YOU were more self-conscious about your father?" you wanted to know.

"Self-conscious . . . I don't know. I started to see the cracks. That was around when he lost his job and stuff."

"His job? What was his job?"

"It was something at an insurance company, when I was little. He didn't like it much in the first place, I don't think. But it was around that time—the time with my friends—that he lost the job. Not that I understood much about it back then. My mom kicked him out when he started drinking a lot."

"Did you understand *that* at the time?" you wanted to know.

"Not really. My mom wouldn't let it get to that point. She told me later that she said to him, 'I don't want that stuff around our daughter.' And he, I think, on some level, kind of agreed. I didn't see much of it. Because he left soon after he fell off the wagon."

"And went where?"

"To stay with his brother in Meriden. So, not far away. He'd visit a lot. And then, after they divorced when I was around nine, he disappeared for a while."

"Disappeared?" you repeated.

"I mean, he was in touch by phone occasionally. He was staying with a girlfriend in Springfield for a while, then back with his brother. My mom married Anthony. But . . . anyway. My dad was back around seeing me a lot by the time I was twelve. Because he was really trying to pull it together. He was working in Campion then, and living near here. And came to see me like three times a week."

"And how did you feel about that?"

"Umm . . . it was nice. It would be awkward when he'd try to joke around with me, sometimes. Like, he remembered what made me laugh when I was eight, and now I was twelve, so . . ."

"And was he still drinking or . . ."

"No. It didn't seem like it. Not at first."

"Not at first?"

"He didn't seem to be doing anything like that until—suddenly—the day he died."

"Do you want to talk about the day he died?"

I remember my heart thudding hard then, at the prospect of having to talk about that day.

Your father.

He took too many pills.

We think he just wanted to go to sleep.

He didn't make it.

It was painful even to remember the excruciating number of softly worded sentences it took my mother and Anthony to get to the word *dead.*

"I'm sure my mother's told you about it," I said.

"A little bit. But I'm more interested in what you have to say about it."

"She told you it was a bunch of pills? Probably just took too many and fell asleep and never woke up."

You hesitated. "Yes."

"That's all you need to know, I think."

You were quiet for a while. I stared at the box of tissues on the side table next to the couch. I made a mental note never to use them.

"We can leave it there for now, if you'd like," you said.

"Okay," I agreed.

HENRY

THE STATE MEDICAL examiner came and took Dr. Fabian away. But before he did, he gave his initial assessment. The doctor had suffered multiple blows to the head, and the time of death had probably been several hours before Caroline Rouse found him.

Once the body was gone, I wandered away from Amy and looked at the At-a-Glance calendar again. The Wednesday calendar started with "Caroline"—at nine A.M. Flipping through, it looked like Dr. Fabian started early on some days and ended late on others. Sometimes both. In any case, I was eager to talk to "Connor," who had the last appointment the evening before. How many "Connors" could there be in Campion? Then again, Fabian probably had some out-of-town patients.

"You dusted the laptop yet?" I asked the State guy doing the prints.

"Yeah."

"We're going to want to try to get into it ASAP."

"We figured. If it's password protected, we ought to send it to Naugatuck. They've got a good computer forensics team there."

"So I hear. Any cell phone here?"

"Yeah," Amy piped up. "We found it in his coat pocket. But it's password protected."

"Henry!" Greg stuck his head in the door. "I've got someone here you're gonna want to talk to. Her name's Melissa Troyer, and she's a therapist in one of the other suites in this building. She came in today around eight."

Greg led me to the outside hallway, where there stood a tall woman in a flowing black skirt and draping purple sweater. She stood so stick-straight it didn't look like she had limbs.

"I'm Sergeant Detective Peacher. Melissa, is it?"

The woman lifted her thin face and stared at me with forlorn eyes. Then she nodded. For a moment I wondered if Greg had been mixed up—that this was a patient, not a colleague.

"It must be a shock that this happened here, in your building."

"Yes," she whispered. And then cleared her throat and said it louder. "Yes. Mark was a kind person."

"Were you friends?"

A skinny hand emerged from all of Melissa's drapery, and she pushed her white-streaked hair out of her face.

"We had some nice chats coming and going over the years, and actually sort of dated briefly . . . I mean, had dinner a couple of times. Years ago. But it never went anywhere. We were friendly, but not friends."

Her voice was confident and soothing. It didn't match her waifish face at all.

"You've both worked in this office building a long time?" I asked.

"Twelve years for me. More for Mark. He's been here forever."

"I'm very sorry. I know this is difficult, but would you mind answering a few questions about what you might have seen this morning?"

"Of course. I mean, of course I don't mind."

"Did you notice anything unusual when you came in this morning? Did you see anyone around the office?"

"Nothing unusual, but I did see someone leaving the building as I was getting out of my car. A woman. I'd guess in her thirties. She looked like she was in a hurry."

"Can you describe her a little more? Body type? Hair color? Was she white, or . . . ?"

"Yes. White." Melissa frowned. "Average height, I suppose. Maybe on the tall side. Long brownish hair."

"Had you ever seen her on a Friday morning before? You don't happen to know if she was a patient of Dr. Fabian's?"

"No. I would occasionally see people coming in and out, but I didn't know who was whose patient. There are two chiropractors in this building, upstairs. Mark and I, and then the two dentists. We all had early morning appointments sometimes, and I know Mark and I in particular often had evening appointments."

"Do you think you'd seen this woman before, the one rushing out this morning?"

"It's hard to say. But I don't think so."

"Did she look like she could've been injured? Any signs of struggle or stress?"

"Hmm. I didn't get a good look at her, but nothing obvious. She looked like she was rushing, though. I said hello as I passed. Which is unusual for me. I don't usually do that. Since I know there's another therapist in the building, I understand people sometimes want to be anonymous or invisible. But the holidays . . . they always put me in a friendly mood. I was listening to something Christmasy in the car."

I hesitated. Coming out of Melissa's pinched little mouth, I thought this might be sarcasm. She smiled uncertainly, and I decided she was being sincere.

"What about yesterday evening? What time did you leave your office?"

"Oh . . . just after six. My last patient was at five."

"And did you see Dr. Fabian at that time?"

"No. I believe his car was still here, though."

"Which vehicle is his, then?"

"The silver gray Subaru."

"Okay. So did you see anyone or anything suspicious in the building, or outside in the lot?"

Melissa shook her head. "No, it was pretty quiet. It usually is at that hour."

"Any cars that you're not used to seeing?"

"I'm sorry. There are enough practitioners in this building that I don't take much notice of all the different patients' cars."

"But you say it was quiet. So aside from Dr. Fabian's car, did you notice that there were any other vehicles left?"

"Hmm. I want to say there were one or two. I can't remember it being completely empty."

"Okay. Do you know of anyone who'd have wanted to hurt Dr. Fabian?"

"Well. No, not specifically."

"Not *specifically,*" I repeated.

Melissa sighed, twisted her hands together, and buried them in the folds of her sweater again.

"We only ever talked very broadly of patients, and very rarely. But I'll assume you're wanting to know if any of his patients were angry with him. And it's the nature of the profession that occasionally you'll have people who *are* angry at you. Or who believe they are."

I tried not to show my distaste at this statement. No wonder I'd always avoided shrinks. I was pretty sure that it wasn't *perceived* anger that bashed the side of Fabian's head in.

"All I mean to say is yes," Melissa hurried to say. "It is quite possible that Mark had a very angry person in his office. There are occasionally really tense situations—like if Mark was asked to sign something about mental fitness to go back to a job, or retain custody of a child. Or, on the other hand, there could've been a psychotic episode of some kind. So, there's all kinds of things you might find, if you *are* going to start looking at his patients—though I think you might have trouble finding out who they all are. But that's another matter."

"Would you mind telling me where *you* keep patient information in your office? Where you keep your appointment information?"

Melissa hesitated for a moment, then nodded. "On my office computer, under two different passwords. One to get into the computer itself, and one to get to my appointment and progress software."

"What's the name of the software?"

"TheraPro."

"Any chance you know if Mark used that?" I asked.

"No idea." Melissa shook her head. "Sorry."

"Okay. But getting back to what you were saying before, he hadn't mentioned any situation like that to you recently? An angry patient?"

"No. In fact, it had been quite a while since we'd talked about anything work-related at all. Aside from the fact that he was retiring."

"Retiring." That was an interesting nugget. "Okay. When?"

"I don't know the exact details. But 'a few months from now' was what he said to me. That was a couple of weeks ago. It seemed rather sudden, but he was in his sixties, after all."

Melissa frowned and combed through her hair with her fingers, looking thoughtful. "Oh, God." She sighed. "Has Linda been notified yet?"

"Who's Linda, ma'am?"

"Linda Dalgaard. His girlfriend. She works at the flower shop on Main Street—you know, across from the little wine shop? The big plan was to travel together after he retired."

"Oh." I wrote this down. "We'll be doing a full check to see which family members need to be notified, but maybe you can help us shortcut to the right people. Linda Dalgaard. So he wasn't married?"

Melissa shook her head. "Long divorced. He has one son

named Brendan. Recently, he'd been living with Mark because he'd gone back to school."

She put her hand to her mouth, closed her eyes, and shook her head again.

"Any other children?" I asked. "Other family around that he talked about a lot?"

"No other children. And other family around? Not that I know of."

There was a sound behind me. A clank-*clunk* that I felt first in my chest, and that seemed to shoot halfway up my throat. A gust of air blew over Melissa and me, and her Cruella De Vil hair whirled over her head for a moment. I whipped around. Because I'd been facing Melissa, I hadn't seen Chief Wheeler approaching the building. The sound was him pushing open the building's heavy institutional door.

He nodded at me and went wordlessly to Dr. Fabian's office.

Melissa's hand slipped down her face and back into the folds of her vast purple sweater-cape. The motion seemed to take longer than it should—as if time had slowed down to suit the silence of this white-walled stairwell. I felt a warm fuzzy sensation begin to prickle my fingertips, and then work its way up my hands.

"Did you have any other questions, Detective Peacher?"

I squeezed my hands tight to work the sensation out of them. I could feel Melissa's urchin eyes studying me. I met her gaze to stop them.

"Not right now, but I'd like to take your number if something comes up. Thanks."

NADINE

FOR SOME REASON my GPS is already set for somewhere out of town, and she's telling me how to get there in such an assured voice. Why wasn't this lady around when I was sixteen? GPS is so much cheaper and more direct than therapy. Turn here, go down this road and not that one. Go forward. No looking back, and no fucking around.

She brings me forty minutes south to East Haddam, to a big blue Victorian house with a sign out front that says THE APPLE BLOSSOM INN in spindly wood letters. At least I remember now what brought me here. When my mother heard my plan to spend a night in East Haddam, she said she thought I'd love this gorgeous bed and breakfast. And while I was sure I wouldn't, it seemed easier than researching a place to stay. It wasn't particularly expensive, my mother had said. *Cute, but not fancy.*

But it's too early to check in.

I open the car window and marvel at the balmy air. What the hell kind of New England Christmastime is this?

THE FIRST TIME you asked me about what I'd done to Mr. Brewster, you didn't ask as directly as you could have. You didn't ask about the *moment* it happened. Instead, you asked how I was feeling when I woke up that morning. How I felt while I ate breakfast and dressed for school.

"Cold," I said, after thinking for a minute or two.

"Cold? Okay. What else?"

"I don't think you understand what I mean by *cold*."

"Okay. What do you mean? Not a literal cold, then? An emotional cold?"

You had a tendency to word things in a decidedly adult manner—I supposed so I would understand how seriously you pretended to take me.

"No," I murmured. "Very much a literal cold."

"Is it very cold in your house in the morning?" you asked.

"No. I just woke up remembering something. Something from when I was around eight or nine. This thing that happened with me and the other kids in my neighborhood."

"Yes?" You put a single index finger to your eyebrow and rubbed it slowly—a tick of yours that was already familiar to me.

"It was a spring day and this girl I knew, Julie, was washing her mom's car with her older brother. And then two other boys from the neighborhood came over. And then we started washing her dad's car, too. It was like a chewing gum commercial, all of us squirting each other and having a great time."

"Sounds nice," you said.

"It was. Now, I don't remember how this thing started. After the cars were clean, we started this little competition.

Each kid would sit in the middle of the yard and see how long he or she could stand having ice cold water squirted directly at their head, from two different hoses. We took turns sitting and squirting. Some kid had a digital watch and timed us all. I don't remember whose brilliant idea this was. Probably one of the older brothers."

Maybe unconsciously prompted by my mention of a watch, you glanced down at your own watch, and kept your eyes there for a moment longer than was comfortable. But I kept talking. It was easier when it felt like you weren't listening, anyway.

"And when we were all done and looked at the times, mine was more than twice as long as everyone else's. Even the bigger boys'."

"And you were proud of yourself?"

"Proud? No. I was . . . surprised. Surprised not at myself, but at the other kids. That they couldn't stand it for all that long."

You sighed and put your hands on your knees. "But how did *you* feel, sitting under the spray of the cold water for so long?"

"Well, it wasn't fun. But it was endurable. Like, with each second that seemed too painful to stand, I just thought. *You can get through this second. And you can get through one more. And look! You're still here. So you can get through another. And now that you got through that second, why don't you stay for another?*"

"Okay. That was what you were *thinking*. But how were you *feeling*?"

"Well, it was *really* cold. It was like a massive headache.

And then—when the water would squirt right in my ear—that hurt. But I'd turn my head a little, and think again. *You can keep going. You can go one more second.* Even when I finally crawled away, I felt like I could keep going. But the other kids were getting bored, waiting for the next person's turn."

You nodded. "Uh-huh." And then you paused, and said, "And that morning—in November—you thought of that cold."

"Yeah. I woke up knowing I was going to do something. Knowing that if I held my breath or held my nose or whatever . . . I would follow through. I'd be . . . different."

"Follow through," you repeated.

"Yeah," I said.

"Do you feel like you're different now?"

I folded my arms and held myself in tight. "Yes."

"How are you different now?"

I squeezed myself tighter and didn't reply. It felt unfair for you to make me explain what a monster and a freak that day had made me. When of course you already knew that.

"Nadine?"

But maybe it was better to be an honest little monster than pretend to be good and innocent.

"Nadine?"

Maybe. I wasn't sure. I closed my eyes so I wouldn't have to look at you.

"Nadine, I know this is difficult, but can you describe how you're feeling right now?"

"Well, I feel *bad.*"

"Bad is a very general word." Your tone was flat. "Can you be more specific?"

I ignored this request but unfolded my arms. "I'm trying to tell you that I feel like there's some connection between what I did in November and that cold water contest. Now that I think about them both at the same time."

"And how is that? How are they connected?"

"They *felt* the same." I took a shaky breath, because we were getting awfully close to the details of that day *in November.* "Like I have this freakish . . . endurance. But I also have this freakish stupidity."

"Can you explain that a little more?"

"The other kids maybe couldn't stand the cold water. But they weren't stupid enough to think it mattered. They weren't stupid enough to endure it, either."

You thought about this for a moment. "What else do you endure, Nadine? Besides the cold water?"

My breath stopped for a few seconds. I didn't know how to answer this question. I was pretty sure I would cry if I tried. And I didn't want to cry—not today, anyway.

"I think I have this uncontrollable pull to finish things I start," I continued. "To ignore the voice that tells you to stop—*stop, this is crazy, this is too much*. I *had* that voice the day of Mr. Brewster. But I ignored it, at least for a minute or two. And that *could* be a good thing, the ability to ignore that voice sometimes. If I didn't also have a warped sense of *which* things are worth enduring. Which things are worth ignoring that voice for."

You nodded hard as I said this, Bouffant. I believed, for a second, there was something in your eyes saying *yes*. For real—not just pretend shrink *yes.* You didn't even mind that I'd ignored your question about what I endured.

"I think this is an interesting point you're making," you said. "And I'm impressed that you're willing to articulate it this way. And I think we should talk more about it. Let's pick up here on Friday."

I knew we probably wouldn't do any such thing, because we never really followed up on anything from session to session. You seemed to forget a lot in the days in between.

You looked at your watch again, and maybe noticed we had a few minutes left.

"I've been meaning to ask you," you said. "I've noticed that you always leave your knapsack in the waiting room. Why do you do that?"

Before I could register any surprise at the question, I answered honestly. "Because it's so heavy."

And it was. I was, of course, still expelled from school at that point. But I was genuinely trying to do well with my schoolwork at home. Plus I was constantly checking out heavy library books on artists like Hieronymus Bosch and Pieter Bruegel, and lugging them around with me everywhere. I hadn't actually been much into art before this but now that I'd done something so crazy it seemed like an art streak might make it more palatable—more acceptable. Without the art, Van Gogh was just a sad sack who'd sliced off his ear. My crazy sad sackery had come first, and now I needed art to justify it.

You hesitated, and then nodded wordlessly. At the time, I concluded that you were a really crappy conversation starter—which was surprising, given your profession. I felt sorry for you, just a little bit. I liked feeling sorry for you, because it convinced me that you were real.

"I've noticed you always bob your head back and forth before you look at your watch," I countered. "Why do you do that?"

You smiled.

"I'm stretching my neck," you said, and then shrugged. "It gets stiff sitting in the same position all day."

I nodded, satisfied. An even exchange. We both had tired backs and necks. We had one tiny thing in common.

On my walk home, it dawned on me what a moron I was. You didn't ask the question because you couldn't think of anything better to talk about. You'd asked it because of the young man who was occasionally—though not usually, and not today—in the waiting room when I fetched the backpack.

This young man looked a little older than me—and definitely wasn't a familiar face from school. He had a thin smile and shiny brown hair, boyishly cut. He usually wore plaid shirt-sleeves that made him look like some kind of missionary, and had a mouth so red I occasionally wondered if he was wearing lipstick.

It was rude of me to leave my backpack in the waiting room, wasn't it? Because your therapy patients weren't supposed to see each other. This was an unspoken rule that I hadn't known because I'd never been in therapy before.

By the time I realized my error, it was too late. I'd seen that guy a handful of times.

But he hadn't seemed to mind being seen. He'd started to smile with recognition, in a way that was almost flattering.

Does he think I'm cute? I hadn't thought to wonder that till now—now that you had brought it up. Had that guy mentioned me to you? I wondered.

Or does he wonder what kind of crazy I am?

And then the counter-question was: *What kind of crazy is* he*?*

And of course it was not any of my business, or his business, or anyone's but yours, Bouffant, that we were crazy at all. The whole physical setup of the office was designed around this principle—to allow patients in and out of the office without seeing each other. And I'd just trampled on that delicate design.

But—did I *like* it that I'd fucked up your system? I wasn't supposed to like it. But wasn't that why I was here in the first place? Because I liked to fuck things up and then watch to see how men reacted to it?

Men—especially older men—were such weird creatures.

Dress shirts and ties masking overgrown bellies. Aftershave masking sweat. Pointy dress shoes over hairy gorilla feet. Older men were meant to be exposed.

Or more like—solved. Solved like a riddle.

Or just broken. Cracked open like a walnut.

CONNECTICUT COURIER

March 8, 2010

REST HOME RAMPAGE STUNS CAMPION

Campion, Connecticut—A gunman opened fire at the Brookhaven nursing home Tuesday morning, killing ten people and wounding seven others.

The alleged shooter, Johnny C. Streeter, is 37 years old and a Campion native. Seven of the fatalities were Brookhaven residents, and three Brookhaven staff. Police have not yet released the names of the victims.

Streeter's rampage lasted approximately twenty minutes before police officer Henry Peacher wounded and incapacitated him after exchanging fire on the third floor of the facility. "Sergeant Peacher was the closest officer to the facility when we got the call, and the first officer on the scene," said Police Chief Brad Wheeler. "He did an excellent job. If it were not for Officer Peacher's quick response to the call, and his quick thinking in the building, this tragedy might have been even worse."

Police believe Streeter entered the facility at 7:13 A.M. and opened fire on the front desk staff before proceeding to a dining area, where several residents were having breakfast. A kitchen worker hid in the supply closet and called 911 on her cell phone at 7:19 A.M. Several other 911 calls were made from Brookhaven before Officer Peacher shot and incapacitated Streeter at approximately 7:35.

Officer Peacher sustained a shoulder injury from a gunshot, but is expected to be released from the hospital shortly.

The assailant, Streeter, was shot in the stomach. His condition is stable, however, and Chief Wheeler says that he has been interrogated in the overnight hours and will be transferred to Eastern Correctional Institution in the coming days.

According to several witnesses, Brookhaven director Dr. Eugene Morrison confronted Streeter outside of the dining area and was shot in the torso and leg. He is currently at St. Michael's Hospital, in critical condition. Morrison is well-known in the Campion community. Brookhaven's state-of-the-art facilities and diverse programs for its residents were developed under his directorship starting in 1988.

In Dr. Morrison's absence, assistant director Michelle Zimmerman made a statement on behalf of Brookhaven Manor.

"Our hearts are broken today. We lost many friends and many hard workers. We do not understand this cruel and senseless act of violence. However, today our priority is not to attempt to understand the unfathomable, but to take care of our residents. Many of them—and their families—are in unimaginable pain today. Our job today is—as always—to take care of them."

HENRY

WHEELER WANTED TO know how things were looking, and I gave him the basics—the medical examiner's initial hunches, the bookends, Caroline, Melissa.

"Yeah. So, with the nature of the injury here, and that probable weapon," I said, "I don't think this was a planned assault. The examiner's confirmed that the body was probably here several hours, so we're looking at tracking down his last couple of appointments yesterday, as a priority. We might have to jump through some hoops to get those names, but I've already got a couple of ideas."

Wheeler folded his arms. "This is going to be your case, Henry. Detective Ahearn will be helping you, and Sergeant Clausen, too, where it's appropriate."

I glanced up at Amy, who was quietly watching the lab folks while standing in the corner, taking in the last of the evidence as it went into paper bags. Upon hearing her name, she glanced at me and rolled her eyes just so.

Wheeler didn't seem to notice.

"What've you got Officer Clausen doing right now?" he demanded.

"Greg is out talking to some of the folks who have offices in the surrounding buildings, and Officer Landon's got the entrance to the lot—letting in people who've got appointments in the other buildings. Planning to hold on to anyone coming in for Dr. Fabian here, to talk to them, just in case they have any pertinent information. When Officer Nesci gets here, he'll be looking to see about surveillance cameras on the Exxon station and the Cumby's. Amy was holding down the scene while I was talking with a possible witness. I've just found out that this guy's not married, but there's a girlfriend and a son named Brendan. Amy and I will be tracking down the son so we can talk to him."

"Okay," Wheeler said, and then wandered into the waiting room to chat with the State guy who was photographing and dusting in there.

Amy came up to me and smiled, raising both eyebrows. She didn't even need to say it: *Why am I not surprised?*

"Sorry," I said. "It may be because you were on that Yarnell Street assault in September. Maybe he wants to go back and forth."

We both knew she should head the investigation here. She had assisted on the occasional homicide case in Meriden, when she was there working primarily in sex crimes. We'd technically been detectives the same amount of time, and I'd been on the Campion force for much longer, but that didn't count for much, as far as violent crime is concerned. Still, misplaced hero status complicates things.

"It's not a problem," she said. "With the shit going on in my life right now, I'd prefer not to be in charge of anything."

"What shit?" I asked.

"Well, the usual. Stuff with the kids, mostly. Christmas always amplifies my domestic incompetence. I haven't done hardly any shopping, and I think tomorrow's the last day I can order from Amazon. So, we're notifying the son together?"

"Yeah. This guy had a girlfriend and I know where she works. I'm hoping she might be able to give us the son's contact information."

She nodded. "Before you go—did you read any of the stuff on this guy's desk?"

"I saw it. The 1997 stuff. Didn't read it. Anything?"

Amy shrugged. "It's odd. That's all I can say for now."

I put my rubber gloves back on and picked up the blue exam book on the desk. I started to read it from the first page.

January 8, 1997

The insurance has kicked back in, but I've grown used to writing these little entries.

You asked me if I was mad at my father. And I think you mean am I mad at him for dying? And I said no. Do you know why? Because I don't know if I really knew him. How can I be mad at someone if I'm not even sure I ever knew him? I don't know what's true and what's not, when people talk about him.

At the bottom of the page someone had drawn a cartoon of a doll and a stuffed *Tyrannosaurus rex* talking to each other.

The doll had tangled hair and one eye stuck closed. Their words appeared in bubbles above their heads:

Doll: *Are you going to break my heart, Talmadge?*
Dinosaur: *How would I do that?*
Doll: *There is part of your story that you've never told me. Are you ever going to tell me?*
Dinosaur: *How can I now, Baby Doll? I'm dead. Not just dead. Meteor dead. Volcano dead. Earthquake dead.*
Doll: *So all I'll ever get is the stories you always told before.*
Dinosaur: *Well. Not ALL.*
Doll: *Still. Tell me one of those again.*
Dinosaur: *Okay, Baby Doll.*

February 5, 1997

What does my anger look like? It looks like a picnic basket. It looks like a macaroni salad. What do you think? It doesn't look like anything. And will I be able to control it going forward? Let me ask you a question. Have you seen me lose control in all these long sixteen months? Have you heard reports from anyone—teachers, my mom, my stepfather, anyone? That I have ever so much as raised my voice?

February 19, 1997

It seems to me there are a few things that you want me to say. And I feel like I've as good as said them, but just for the sake of thoroughness . . . Yes, I am angry about what happened to my father. No, I am not willing to say it is all his fault. I am angry that life can do something like that to you at any point, without warning. It scares me. It also scares me how I look at other kids my age sometimes. They don't know. They don't know that the universe can just drop a piano or a lightning bolt on the person or thing they most love, whenever, and with no explanation or consequence. I hate myself for sometimes thinking Just You Wait. And yet, I didn't invent the ways of the universe. I just experienced them earlier. Just You Wait, *old friends.* Just You Wait. *I try not to be too eager on their behalf. I really do try.*

P.S. You might not think it. But I really miss my friends.

There was another cartoon at the bottom of this page.

"Hey," Amy said, before I had a chance to read it.

"Yeah?"

"I didn't mean to distract you. You probably ought to go talk to the girlfriend. I'll be here as long as you need me to be. I think this can be on your list for later."

I closed the book and handed it to her. "Save it for me, will you?"

"No problem, Henry."

NADINE

TRUTHFULLY, BOUFFANT, I'D wondered—from the very first appointment—if I'd end up wanting to mess with you like I'd done with Mr. Brewster. We hadn't talked about it yet, this habit of mine—of trying to mess with older men's heads. I wasn't sure I wanted to talk about it—now or ever. Because *until* we talked about it, you were still fair game. And having fair game was more fun than talking.

I'd already set my clumsy foot into the sand castle, by going into the waiting room for my backpack after my appointment. Why not have a little fun, and wiggle my toes in the sand a bit?

So I kept leaving my backpack there—every Tuesday and every Friday afternoon. For several weeks, until the young man in plaid shirtsleeves—the occasional appointment after mine—finally appeared again.

He nodded when he saw me, and whispered *Hi*. There was a bulginess to his eyes when he smiled, but it disappeared quickly, and then he looked cute and boyish again.

He'd never said anything before. It was almost as if *he* was waiting for *me*.

"I hope you're ready," I murmured. "He's on fire today."

I'd practiced this line. But it didn't come out as savvy as I'd imagined it.

His smile grew wider—disbelieving. *"What?"*

I took a step back, regretting my words immediately.

"Just kidding," I mumbled.

He stuck out his hand. I let out a breath.

"What's your name?" he asked.

"Nadine?" I said.

"I'm Johnny," he replied.

I picked up my backpack and threw it over my shoulder.

"Hi, Johnny," I said, and turned to leave. "Bye, Johnny."

HENRY

I FOUND FABIAN'S GIRLFRIEND Linda on her lunch break at Flowers by Rory, brought her down to the station and gave her tea and tissues. After a half hour, she tidied her hair behind her ears, wiped her strong aquiline nose, and was ready to talk.

"Can you think of anyone who'd want to do something like this to Mark?" was my first real question.

"No," she said.

"No conflicts with family, or patients?"

"Family? No. He just has Brendan, and that's going fine. He never tells me much about his patients—you know, confidentiality."

"So he didn't indicate any potential trouble with patients recently. Even vaguely?"

Linda folded her tissue and dabbed at her nostrils. "He was slowly trying to cut ties with his patients. Some of them had been with him for years."

Linda sniffled loudly and looked up at me. "I wonder if that became too difficult of a situation for someone."

"So he was in the process of dropping patients?" I asked.

"Well . . . dropping. He wouldn't have put it that way. He was retiring. He'd just started to tell his clients recently. But he'd decided to give it six months, to help his clients adjust to new arrangements."

"He'd made the decision to retire recently," I said.

"Yes. The decision was abrupt, but he didn't want it to be abrupt for his patients."

"Why was the decision abrupt?"

"Well . . . he'd previously been thinking he'd go on at least a few more years. But then something happened. There was a problem with one of his patients that made him think he was getting too old for the job."

"Can you describe that a little more?" I asked. "This problem?"

"Well, the way he put it to me was that he 'slipped.' He didn't give me the details, of course. But he told me that he said something to a patient that he shouldn't have. Not like something hurtful or insulting, exactly. It was a situation where he'd forgotten who'd told him what, and gotten mixed up, and revealed something he shouldn't have."

I thought for a moment, trying to imagine such a scenario. "Like, in a situation between spouses, or something?"

"Yes." Linda nodded. "It must have been something like that. He admitted to me that he felt his memory was failing, and it could be potentially damaging to his clients."

"His memory was failing. Okay. Did he have some medical condition that was causing this, or . . ."

Linda sniffled and then sobbed.

"Take your time," I said.

"I don't know." Linda wiped her eyes and straightened her posture. "He didn't go to a doctor for it, if that's what you're asking. I think he wanted to retire first and ask questions later. Have some fun. Do some traveling. See, I'm already semi-retired. I used to teach. The flower shop is just to keep busy."

"Okay," I said.

"Anyway, I believe his thinking was that he would hold off on trying to pursue any medical diagnosis. I very much doubt he was really developing dementia or anything. He said to me, 'Linda, I think I'm just getting too *old* for this.' This slip he had, I think it was a sign that it was time to stop."

"Did he say if the patient involved in that slip . . . if he or she was angry?"

"Yes. I think there was some disappointment in Mark there."

"But anger?" I asked.

"I'm not sure. You realize Mark never spoke about his work on very specific terms. I can't tell you any more than what I've said. He didn't even say if it was a man or a woman."

"Alright. Okay. But . . . going back to my original question about whether you knew of anyone who'd want to hurt Mark. From how he talked, could this person have been *that* angry with him?"

Linda shrugged. "I don't know. It was a couple of months ago. And Mark never expressed any *fear* about the situation. Just regret. But it's possible he wanted to downplay it."

"And you say his relationships with his family were good?"

"Yes. He was enjoying having his son around lately. Aside

from Brendan keeping odd hours sometimes. Coming and going, partying with friends. He's still young, you know?"

"But were he and his son getting along generally?"

"Yes, absolutely."

"Okay. Do you have the son's cell number, by chance? Any contact information?"

"No. But I know he works at Wiliston-Buckley during the day. You know, the special school in Eastbury? He's a paraprofessional there, and takes classes at Quinnipiac at night."

"Okay. Other family we should know about, that you can help us contact?"

"Uh, let's see. Mark has a brother, Ryan, in California, and they chat on the phone occasionally. They're not especially close, but they get along."

"Okay," I said. "So, when was the last time you saw Mark?"

"We had dinner Monday night." Linda's face crumpled and she clutched her tissue to her nose. "We were going to go to Italy. That's where we were going to go first."

"I'm sorry for your loss," I said, and then felt awkward for saying it. As if I was implying that the trip to Italy was the main thing she'd lost. After she recovered again, I asked, "So, you didn't talk to him at all after Monday?"

"Umm . . . let's see. I called him to check in yesterday afternoon. He said he was a little busy and couldn't talk long. We confirmed we'd have dinner on Saturday. Said we'd eat at the Mexican place. That's it."

"And where were you last night?"

"With my grandkids in Hamden. That's a regular thing for me Tuesday night."

"So you wouldn't have had any reason to expect to hear from Mark last night."

"That's correct."

"Linda, did he ever mention his laptop password to you?"

Linda shook her head. "Sorry."

"Did he ever talk to you about how he kept track of his patients? We've got a calendar of appointments. All it has is first names."

"I see. I . . . don't know anything about his laptops. I know he had a work one and a home one and never brought the work one home. I'm not sure how many patient notes he really kept, though. I'd asked him once if he took a lot of notes on his patients, and he said no. He'd write up a report, or whatever, if insurance needed some minimal statement. And he told me he kept weekly notes for himself, just jotted stuff down after appointments, if there was something he really needed to remember for the next time."

"Any idea where he kept those?"

"He didn't."

"He didn't?"

"No. He threw them away every week or so. He said they were just personal notes. He didn't want anyone ever asking for them. He felt it was a liability to his patients, and to him, to have extra material on them that someone could potentially ask for—like, in a legal situation. But no one can ask for what you don't have."

"I see," I said. "Were these something he stored on his computer?"

"Just handwritten notes, from what I gathered."

MAJOR CRIMES WAS almost finished when I got back to the office building. Amy gave me a brief update on what they'd found.

There were lots of different fingerprints all over the consulting room, waiting room, and bathroom—obviously various patients that had been through the office recently. More notably, there were a couple of partial bloody fingerprints on the couch. Lucky that, otherwise the perpetrator hadn't seemed to have touched much on his—or her—way out. Maybe wiped their hands on their clothes. In any case, the prints were being run through the FBI database, and we'd get a report on that in a couple of hours. They found a long dark hair on Fabian's sweater.

"Seven inches long," Amy said. "So, a woman's . . . or a guy with really long hair."

"Hmm." Hairs can stick to sweaters for weeks. "Okay. Something came up while I talked to the girlfriend. Did they find handwritten notes of any kind, by any chance?"

"Not out in the open. But if you go into the bottom drawer of the desk there was something like that."

I nodded and opened the drawer. Inside it were a bunch of half-empty boxes of Twinings tea. Beneath them was a thick pile of yellow legal pads. They were all blank and brand new. But shoved to the side of the pile was one with some writing on it—just a few pages.

"Find what you're looking for?" Amy asked.

"Maybe," I said. "Any shortcut we can make to the patients, really."

It looked like Dr. Fabian started a fresh page for each day. Unfortunately, still no last names:

MON

ELIZABETH: Reports sleep difficulties. Discussed calling Metcalf for adjusting meds. Follow up 12/17.

ALEC: Resolved to attend group meeting.

NADINE: Find old file.

PHOEBE: Does not recall retirement discussion? Possible it didn't occur? Tearful upon leaving.

TUES

MARISA: Forward records to B. Townsend.

JAKE: Brother-alcoholism. Ran out of time. Follow up 12/22.

ANGELA: Husband's name is Paul. Paul. PAUL. Good grief.

LIAM: Call parents. Termination meeting after holidays?

I turned the page. The following page had no day or name scribbled on it. Just these words:

TR 4/12/91
Patty—Patsy
Greensomething?
Brookhaven 2001

I compared the legal pad notes to the calendar. They matched up generally, although it didn't look like Fabian took notes for every patient, every session, every day. In a vague way, the notes supported the idea that something happened with Connor, the last patient of the day. Fabian never had a chance to write anything about him. But then, maybe he wouldn't have anyway. Apparently he didn't write notes about *every* patient.

His Monday note about "Phoebe" really caught my eye, though. Really? Poor Dr. Fabian, and poor Phoebe. It confirmed Linda's thoughts about his memory loss. In fact, it made me think things were even worse than Fabian had let on to Linda. Same with the note about "Angela" on Tuesday, although I could imagine it might be hard to remember the names of everybody's faceless spouses and girlfriends.

"Anything good?" Amy asked.

"Not much," I said. I handed her the legal pad so she could look, too. "We'd better go talk to this guy's son."

CONNECTICUT COURIER

March 13, 2010

NEW DETAILS EMERGE IN BROOKHAVEN SHOOTING: NURSE WAS TARGET, INVESTIGATORS SAY

Police are releasing new details about the shooting last week at Brookhaven, Campion's elite retirement facility. Jonathan Carl Streeter, 37, is being held without bond at Eastern Correctional Institution for the shooting, which left ten dead.

In the days following the shooting, it was widely reported that Streeter's father, William Streeter, is a resident of Brookhaven Manor. He has resided there for four years—three years in the facility's Alzheimer's unit. According to a statement by the Brookhaven facility, the elder Streeter is uninjured and "unaware of his son's rampage."

"It appears that his father was not the intended target," said Campion Police Chief Brad Wheeler in yesterday's press conference. "We initially thought that, because after shooting for several minutes downstairs, he went up to the third floor Alzheimer's unit, where his father was, and resumed shooting. He skipped the second floor. But after Detective Gagnon's interview with Johnny Streeter, we ascertained that the main intended target was a nurse on that floor, in whom Streeter had had a romantic interest. The particular nurse was not on duty the morning of the incident. But I believe he thought she would be."

Investigators are not releasing the name of the nurse at this time, but Wheeler disclosed that Streeter had attempted to make several calls to her cell phone on the night before and the early morning of the shooting. "We believe they were unwanted phone calls," Wheeler added. "She did not pick up, because she did not wish to speak to Mr. Streeter. He left some obscene and threatening voice messages."

NADINE

I THINK IT WAS around then that you sensed I was having a little too much fun. And that I was kind of fiddle-fucking around with the institutions of your waiting room and your couch.

So you finally, after several months, came right out and said it.

"I think we should talk more about what happened with your teacher in November."

I liked you by then, so the request felt a bit like a betrayal. But I knew, nonetheless, that this was what my parents were paying you the big bucks for. To get to the bottom of the thing I'd done to Mr. Brewster. And so, at long last, I sank deep into the couch, rested my head, and surrendered to the topic as best I could.

Mr. Brewster.

Some of the kids called him Brewski. I suppose because Brewski is beer and the kids also liked beer—or wanted each other to think they did—and they liked Mr. Brewster and this was Campion, after all, so rebellion was straightforward and uncomplicated and ultimately innocent.

Anyway. Mr. Brewster had the requisite ponytail of a cool teacher of the era. He was clean-shaven and crooked-nosed and blue-eyed. The blue eyes were always sparkling, always laughing just a little—like he found us all amusing. We were a way to pass the time until he went off and did something more interesting every day after three o'clock. What that interesting thing was we could only speculate. Punk band in New Haven? Bongo drums? Righteous girlfriend with high hair and hoop earrings?

Whatever it was, he drove off in a vintage black Mustang to do it. I mean, *really*.

He let us sit on our desks and swear in class. As long as we were having "passionate" discussions about American politics. A bunch of well-off, white-picket-fence kids talking about the partial-birth abortion ban. He'd sit back in his squeaky swivel chair and put his feet up—and surely he fell asleep at least one period a day, just to keep from strangling himself with his bolo tie.

For me, the attraction was to his distance. The noncommittal look in his eyes that said *break me*.

My father had taught me how to talk to adults. And I had learned on my own how to shine in a class discussion. Listen for three to five minutes before speaking. Find the one thing that no one else is saying. Take a minute to formulate it. Raise your hand. Say it humbly and succinctly, using full sentences without ums or likes.

Teachers and parents always remarked at how thoughtful I

was. But usually, when I spoke, Mr. Brewster just nodded and said, "Okay." And then he'd point at someone else to speak. He treated everyone the same. He rarely said much about anyone's comments except to ask the occasional Socratic sort of question.

He didn't single me out in any way. He never remarked on my thoroughness, my eloquence, or my thoughtfulness. Not on written work or even on a report card. He gave me A minuses. He gave half the class A minuses.

Break me.

Oh, I will, Brewski. *I will.*

One night, in my room after a spaghetti dinner, I was writing a social studies essay and found my mind wandering to my father. My real father, who died when I was twelve. Not the soft-spoken and kitchen-ready fellow my mother married when I was ten, a couple of years after the divorce. The real guy. It seemed many weeks—a surprising number of weeks—had gone by since I had last thought of him in any more than a passing way.

And I started to wonder if it was because of him that people had previously thought I was so sensitive and so special. A lot of teachers and kids and parents knew of my father's death. Maybe that was why they seemed to regard me with admiration. Maybe it was just a thinly disguised type of pity. I was always aware of this possibility, but Mr. Brewster made it far more stark.

And if that was the case, I liked him for it. But still I needed to break open his honest apathy a little bit. I wanted to understand its causes and its limits.

And maybe this need to be special had always been a little sick anyway. It just hid something deeper and darker that I'd felt vaguely since my father died, but rather keenly this particular year. I did not have a word for it, but *futility* felt close. Whatever it was, it oozed out of me in quiet moments like this one, while I was doing my social studies homework to an old Simon and Garfunkel tape in my Walkman.

This essay I was writing—what was it about? The death penalty or some such? It would never get Brewski's attention—not the way I wanted it to. It would get me an A minus, and minimal comments. So on its last page—half-blank after my tidy final paragraph—I doodled a picture of a fluffy white bunny with an arrow piercing its belly.

When Mr. Brewster handed it back to me a week later, it had an A minus on it. After the final paragraph, he'd written, *Well-organized, staunchly defended thesis.* He hadn't touched my drawing. Had he even seen it? Maybe I ought to have drawn blood drops trickling from the bunny.

The very next day in social studies, I asked for a bathroom pass and sat in a narrow yellow stall for a while, crying. I wasn't sure if I was crying because of that familiar old pain or my uncomfortable need for Mr. Brewster to witness it. I came back to class red-eyed and still sniffling. Brewski didn't look at me.

I couldn't sleep that night, because *how dare he not look at me?* What was he playing at? And how could I break him if I couldn't get him even to *look*?

A few days later I convinced my mother to let me take her car out after school. I'd gotten my license that summer, and was allowed occasional use of her car. It was a Thursday, and I knew that on Thursdays Brewski stayed late with the Amnesty International kids. (Why didn't *I* join Amnesty International? In which I could hang out with Brewski after school hours and send my thoughtful words to cruel and corrupt foreign leaders? I don't recall now. Maybe it just sounded like too much effort.) So his Mustang was still there in the staff lot. I waited from the safe distance of the student lot until he came walking out.

And then I followed him. I was relieved when he stopped at the nearby Rite Aid. Because I realized I didn't want to follow him *home.* I wasn't that nuts—not really. It would be nice just to run into him in real life. And better yet, run into him while he was off guard—buying deodorant or some sort of embarrassing ointment. I was curious what he looked like when he was surprised. (Surprised was about one-quarter of the way to broken.)

When I went into the store, I found him in the shampoo aisle, then hid in the next aisle over. It didn't seem to me that he could be surprised or embarrassed buying hair care products. (Though it depended on what and how many. Hair gel—maybe. Shampoo—no.) So maybe *I* was the one who should be buying something worth noticing. Something to *exhibit.* But what?

A big rainbow-colored lollipop to stress my innocence and vulnerability?

Or the opposite?

Condoms would be overdoing it. Tampons would be gross.

Something symbolic of pain?

Bandages? A giant bottle of aspirin?

Brewski didn't seem very perceptive of subtleties, and would likely miss the symbolism entirely.

But I didn't have a lot of time. I ran to the shaving products aisle and found a straight razor. Yes! They only had one kind. I wasn't sure I had enough money but it wouldn't matter if I was in line *after* him, not before. I peeked into the shampoo aisle. He was heading toward the front of the store with a baby blue bottle of conditioner. I hurried toward the registers and grabbed a *Time* magazine, then retreated behind a rack of paperbacks.

Then I timed my approach to the registers just so. Just so I'd practically run into him.

"Oh!" I gasped as we nearly collided.

"Hi, Nadine," Mr. Brewster said.

"Oh, hi," I said, lifting the straight razor to eye level and then hiding it behind the *Time* magazine.

"After you," he said, waving toward the register.

"Oh . . . well, no. You go ahead. I forgot one thing."

"Okay. You have a good night, now," Mr. Brewster called after me as I scurried away toward the toothbrushes and toothpaste.

I waited for him to check out and leave the store. Then I put the razor and the magazine back and went home.

HENRY

AFTER I UPDATED Amy on the status of things, she picked up my iPod. "Can we listen to something, maybe?"

We were in my car, only halfway to Eastbury.

"I don't know if we should listen to anything on the way to this. Kind of grim."

"I won't pick anything too happy, alright?" She flipped through my music options. "No. No. No. How much Radiohead does one man need? Now, what's 'Hans'?"

"Uh, that's not music. It's an audiobook for my girls. Or, it was supposed to be. They didn't like it."

"Too bad. *Hans.* I thought it might be some kind of German industrial techno or something. I thought I was going to learn something new about you today."

"It's Hans Christian Andersen."

Amy hit Play.

For a few minutes, we heard the somber male narrator tell the opening of "The Red Shoes." The girl in the story, "Karen," wore her red shoes to church, and couldn't stop looking at the pretty shoes instead of listening to the prayers. Later, the shoes started dancing against her wishes, but she couldn't take them off, so she was forced to dance day and night, through "field and meadow," and eventually into the churchyard.

Amy paused the story.

"You really drive around with the kids listening to this?"

"No. They didn't like it. I downloaded it on this iPod a couple of months ago and then—"

"Put the fear of God into the kids. I like that."

"Olivia's into this kind of thing lately. Fairy tales. So I downloaded some Hans Christian Andersen stories. But they didn't go over that well with Sophia."

"I wonder why," Amy said. But she hit Play again and we listened in silence as I drove. Karen had an executioner cut off her uncontrollable feet, but they continued to dance without her, taunting her when she'd try to go to church with her crutches and wooden prostheses.

"Oh, for the love of God," Amy murmured as I pulled into the Williston-Buckley parking lot. I let the car run for a minute more so she could hear the ending.

"And the moral of the story is, don't be thinking about fancy footwear when you're supposed to be thinking about God," she said as I shut off the car.

"You've never heard that story before?" I asked.

"No."

"Did you like it?"

"You know, I'm going to have to give it some thought." She turned and gazed at the front entrance of the school. Her unusually pale face, thin features, and tidy ponytail often made people do a double take, like they were seeing a child in a cop's uniform. "I've never been a shoe girl."

"Fair enough," I said.

"I'll do most of the talking if you want me to," she offered. "I mean, I can give the actual news if you want."

"Thanks," I said. We both knew she was better at this sort of thing.

WE HAD TO have a secretary pull Fabian's son out of a class, and broke the news to him in a teachers' break room. After Amy told him how his father had been found, he was silent for a minute, his dark bangs in his face, shielding his initial reaction from us.

Then he turned beet red, stood up, and flung the drinking glass he'd been holding, smashing it on the floor.

Amy rose and touched Brendan lightly on the arm. He fell back into his chair and grabbed at his hair. For a moment I thought he was going to pull out a handful.

"His *patients,*" he wailed. "It was one of his patients."

"Did he mention a problem with a particular patient?" I asked.

"No. He never discussed patients with me. Ever." He stared down at the broken glass on the floor. "Shit. The kids probably heard me."

"Don't worry about that right now," I said. "So, talking about his patients . . . it's not allowed in his line of work?"

"Correct."

"And yet you're sure it was a patient?"

"It was in his office, wasn't it? Fuck!" He stood up again

and glanced around the room, as if looking for something else to grasp or throw.

"Listen," Amy said. "We know this is hard. And we're going to give you some time to process this, bring you home if you'd like. But if there's anything you can tell us right now that you think would help us, we'd appreciate it. Is there anyone you know of who might've wanted to hurt your father for any reason? Anyone *besides* patients? Anyone there'd been any disagreements with?"

Brendan shook his head.

"His patients," he growled. "Go after his *patients*."

After Amy and I cleaned up the glass shards, Brendan told us he'd slept over at his girlfriend's place Tuesday night, so hadn't noticed his father's absence from home. Then he started crying.

"Can you tell us your girlfriend's name?" Amy asked gently. "And where we might find her? Maybe we can call her so she can pick you up?"

Nice. We'd also be confirming his story before we had her do any such thing. Amy might've picked up the same vibe that I had—that Brendan was a little odd. Not that anger or shock or sadness were unusual reactions—but Brendan seemed to rotate between all three very quickly, almost as if trying to decide which to go with.

"She works here. She's a teacher. Her name is Brit."

Well, that was convenient.

Amy fetched her and talked to her in my car while I sat with Brendan. He gripped his hair again and then flexed his fingers.

"I want to scream but I'm afraid the kids will hear."

"My colleague already notified your principal you'll be leaving. You'll be out of here in just a few minutes."

Brendan didn't reply. For the next minute or two, I listened to his shaky breath and left him alone.

"The last night I saw him," he said, "we had some bourbon together."

"Sounds nice. I don't think I've ever had bourbon with my dad."

"This was the one time for us, actually. My dad barely drank, my whole life. Except in the last few years."

"The last few years?" I repeated.

Brendan shrugged. "His standards for a lot of things . . . loosened. In the last few years. Maybe something about turning sixty."

"Hmm," I said. "Maybe."

Amy came back and pulled me out of the break room.

"She seemed genuinely shocked. She confirmed she'd been with Brendan. And she gave me the name of a mutual friend who'd come over to watch a movie with them."

"I'LL HAVE GREG check on the friend," I said as we drove away. "I'm already having him check Linda's alibi."

"Okay," Amy said.

"Do you want to listen to more Hans on the way back?" I asked. "There's a great story on here about a snowman who sees a wood-burning stove through a window, and falls in love with it."

"Not right now, thanks," Amy replied.

NADINE

AND NOW I'VE been sitting here in my car for way too long. I know this because a white-haired lady is slowly making her way down from the front porch of the Apple Blossom, squinting at my car. I get out and meet her on the walkway so she doesn't have to hobble all the way to me.

"You don't have a reservation, do you, ma'am?" she says.

"Oh. No. Are you filled up at the moment?" I say it with some relief. After loitering in her driveway for so long, I ought to reserve a room. But I'm not sure I actually want to be here.

"Oh, no," says the lady. "I barely get any customers in the winter. I don't have *any* reservations this week, is why I was asking."

"Oh," I say.

I stare at my hands for a moment. There is something red in the overgrown pinkie fingernail of my right hand. Blood? I don't know, and I am afraid to put it close to my nose or my mouth to find out. I can't remember how I drove here. All I remember is the square white back of a semitrailer and *Not again. No. Not again.*

I'm not sure where I could go next even if I *could* manage to keep driving. The GPS had told me I had arrived, and then gone silent.

"Is it too early to check in?"

"Not today," the lady says. "Nobody here now. Makes no difference to me."

I pay for the room in cash and tell her my name is Lisa. She shows me the room on the second floor, which is covered in a dusty blue wallpaper with pale pink bunches of roses. The pink matches a quilt on the four-poster bed.

"It's kind of like a honeymoon room," the lady tells me.

"It's lovely," I say, but she sort of snuffles in response, as if to communicate to me what she really thinks of honeymoons. Or loveliness. Or me.

"Enjoy it," she says as she makes her way back down the stairs.

She seems like a nice old lady but I'm glad she's gone. I wash my hands in the tiny bathroom. I don't look in the mirror.

The room is claustrophobic with the curtains closed, but with them open I can pull the reading chair to the window and look out into the small sunken garden in the back. All of the flowers are dormant for the winter, but tidily trimmed and mulched.

If I leave the lights off, the crazy-making wallpaper fades into the background.

I can still think.

I can still remember.

WHY A STRAIGHT razor? I wondered this for days.

I really wasn't a girl who romanticized wrist-slitting or anything of the sort. Maybe on account of my father's death—it just wasn't *me*. And yet, a razor was what I'd run for, and instinctually grabbed, to get Brewski's attention. Was it a subconscious thing? My subconscious lacked imagination? Or maybe it was simply more practical than the conscious me. Smarter about the bottom line: *There aren't many ways to get these people's attention. Not really.*

I mean, I'd tried subtlety and I'd tried well-spoken maturity. But flashing a straight razor—that was crazy.

Crazy but—potentially effective? I puzzled over this for a while. I read through all of my old *Sassy* magazines until I found some bits about girls who cut themselves. Someone had written a letter about it to the advice column. And in another issue, there was an anecdote from one of the cool editors' personal experiences. So it was real. I hadn't made it up in my head. People did this. I wasn't sure why but maybe it didn't matter.

And maybe I didn't need to do *that* exactly, but just something like it. Something equally, painfully shocking. After all, I'd waved a straight razor at the guy and naturally I needed to finish what I'd started—whatever that might require.

Hold my breath. Hold my nose. *Follow through.*

And on that cold morning, I skipped breakfast and rummaged through the bathroom cabinet and scanned the kitchen to find the right instrument for this purpose.

A chopping knife? Dramatic—but probably obnoxiously so. I needed precision and discretion.

On the wall above the utility drawer is a little nail with three keychains. One to the house. One to my mom's car. One to my stepfather's. Anthony was absent-minded and lost his keys and stranded himself at work or the grocery store all the time. Mom stopped finding it endearing after about a year of marriage to him, and nailed up extras of everything. But what kind of damage could I do with keys, anyway?

I was going to miss the bus if I didn't decide quickly. And if I didn't decide quickly I'd have all of today and tonight to change my mind. It had to be today. I'd known that when I'd showered this morning. The hot water was on the fritz. The cold reminded me who I was.

I opened the utility drawer. The yellow plastic of my stepfather's X-Acto knife popped out at me. I grabbed it and put it in my backpack. And then I headed out to catch the school bus. All the way to school, I listened to my friend Julie talk about how late she'd stayed up studying for the chemistry test, and how bad she was going to flunk anyway, because she didn't really understand what she was studying. This felt like bullshit to me, because I knew she'd probably spent half the night talking to her boyfriend on the phone, and then started studying at ten P.M., at which point she realized she was probably going to flunk.

Either way, I'd forgotten about the test altogether, and felt a little freedom in the forgetting. Funny, the box cutter in my bag might just free me from everything.

"We'll both do fine," I mumbled to Julie, as the bus pulled up to the school.

Brewski's social studies class was second period. Right before it, during the passing period, I locked myself in a bathroom stall and played with the length of the blade and murmured to myself. *It'll be fine. It'll be quick. Go ahead. You'll be fine. We'll all be fine.*

When the bell had rung and we were all seated in Brewski's room, he gave the class a response prompt to work on for five minutes while he took attendance and collected our homework.

Perfect. I didn't have my homework, but he would walk right by my desk either way.

As he approached my desk, he said, "Nadine? No homework this morning?"

I didn't respond. That's when he saw the box cutter. I could tell by the look in his eyes.

"Nadine. Is that . . . ?"

I stared at the top of my arm, where a spare constellation of freckles formed its own Ursa Minor. Right there. It wouldn't hurt much, would it? Not like a wrist would. I could stand it for a second or two or three. Just like I could stand the cold water.

"Nadine, give that to me."

But who *were* those girls who did this sort of thing? Not me. Why did I need to follow through on something that wasn't really *me*?

Fuck those sad girls. And fuck him. Fuck him for not paying any goddamn attention to anyone. Fuck him for being so preciously enigmatic. And fuck him, finally, for reducing me to this.

But then—Fuck it! I wouldn't do it! I wasn't one of those sad girls. Not at all. *Fuck him.*

It took only a second for my indecision to turn to rage.

"NADINE."

Mr. Brewster's hand was planted on my desk now. His other hand reaching toward me. I gripped the box cutter tight.

Cold water. Head aching. Follow through like the other kids can't—like the other kids don't know how.

Fuck him.

I jammed the blade into flesh and ripped it back and forth like I was cutting a tough piece of meat.

It was too easy. It didn't hurt at all.

Because it was someone else's flesh. Someone else's arm.

The other kids were stunned and staring. Somebody screamed.

I let go of the box cutter. I heard it fall on the floor. I felt a certain relief in knowing that I had made something happen. But then nausea in the realization that it hadn't been exactly what I'd planned.

And there he was. Mr. Brewster. Screaming. Swearing. Bloody.

Finally—broken.

HENRY

March 12, 1997

You asked me if what I did to him was maybe a way of me showing the other kids the tragic unpredictability of life. Giving them a taste of what I've had, and what's eventually to come for them. That's a very interesting idea, and one I've given a lot of thought since you said it. And I think the answer is no. For the sake of going forward, I wonder if you can trust me when I tell you I don't want to hurt anyone. I wanted to hurt myself and I turned coward at the last second. I have no voices. I have done wrong and I have suffered consequences. I believe I have real remorse but I can't make a maudlin show of it for you, because that would make me feel crazier than having done it in the first place. So this week, can we please talk about the future?

May 7, 1997

I'm sure I won't forget to tell you that I've decided to go to Northern Arizona University. I like the idea that I'll be near the Grand Canyon. And the feeling, when I look at pictures, that I'll be going almost to another planet. I think decisions about where to go to college have been made on a lot less—pretty brick buildings with ivy, girl-guy ratio, proximity to one's high school sweetheart. These past few months I've mentioned feeling older than I am. To me, such a weird and faraway place could mean erasing some of the years I feel. Please don't say "Wherever you go, there you are." That's the one thing you're not allowed to say. Okay? You've said it twice before, and I'm tired of it. (Those lines make you seem a little robotic, by the way.) Just wish me well and ask me for a Grand Canyon postcard.

July 12, 1997

Am I supposed to like having a tongue stuck into my mouth? Is that supposed to be practice for having a dick in there? Could you explain this to me? Because I'd really like to know.

August 13, 1997

I think it will feel weird to go through the motions of talking for exactly one hour this one last time. Can we talk about Star Trek *again this time? That was my favorite session ever.*

I want you to know I've never lied to you, but I have left things out and put extra stuff in. If you listened to about every other word, you'd be close to the truth.

P.S. I got you a good-bye present. Don't let me walk out without giving it to you. Thanks.

I READ THE LITTLE blue notebook a couple of times, for lack of anything else to do. It was nearly nine P.M. and there wasn't much reason to stay in the office, but I couldn't bring myself to go home yet. The fingerprint database request hadn't turned up anything. I had put in a warrant for Fabian's phone records, but we weren't going to see them until tomorrow. I had also called Caduceus Billing to get information on that patient "Connor" and everyone else Fabian had seen on Tuesday. As I predicted, they said they wouldn't release anything without a subpoena. Our DA Carly Dayton had gotten on that right away. (Not before saying to me: *Brace yourself, Henry. With HIPAA, and no one officially in charge of the victim's records, getting what you need might be kind of a clusterfuck for a little while.*) But we weren't going to hear back from the Caduceus folks until tomorrow at best. It wasn't clear if they even had any information on Connor.

Greg had talked to several of Fabian's neighbors in the afternoon. They hadn't expressed much besides shock. An elderly lady from next door said that a young man in a "nice" black car (she didn't know the make or model) had approached his house early yesterday evening, and had knocked on the door. She also said that young men were often pounding on Fabian's door—friends of his son's who fetched him and then careened off in their cars—to bars or parties, she assumed, because Brendan was young, and because he would often get dropped off at all hours of the night.

"She also wanted me to know she had never gone to a shrink herself, and never would," Greg had told me as he scarfed down a particularly smelly Subway sandwich. "In case that's useful information."

We'd also nabbed a couple of Fabian's patients over the course of the day—one of our officers manned the yellow line and asked people who drove or walked up which practitioner they'd come to see.

Both patients were coming in for weekly appointments—so neither had seen Fabian since last Wednesday. Both—a college-aged girl in yoga pants and a newly retired guy with a bald head and a cashmere sweater—appeared genuinely shocked. Their first names matched the ones scribbled in Fabian's appointment calendar for today—Megan and Theo. The girl cried when she heard the news, and said Fabian seemed a little sad lately. The guy said Fabian seemed more laid-back since he announced his retirement. Neither knew the names of any other patients.

The story had made the local evening news, but we hadn't given a press conference yet. We thought we might at some point ask patients to come forward if they had any information. But we also thought it would be good to hold off on that, for now. We'd see what Caduceus and the phone records gave us tomorrow. We'd also get a preliminary autopsy report in the morning.

So I didn't have much to work with tonight besides the

ramblings of this 1997 girl. Girl, I was guessing, because of the July 12th entry in the little book. And if this girl was going off to college around August of 1997, she was exactly my age. Off the top of my head, I couldn't think of anyone in my high school class who'd gone to Arizona for college. But then, I had a class of about two hundred kids—maybe a little more. Although I definitely qualified as a townie, I didn't know *everyone.*

I looked again at the doll-and-dinosaur cartoons drawn on the pages of the booklet. Aside from the long one I'd seen in Fabian's office, there were two more. One went like this:

> ***Dinosaur:*** *How many more dinosaurs do you think you'll know in your life?*
>
> ***Doll:*** *Maybe many. Maybe none.*
>
> ***Dinosaur:*** *Will you know a dinosaur when you see one?*
>
> ***Doll:*** *How could I not?*
>
> ***Dinosaur:*** *Because one of your eyes is broken, Baby Doll.*
>
> ***Doll:*** *Who cares, anyway? Probably I'll find more interesting company than a dinosaur.*
>
> ***Dinosaur:*** *Let's hope so.*

The other was opposite the last entry of the booklet.

The doll was holding a small present with a bow on top, saying, "This one will last. Our secret. Forever." The dinosaur was saying, "You shouldn't have."

In the next frame, the doll's eyes were both open, and she was saying, "Please, look, look, Talmadge! At last, page last! One good-bye! Oh, good-bye! Two good-byes!" The little gift was on the floor at the dinosaur's feet, and he was saying, "I'm not sure if I can accept this, Baby Doll."

I wondered if, since Fabian had a PhD in this stuff, he understood what all of this dinosaur business was supposed to mean. In any case, it was curious to me that he would have been looking at something written by a patient nearly twenty years ago. Was she *still* his patient? Had she come back from Arizona and re-upped on the therapy? Or was Fabian going over all of his files recently, reminiscing in the days before his retirement? Why did that feel slightly wrong to me? And was there something special about this patient that made him go back and look?

Katie called right as I was about to reread the legal pad notes.

"Still working?" she asked. I'd talked to her in the early afternoon and told her what was happening.

"Trying to," I said. "There might not be much more we can do till tomorrow."

"The girls are asleep. Olivia missed you. She wanted you to read 'The Snow Queen.'"

"Oh. Right."

"She wouldn't let me read it. She says I read it wrong."

"Ah," I said, staring at the dinosaur-and-doll drawings.

"You wouldn't happen to know what she means by that, would you?"

"Not sure," I lied. "Listen, I'll be home soon."

"Yeah, you ought to. You may as well sleep for a few hours."

"Right," I said. "See you in an hour or so."

I hung up the phone. I missed the girls, but lately Olivia had been getting me in trouble when I read to her. Recently, Katie's crazy aunt Jeanie had fed into Olivia's fairy tale obsession by bringing home an old library discard she'd found at a tag sale. It was a creepy fairy tale collection from the seventies—full of dark forests and haggard-looking medieval characters—that didn't pull any punches.

Olivia had conned me into reading its version of "Snow White" one night, and I'd assumed that Aunt Jeanie had already read it to the twins. Sometimes I'm really tired when I'm reading to the girls—don't really hear the words coming out of my own mouth. Before I knew it, I'd said something about the stepmother wanting the huntsman to bring back Snow White's lungs and liver for her to cook up and eat.

"What's a liver?" Sophia had demanded, her hands clasped tightly over her tiny white chin as she rose in her cupcake nightgown and jogged up and down on her toes. "WHAT'S A LIVER?"

"Uh . . ." I said. "Didn't Aunt Jeanie tell you?"

"She didn't read that part, I guess," Olivia had said, taking the book from my limp hands. "I don't know what a liver is. But I know what *lungs* are."

"So do I!" Sophia screamed. I wasn't sure if it was horror or competition in her voice. "You breathe with them and that's why you shouldn't smoke."

"Wow," Olivia said. "Daddy, read the *whole* thing."

"No," Sophia moaned, and grabbed my arm. "*Don't.*"

"Olivia, Sophia doesn't want to hear a scary story right before bed. I think that makes sense."

"But you said you'd read it. You said I could pick one and she could pick one."

"How were they gonna get her lungs?" Sophia shrieked.

"If you would *let* Daddy read it, maybe you'll find out," Olivia said quietly.

"How were they gonna get her lungs?" Sophia repeated.

"Now, it's just a story, honey."

"Why did you *say* that?" Sophia looked like she might cry.

"I just . . ." I considered saying that I just *thought* that's what it said . . . that I was mistaken. I thought Sophia might accept a lie for the evening—not because she was any more gullible than Olivia, but because she accepted comfort a little more easily. But I knew Olivia wouldn't want or try to believe me. And I didn't like lying to the kids, either way.

"People like to tell stories in different ways," I said. "In some versions of the story, the queen is meaner than others."

Sophia started to sob.

"Mommy!" she screamed as she ran down the hall.

I got up to go after her. I didn't want her to bother Katie while she was watching her show.

"You could read it while she's with Mommy," Olivia said quietly. I turned and looked at her pulling her cowgirl nightgown over her knees with a wide-eyed shrug.

And then I read the whole damn thing to her, and didn't bother to leave out the sadistic details. At the end, the evil queen has to attend the wedding of Snow White and the prince and dies dancing in some red-hot iron shoes. (What is it with fairy tales and rogue red shoes?)

"Well, how about that?" I'd muttered as I closed the book. I didn't remember any of that from when I was a kid. But then, I rarely read anything I was supposed to when I was a kid.

All the way up through college. And that's probably why I dropped out of law school.

A couple of weeks later we got a report from the speech specialist at the girls' kindergarten, who had insisted upon screening Olivia for possible speech therapy because she supposedly wasn't always saying her *s*'s and *sh*'s right. In her report, the teacher had typed up direct quotes from Olivia, highlighting where she made sound errors.

*The stepmother cook***th** *up her liver and eats it,* was one of the quotes.

"She said it right when she said *eats,* though," I pointed out.

"Jesus, Henry," was all Katie had said about it.

Now I stared at the doll-and-dinosaur cartoons and wondered about the parents of the girl who drew them. Did they have any idea what was in their kid's head? Was she really messed up or did her parents, like many Campionites, just have a lot of extra money to spend on something like a shrink? Either way, of course the endeavor not to fuck up your kids is essentially futile—everyone knows that.

"Right?" I mumbled out loud.

Who was I talking to, exactly?

I thought about Fabian—his long, lined face, bloodied on one side. His soft gray sweater seemingly picked out to match his hair. His quiet office, so clearly designed to put people at ease. I wondered if he was someone I'd have felt comfortable talking to. Or if he'd have made me feel like I was being observed more than listened to—like his colleague Melissa did.

I read through the legal pad notes a couple times more, and then went home.

NADINE

THEY DIDN'T ARREST me after I stabbed Mr. Brewster's arm. Not exactly. I was taken away in a police cruiser. But my mother was at the station about ten minutes after I got there. I don't know whose idea it was to bring me to Barnes Memorial Hospital, where several nurses and a gray-bearded doctor all asked me if I'd been hearing voices. I answered no each time, but I was admitted anyway.

It was an adult psych unit. There was apparently a children's unit there as well, but at sixteen I was above whatever cutoff age there was for that. These days there probably would be an adolescent unit, but not then. The place was surprisingly quiet—full of elderly people with dementia, and people who'd recently made suicide attempts. It wasn't like a full-blown mental hospital—more like a holding pen for patients they weren't sure what to do with yet. I was the youngest person there. The second youngest was a tall college kid with a buzz cut who kept slowly pointing at the ceiling and saying "Dominion? Authorization? Domination?" But who laughed at all the right moments when we'd watch *The Simpsons* together in the TV lounge.

A whole week passed, and the questions persisted about voices. It was like no one could think of any more creative reason for a studious high school girl to have a violent moment than *because someone told her to.* I was consistent with my answer. *No.* I knew that everyone was expecting me to explain what I had done, but lying about voices in my head seemed like it could be a one-way ticket to a hard-core institution.

The bearded doctor chatted with me for about a half hour every other day. I cried a lot during these "sessions." Cried mostly in real disbelief of what I'd done. When he asked me why I'd done it, I sobbed harder and said, "I don't know." Did I have a reason to be angry at Mr. Brewster? "No." Why had I brought a knife to school? "Because I was thinking of cutting myself. Maybe cutting my wrists." And then what happened? "I don't know!" And then more sobbing.

My stepfather stepped up. He's the one who found a shrink who could immediately start up with me three afternoons a week. That would be you, Bouffant. He talked to the bearded doctor. To Mr. Brewster. To the school board. To the police. I wouldn't be told for some time exactly what their action plan was. Mr. Brewster would not press charges. I would be tutored at home and receive intensive therapy for the rest of the school year. During the summer, everyone would assess whether it was appropriate for me to attend the regional alternative school. I would never contact Mr. Brewster or set foot in Campion High School again.

This whole plan was to avoid my having to go to either juvenile hall or a long-term adolescent facility. At all costs, my mother wanted me home. In truth, my stepfather arranged a far better situation for me than I deserved. Neither my mom nor I had any idea what an artful negotiator he was until then. I believe he wanted to prove he could and would stand up for me as well as a real father might have, and outdid himself. Even if I scared the living fuck out of him from that day forward.

I stayed at the Barnes Memorial psych ward for about three weeks while all of this was being negotiated, watching attempted suicides come and go. When the plan was in place and my release date was set, my worry about what would happen next began to lessen, just a little.

And this is one of the things I could never bring myself to tell you. When some of the worry left, there started a twinge in my chest that felt like warmth. It scared me, and I didn't exactly want to feel it, because I started to realize that this was *pride.* Not pride in what I had done, specifically. (I did not like to think of Brewski's many stitches or the blood on the floor.) But pride in the more general fact that I had made something happen. Something for which most people did not have the stomach or the heart or the follow-through. The specifics were unfortunate, but the general fact of it felt like a gift and an ache at the same time—to know I could do something like this, if I ever needed to again. I would keep it hidden, try not to treasure it too much, and only ever take it out again if absolutely necessary.

This was mine. I would always have it. It was planted inside me so deep that no one could dig it out. Not me, and I would come to discover—not you, either.

So with my release day three days away, I finally unpacked the Walkman and tapes my mother had brought me on my second day in the hospital. The Simon and Garfunkel tapes were from my dad—the rest from the mall. When I put in the Simon and Garfunkel, "The Only Living Boy in New York" was what came out. It felt like a sign. I felt like the only living person for miles, because I knew what it was like to take an impulse to its limits.

We had a secret, my dead dad and I.

I sat in the third-floor window of my room, knees to my chest, and watched doctors and nurses walk by—to the corner deli and the Dunkin' Donuts across the street. I hummed along. I rewound. I listened again.

IT'S DARK NOW. I close the blinds and turn on a lamp. The light is dim and yellowish. The Apple Blossom lady apparently favors a low wattage.

As I examine the contents of my backpack, I catch sight of myself in the large mirror mounted over the dresser against the wall. In this light, from several feet away, I can't see my crow's feet or the lone gray hairs that I recently gave up plucking from my widow's peak.

I look young in this light. I look the same as I did when I'd catch a glimpse of myself in that hospital window—when the sky darkened in the evenings after I'd eaten my hospital turkey and mashed potatoes with a plastic spork.

I check the time and see that it's not too late to bother the Apple Blossom lady. I call the number listed for "Front Desk" and she answers. I ask her if I can borrow a pair of scissors.

HENRY

I BARELY SLEPT. INSTEAD I lay awake thinking about Dr. Fabian.

I don't think all that much about the afterlife, so it's not like I was thinking he was watching me from a seat in the sky. But it seemed to me there could be some sort of cartoon cosmology that allowed a murder victim's soul to linger and follow his detective around for a while, and possibly cast judgment on the investigative process. I worried that so far, Fabian probably wasn't all that impressed.

So I felt I had to reassure him—to explain some things to him.

Yes, this is my first homicide case. But no, that doesn't mean you're getting some kind of a raw deal here.

I've been a detective for a few years. It's just that there aren't many murders in Campion. But I know this town like few people do. I grew up here. People know me. People talk to me. Probably as much as they talked to Fabian. Maybe more. And that was true even before Brookhaven. Before I became their sunshine boy. Before I became a detective. Before all of that, I had little desire to become a detective. But after Brookhaven—after Detective Gagnon's interview of Johnny Streeter was on *Dateline* and made him famous for a while before he got a job with the state police—the chief was itching to promote me and Katie was eager for me to finally move up in the world. So I took the required exam. We were raising twins, after all. Two college tuitions looming at the exact same time.

I've been on the force since 2003. September 11th happened shortly before I dropped out of law school, and I took it as a sign I was supposed to join the armed services. My father worked on me until he'd convinced me that I'd do *just as much good here at home* as I could in Afghanistan. I'd never meant for *here* to be so literal—back in the intensely idyllic Campion, with its streets lined with cute front gardens and glutted with giant SUVs zipping from gymnastics to soccer to SAT prep. But there was an opening right after I'd finished at the police academy, and it seemed a sensible place to start. I am the kind of person for whom inertia just tends to happen, so I won't go into how I ended up staying.

Anyway, the Campion police generally do what you'd expect. A lot of traffic monitoring and breaking up of noisy adolescent parties. Our last homicide—before Brookhaven—was the 2007 shooting death of a fifty-two-year-old woman by her boyfriend, who confessed at the scene. Gagnon was in charge of that, although Greg and I did assist on that some.

All of that was pre-Brookhaven, pre-Johnny Streeter.

Johnny Streeter is currently residing in Eastern Correctional—a mere thirty minutes from my house on a good traffic day. There was no trial—just a hearing—because he pled guilty on all counts, and because Connecticut's death penalty hadn't been abolished yet—that happened one year later—and his lawyer was apparently trying to avoid a death penalty show trial sort of mess. So Campion was spared that, but nonetheless I know everyone wishes my aim had been better.

Streeter was a townie, too—and about my age—but no one seemed to know him very well. For most of his thirties—up till the shooting—he had worked at an electronics store outside of town. His long-time live-in girlfriend was not from Campion originally. And before all that, he went to Catholic schools in Meriden, not Campion public schools. People around town like to theorize that his parents knew he was fucked up from the very beginning, and hoped Catholicism would set him straight. It didn't work, obviously.

But I tried to put Streeter out of my head, because I'd never be able to sleep with him there. I focused on Fabian instead. And then I thought of the raw beef wound on the side of his head. So I averted my gaze to a different part of that morning's memory. His bookshelf. Several books had fallen to the floor. But one of the books still on the shelf was quite visible. *JUNG* it said down the spine.

I was supposed to read some Jung in college. I think I may have read some of the assignments, or conned a studious roommate into telling me enough about it to get by—because I remembered a little bit. I remembered that snakes were a big deal. And so were heroes. Heroes ad nauseam. What were some of the other archetypes? Magicians? Mothers? I couldn't remember. I'm guessing Jung and a lot of those books are just required in a shrink's office. Along with the diploma. To let patients know: *Yes, you are in a shrink's office. Start talking, because this is expensive.*

It could be a calming exercise to try to remember some of the archetypes—like counting sheep. What was that one the professor loved to talk about? The wounded healer. That would be Fabian, wouldn't it? Well, maybe not. Not the wounded healer. The dead healer. That doesn't have nearly as powerful a ring to it.

What else was there? The trickster. The warrior? Or was the warrior the same as the hero? Was the father one of them? The clown? The magician?

I WAS JOLTED from sleep by a little hovering shadow by the foot of our bed, waking up with a holler that scared even me, and the little shadow started screaming in turn. I don't know how long we were both screaming.

My heart raced. I tried to remember the shadow's name.

I opened my mouth but all that came out was a wounded dog sort of noise.

I tried again. "Oh!"

The shadow raced to the other side of our bed.

"Olivia!" I said finally.

And by then Katie was up and out of bed, moving toward Olivia to give her a hug and say, "What is it, honey?"

"There's a blue witch in the house," Olivia sobbed. "And I think Daddy just saw it, too."

"A blue witch? You had a bad dream?"

Olivia was into witches. And ever since we had let her watch a snippet of *The Wizard of Oz* on YouTube, she'd been obsessed with the color of witches' faces. She's told me that different witches have different color faces, depending on how bad they are. Blue witches are the worst, then green, then red, then purple. Orange witches think they're bad, but aren't really. Yellow witches are sad. Pink witches are stupid.

"It wasn't a dream."

This reminder of the witch categories made me think of Fabian's skinny colleague in her purple sweater cape. A purple witch?

"You probably saw something in your room. The dollhouse has such a pointy roof, you probably mistook it for a hat in the dark."

"No," Olivia said firmly, suddenly indignant and in control of her tears. "She had taken her hat off and she was holding it in her hand and she had spots on her head where she was bald."

I sat up in bed and tried to look calmly quizzical. Olivia's late-night specificity always scares the shit out of me.

"Let's go back to your room," Katie said. "I'll lie with you for a little while."

"Not a little while," Olivia whispered. "A lot of while."

"We'll see, okay?"

"Daddy's awake. Maybe he can read me 'The Snow Queen.'"

"No. He needs to sleep."

Katie dragged Olivia back to her room. I breathed in and out carefully. The cat was at my feet—unmoved by my outburst. I petted her and said, "Hi, Snow Princess," just to try out my voice, and make sure it had recovered.

Snow Princess. Olivia and Sophia named her that. They agree on little but their love for the cat and a preoccupation with princessry. Sophia wasn't into fairy tales like Olivia, but was game to put on a princess outfit whenever the opportunity presented itself. Sophia would sometimes sit with me in a fluffy violet dress while I watched baseball. Her quiet concentration impressed me. She'd wait until commercials to ask "Are the Red Sox going to beat on them?"

Maybe it was the frequency with which the girls donned tulle that made them seem such strange and ethereal creatures to me. Strange in a good way, don't get me wrong. Maybe if I'd had sisters they wouldn't seem so strange. Or maybe it was that there were two of them—they seemed to overwhelm the house like Thing One and Thing Two in their *Cat in the Hat* book—these two small, messy-haired, wild-eyed little people who showed up in our lives a mere month before Brookhaven. I worry occasionally about the juxtaposition of these events. We've never mentioned it to the girls, but sometimes I'm sure Olivia sees it in my eyes—a dark story that I'm keeping from her. I can tell she's determined to get it out of me, one way or another.

NADINE

OUR SESSIONS MOVED along, leaving Mr. Brewster in the rear view. You maybe knew I couldn't explain what happened *in November,* so you were content that I'd at least described it, thereby owning it to some degree. Maybe you thought that was all I was capable of, for the time being. So you let it drop for a while.

You asked me how I was getting along with my mother and stepfather, now that I was home so much. I said that I didn't see them much more than I had when I was in school, because of course they still worked.

I answered truthfully that I didn't know how to deal with their fear—their fear of me. My latest strategy was making dinner. See harmless little old me, being helpful? Just the good girl you've always known, making dinner. New and improved me, in fact. I started watching cooking shows and getting cookbooks out of the library. I tried an Italian cookbook and made carbonara. I got out a Jewish cookbook and made knishes. I bought copies of *Martha Stewart Living* and quickly gained an appreciation for her misunderstood perfectionism. It made complete sense to me, overcompensating for one's dark soul with tres leches cupcakes and clafouti.

"It helps me to pass all the time by myself," I said. "But I think sometimes they feel guilty that they might be enjoying the food too much. Like the food is made of my depravity or the blood of my social studies teacher, or something."

"They let you use kitchen knives?" you asked.

I gave you a funny look. What the fuck was wrong with you?

You shrugged—almost self-consciously, I thought.

"No, I have to cut everything with emery boards and grapefruit spoons," I said finally. "It's very frustrating."

You cracked a smile. "I'm sorry. I didn't know how strict your parents were being with that sort of thing."

"You didn't discuss it with my parents at all?" I asked. "Whether or not I should be allowed near knives and things?"

You shook your head. "No."

"How much *do* you talk to my mom and stepdad?"

"I respect your confidentiality, as we've discussed before. I wouldn't tell them anything you say unless I think you or someone else is in danger."

"I know, I know. But how much do you talk to them? How much have *they* told you?"

A decidedly quizzical expression. "Told me about what?"

"I don't know. About how I act at home. About what I was like when I was younger. About my family."

"Just the basics, Nadine. Mostly I was told about the trouble with your teacher, and your subsequent hospitalization."

Subsequent. You had this thing about using formal words when it was entirely unnecessary. I always wondered if it was to sound deliberately clinical, to remind me that we weren't friends.

"But what do you know about *before* all of that?"

I studied your face, searching for signs of nervousness or pause. I saw a subtle head cock, but nothing more.

"Very little that you and I haven't discussed directly. Basic family information. When your parents split up, when your mother remarried, when your father passed away. Things your mother thought I ought to know."

Was that last phrase code for something? I tried to decipher this in my head, but gave up and asked, "And were there things included in that that we haven't talked about at all?"

"Is there something she should've included, that you'd like to talk about?"

"No," I said. "It would just make me feel stupid, telling you stuff you already know."

"The basic facts your mother tells me aren't really that important," you said. "How you feel, and how you deal with those feelings, is what we're concerned about here."

I snorted.

"Is that funny?"

"It's tedious," I said, maybe wanting to counter your *subsequent.*

"It's important," you murmured.

Your voice was flat and unconvincing. I appreciated that you weren't going to try too hard. You weren't going to fake it, not really. It wasn't *that* important, how I felt. We all just had to pretend it was, so I could get back to something like normal life, and you could get your ninety dollars. There was a precious honesty in our exchange.

I decided that the next time I tried a new recipe, it would be some sort of cookie or sweet bread. I'd bring it to your office with a generous smile and see if you'd eat any of it with me. Yes, of course it was a way to mess with you. But it was also a way to let you know that your presence had quickly become my favorite place. So favorite it hurt. So favorite I knew I might never get over it.

I BROUGHT A small tin of cardamom crisps to our next session. I'd decided on that recipe because it was slightly sophisticated without having a lot of expensive ingredients. Of course, you looked horrified when I offered them to you.

"I made a ton," I said. "I'm giving them out."

"Who else have you given them to?" you wanted to know.

"My tutor," I lied. "I'd give some to my friends if I had any friends left."

I balanced the open tin on the thick arm of your leather chair, and retreated back to the couch.

I don't remember what we talked about while I gobbled my cardamom crisp, but somehow the conversation rolled around to my father—as it did every few weeks.

"Sometimes I feel like I killed him," I admitted. I'd say anything to make you eat one of those goddamned cookies.

"Can you explain why you'd feel that way?" you asked.

"Because he was perfectly happy being a hippie until my mom remarried and Anthony started becoming a little bit of a father character in my life. Then suddenly my dad wants to live near me again, wants to come back and work at Brookhaven and pretend to be a regular guy with a nine to five."

"Brookhaven?" You looked understandably surprised. "Along with Anthony?"

"Not along with. Anthony's the finance manager and my dad was doing groundskeeping. I think Anthony actually put in a good word for him to get that job, although no one ever said that directly."

You nodded, then looked like you were about to ask more about this curious workplace proximity of father and stepfather. But instead you asked, "How do you know it was pretending, for your dad?"

"Because he was kind of miserable."

"How do you know that?"

"The death by overdose kind of gave it away."

"Alright, yes. But before that?"

I shrugged. "I don't know. He seemed kinda tired a lot. Especially the last couple of times I saw him."

"It was hard work he was doing, wasn't it? Hard physical work? Groundskeeping at Brookhaven?"

"Yeah."

You paused for a while, and then said, "Did you see him the week he died?"

I shook my head. "We were supposed to have dinner and then he called to say he wasn't feeling well. He died the next night."

Another pause. "I'm sure that was very painful for you. I'm sorry."

"Thanks."

"Do you want to talk about how those first few days were?"

"Not really. They were terrible. They were sad. I don't want to talk about it."

We were quiet for a while.

"I want to get back to this thing you said about feeling like you killed him," you said.

"I shouldn't have said it. I didn't mean it. Sometimes I come here feeling like I need to say something complicated."

Your mouth and eyelids worked up and down until they settled into a decidedly bemused expression. "But I wonder where that thought comes from? Is it fair to say you felt guilty when he died?"

"Yeah. Sure."

"Can you explain what you felt guilty *for*?"

"I just did. That he didn't like his life, because he was doing all of this stuff he hated on account of me. Working a shitty, conventional job that left him too exhausted to do anything creative or meaningful with his life. And that's what made him decide to end it."

"This was your twelve-year-old self thinking, or this is your thinking now?"

"More then than now. It was easier to think someone killed him than that he killed himself, accidentally or on purpose."

"And who better to blame but yourself."

"A twelve-year-old might not understand the situation well enough to think of anyone else to blame, right?"

You nodded. You liked this for some reason.

"Right," you said. And you stared at your hands and worked them against each other as if applying imaginary lotion. As you did so, I noticed you were no longer wearing a wedding ring. Before I had a chance to absorb this observation, you took a cookie from my little red tin and nibbled around the edges.

"I don't want to be presumptuous," you said, after a while. "But don't you think it's fair to suppose that everyone has dark moments—dark nights of the soul—that have little to do with those around us?"

"Yeah," I offered. "That's fair. So am I supposed to try to understand his dark moments? Step outside of myself and understand his pain as something totally separate from me?"

"Well. You can try, certainly. But there may be a point when you have to accept that there's only so much you can understand. Of another person's suffering, that is. Especially if that person is no longer with us to describe it himself."

We were quiet then, and I wondered what you meant by *dark moments.* I wondered if you and I were thinking about the same thing. If we were finally going to get real here, about my father and about me.

"You work at Brookhaven sometimes, don't you?" I asked.

You looked startled. "Well . . . yes. I do some counseling there, part time."

"And that's how you know Dr. Morrison?"

You were tight-lipped now. "Well . . . I've known him quite a while, actually. Does this matter?"

"I know you know him because that's how my mom and stepdad got your name as a recommendation when I was in the hospital. Through him."

You nodded. "I see."

"So since you know him, and since you've worked at Brookhaven some, I wonder if you heard about my dad already?"

"Heard about him?"

"Well . . . for one thing . . . that he stole some drugs from Brookhaven. Right before he died."

You looked genuinely surprised. "I didn't know that."

"Oh. Okay. You didn't?"

"Nadine, I never knew of your dad before you became my patient. And I just started counseling there recently, so I never met your dad. If I had, I'd have told you. It wouldn't be appropriate for me to keep something like that from you."

"I know . . . I know *that.* I just wondered if anyone talked about him after the fact."

"Well . . . not to me, Nadine."

I stared at you, wondering if I could break you if you were lying. You were probably used to lying to patients. At least, lying by omission.

"Okay," I said reluctantly.

"You've been wondering if I knew that? About the drugs?"

"Yeah."

"Um . . . You know, Nadine . . . in a place like that, where everybody's busy taking care of patients who have so many daily needs . . . I don't think rumors last long. I don't think people have much time for gossip that's a few years old."

I was silent.

"And I think it's true of most situations," you continued, "that people are usually just trying to get by and do their jobs . . . don't have time to think and talk about other people as much as we *think* they do."

And then you gave me this patient, reassuring smile. It was early summer by then. The smell of fresh mown lawn was wafting into your office from the front landscaping of the building. Mown lawn smell had, in fact, used to make me think of my father.

Ah, grown-ups! I was supposed to think. *Just getting by. Shucks! Just taking care of business. I'd learn. I'd learn life was not all about me. About people looking at me and talking about me. When I learned that, I'd probably stop stabbing people.*

I wanted to get back to *dark moments.* To maybe clarify what those were. Tell you something you didn't know. But then, there was such comfort in *this* moment. In the smell from the window, and the gentle breeze that brought it. You pretending to teach me something, and me pretending to learn something. Us sharing that in this sweet, avuncular quiet.

DECEMBER 17, 2015

HENRY

I CALLED THE NAUGATUCK computer forensics folks first thing in the morning. They put me in touch with the officer who'd been working with Fabian's computer, and she told me that she'd had some luck opening the desktop, but not the e-mail account or the TheraPro software he'd apparently been using for his patients.

"It looks like it's double password protected."

"I'll be seeing his son later today. Long shot, but I'm thinking he might know some of his dad's passwords," I said.

"Here's hoping on that one. We'll keep working on it. I'm going to try to talk with someone at this TheraPro company and see if we can get anywhere with that. In the meantime, there was something interesting on his web browser. He'd done a Google search for this news article the last time the computer was on—on Tuesday. If you give me your e-mail address, I'll forward you the link."

"Thanks," I said.

So, no listing of patients' last names yet. It seemed to me the key to all of this was the patient roster, and if we didn't get a sense of that soon, we were kind of fucked.

The Naugatuck officer's e-mail came in about a minute later.

This was up on Mark Fabian's web browser, it said, and then there was a link to a news article from the *Connecticut Courier,* written in 2013:

SECOND ASSAULT ATTEMPT RAISES CONCERNS ABOUT CARRICK CENTER

For the second time in three months, a sexual assault has been reported in downtown Westford.

The first assault occurred on October 25. A Westford resident in her 40s reported that when she was approaching her car in the lower parking area at approximately 8:45 P.M. a masked man wielding a knife forced her behind a car, where he groped her and tried to force her to perform a sexual act.

The second assault occurred on the sidewalk outside of Trout Brook Park. The second victim, a 20-year-old from East Haven who was housesitting in Westford, says that a man followed her from Cumberland Farms, grabbed her, and tried to pull her into the park. She reported that she scratched and kicked him and managed to escape.

"He was wearing a baseball cap and winter scarf, so she did not get a good look at his face," reports Detective Lupton of the Westford Police. "It was also very dark. But we are looking for a tall male, probably in his 30s or 40s."

Both assaults have occurred within a mile of the Carrick Center, an inpatient and outpatient drug rehabilitation facility that opened its doors in 2009. Westford residents who live in the vicinity of the assaults have expressed concern that the location of the clinic is increasing crime in the area.

"I've always been a little wary of that place," said Travis Farber of Trout Brook Lane. "How closely are they monitoring who is coming in and out of there?"

"I have two daughters," said another Trout Brook Lane resident who did not wish to be named. "Can I let them walk to the store anymore?"

"There are perverts everywhere," disagrees his neighbor, Nathan Mordecai. "I wouldn't be surprised if this guy was homegrown."

Alese Prater, the director of the Carrick Center, echoed this sentiment. "Sexual violence and addiction are entirely different issues. People come here because they need help.

"The first step here is to look at the facts objectively and not make any snap judgments. There is no evidence that the perpetrator of either assault was in any way associated with the Carrick Center. We know nothing about the perpetrator of this crime. We are concerned about these incidents as well. Our patients are as vulnerable as anyone else who spends time in this area—if not more. It sounds like there might have been two perpetrators. I would hope that we can all work together to make this place safer."

> The Westford Police Department will be holding a town meeting at 7 P.M. on Tuesday. "This will be an opportunity for Westford residents to hear the facts of these two incidents, to inform themselves as to the steps we are taking to ensure their safety, and to voice their concerns," said Detective Lupton.
>
> The department is also planning to offer a RAD self-defense course to Westford residents in the near future.
>
> "This is only one of many plans we are putting into action in response to this very serious matter," said Lupton. "All concerned citizens should attend the meeting."

I considered the article for a few minutes before sending back a "Thanks," and then approaching Amy's desk with it. She was twisting an earring with one hand, holding a paper coffee cup with the other.

"Take a look at this," I said. "Remember when this was happening in 2013 in Westford?"

She read it. "Yeah, I remember. They never caught the guy, did they?"

"No. I'm pretty sure they didn't. But I ought to check on that. And I'm thinking about why Fabian would've cared about this now. As a shrink, he might've had patients who go to this clinic . . . or who had in the past."

"Or maybe one of his patients was one of the victims," Amy said. "Of one of these assaults specifically, or one like it."

"Right," I said. "That, too. I'm thinking we should contact Westford and see if we can ask them to talk to those victims to see if there's any connection to Fabian there. And work on seeing if he had patients who also did drug rehab at the clinic."

"How do we go about that, exactly? When we don't even know who his patients were?"

"Well, we can go to the clinic and see if they can tell us if any of their patients are also *his* patients."

"Of course that will require more warrants." Amy sighed. "Which will be complicated if we don't have names of specific patients."

"We'll see what we've got by the end of the day. Can you call Westford for now? I've got an interview in a few minutes and we'll talk after that."

"Sounds good."

My interview was set up for nine o'clock. Dr. Eugene Morrison called the department at about seven A.M., asking if he could come in and talk about Fabian. He said he'd talked to Fabian recently. I wasn't surprised that Dr. Morrison knew Fabian, because he seemed to know everyone. So many Campion people had worked at Brookhaven over the years, as its size and reputation had grown as one of New England's best eldercare facilities. I, on the other hand, knew him from various memorials and ceremonies we'd both attended in the months following the shooting.

I liked Dr. Morrison a lot. At first I wasn't sure how to talk to him because he was a fancy doctor, because he'd been far more heroic than any of us, and because he sometimes wore a bow tie. But once, a few months after the shooting, we both attended a town event at which we were "honored" in the high school auditorium, with a bunch of town dignitaries present.

Afterward there were crackers and cheese and cookies in the lobby by the old trophy cases. He came up behind me while I selected a second oatmeal cookie.

It feels like we're at a really nice dog show, he murmured in my ear, practically falling into me as he steadied himself on his cane. *And we're the dogs.*

Then we ate our cookies in silence, because not much else needed to be said.

Now, when I checked the front lobby he was already there—I recognized his bald head and slouched posture. He was sitting with a George Clooneyesque sort of guy—tall, salt and pepper hair and a white dress shirt with purple suspenders—who was looking at his phone.

"Dr. Morrison. Come on back," I said, approaching him and shaking his hand.

The dapper fellow helped Morrison up. "I'm Scott Morrison," he said, and also shook my hand. "I think we've met before. Maybe at the one-year memorial."

"Yes. Right," I said, although I had no recollection of him. "Good to see you."

"You want me to come in, Dad?" Scott said.

Morrison shook his head as he lumbered toward me.

"No," he said, taking my outstretched arm. "I know you need to get to work."

"My sister's picking him up in about an hour," Scott said. "I mean, it's fine if you need longer than an hour, but that's what we worked out, because I have to go."

I nodded. I knew that Morrison couldn't drive at all after the shooting. I felt bad for him, and tried to think of something to momentarily lighten the mood.

"You shaved your mustache," I said, closing the interview room door.

Morrison seemed stunned by the observation—though just for a moment. He leaned forward and folded his hands on the small white table in front of him.

"Yes," he said softly, and then grimaced. "A couple of months ago."

I realized then that I'd been glib. He'd lost a colleague—maybe a friend—so the thing about the mustache wasn't the right way to start.

"I'm sorry. I'm sorry for your loss, Dr. Morrison."

"*Eugene.* Henry, please."

"Dr. Fabian was a close friend?" I asked.

"A colleague, and we were on friendly terms. I've known him for years. So it's a shock."

"Thank you for coming in. I'm sure it's difficult. Do you want a coffee before we get started?"

Morrison shook his head. It was easy to forget that Morrison was technically a shrink. He had been the director of Brookhaven since its opening in the late eighties until the shooting in 2010—after which he'd retired, partly due to his injuries. And I'd known him from around town long before it had happened.

But Morrison *was* a trained psychiatrist, and maybe that

made him even more of a shrink than Fabian, since he had an MD. Or did that make him less of a shrink? I wasn't sure.

"So when you called, you said you talked to him on Tuesday."

Morrison nodded. "I'd have to check my phone again for the exact time. But yes. Tuesday. Oh my God."

Morrison rubbed his bald head, looking distressed at the memory of the conversation.

"What did you talk about?" I asked.

"He was having some difficulty . . . you know, we were often mentors to each other. He had a situation . . . he wanted my take."

"What kind of a situation?"

Morrison hesitated. "I can't give you names because he didn't give me any. I would if I had any."

"But what was the situation?"

"He was having difficulty with a former patient."

"A *former* patient." I paused before writing this down. "Are you sure about that?"

"Yes." Morrison closed his eyes and sighed. "This person was harassing him and he wasn't sure if taking precautionary action would escalate the situation unnecessarily."

I wondered, with Fabian's retirement coming up, if very recently dropped patients would also be considered "former" patients.

"Was it a man or a woman?" I asked.

"He didn't say, actually. One grows accustomed to seeking professional advice in this very general way . . . revealing as few details as possible, for the sake of the patient's confidentiality."

"Okay. Then did he specify what form this harassment took? Calling him? Showing up at his home? What?"

"There was an unexpected office visit, and also a note of some kind."

"Did this patient threaten physical harm?" I asked. "What did the note say?"

"I believe it was something like, 'I wish things had been different between you and me.' Something of that nature. I can't recall the exact wording. There was an expression of dissatisfaction. No direct threat of physical harm, but it was implied. That's why he was eager to consult me and, I assume, other colleagues. It was a 'gray area' kind of situation."

"I see."

"In my position at Brookhaven I never experienced much of that, for obvious reasons. You know, they were all elderly inpatients. But in a more conventional therapy situation, it's fairly common for a patient to become confused about a situation . . . to cross a boundary, you know? As the therapist, one often needs to figure out how to remedy the situation without overreacting, because in overreacting we potentially harm the patient, and betray their trust. That's why it's often important to consult colleagues . . . to check yourself. To make sure you're not responding inappropriately."

It seemed like *inappropriate* was a very important word in the therapy world. Which is kind of sad, in a way—considering what happened to Fabian. It's all very inappropriate in the end, isn't it?

"Were there any phone calls from this individual?"

"Well, the unexpected visit was what really concerned him.

But I believe he said there was a phone call as well. I can't remember for sure. It was more the note that he most wanted to discuss."

"Okay," I said. We were still waiting on phone records, but I was expecting them by the end of the day. "Did he mention if it was a recent patient, or . . ."

"He didn't say. You know, in this line of work, patients come and go. Sometimes a few years later, someone will come back if they find themselves wanting to talk to you again. If they have some new difficulty, you know? Some new life challenge. That in itself isn't all that unusual."

"Okay," I said. "But in this case, this wasn't just regular contact. It was in the 'gray area,' you said. Meaning it bordered on harassment?"

"Yes. That was my understanding."

"I see. Okay. And did he give any other details?"

"No." Morrison took off his glasses. "He asked for my opinion. And I said that I thought that at this stage it was a matter of instinct. How well did he know the patient from the past? Was there any sense of danger back when he was treating him or her? Was this perhaps the patient's way of getting him to take them seriously? And little more than that? We really just chatted along those lines for a few minutes. We left it that we'd give it a couple of days, and maybe meet and talk more extensively next weekend if the situation escalated."

Morrison slid his glasses back on and leaned forward in his chair, clasping both hands together tight. He stared at his fingers for a minute.

"Henry . . . I know you share this feeling with me. Of that day. Wishing we could do it over again, in a different way."

He was speaking so softly I had to lean in close to hear him. "That if I had done one thing differently, the count would have been nine or eight or seven."

I stared at him, my face still up close with his. His square black eyeglass frames were probably selected to disguise the softness of his face—to make himself look more clinical and more severe than he really was. Beneath them, his cheeks were pink, his jowls plump, his eyes bright but drooping at the outer corners. There were some unshaven white whiskers on his chin.

"Less than ten would've been nice. Less than ten might have kept the press a little more under control."

I stood up and adjusted the blinds, so the morning sun wouldn't hit him right in the face. "There would've been just as much press," I said. "No matter the number. It was the setting that shocked everyone."

Morrison was still for a few moments. I wasn't sure if he'd heard me. He pulled off his glasses again, wiped his eyes with the backs of his hands, and then fixed his gaze on the ceiling.

"Can I get you anything?" I asked.

"No," Morrison said. "I should have done something or said something different, Henry. I mean, with Mark. With what I've experienced, why wouldn't I advise to assume the worst-case scenario, from now on?"

I shook my head. "On the face of it, what he said about this former patient doesn't sound *that* extreme. And we don't know what happened yet, Eugene."

"If I'd given him better advice, maybe . . ."

I didn't know what more I could say. Or what more he could have done.

At Brookhaven, Morrison was the one who practically threw himself at the gunman. And unlike me, *he* did it without a gun.

"You did everything you were supposed to," I said.

"That's kind of you to say," Morrison said, looking past me. Recognizing my reassuring bullshit, probably, for exactly what it was. Just as I recognized it when other people tried it on me. I should know better.

"You have your phone on you?" I asked. "Can you check the time that he called? We'll be accessing all of his records, of course, but if you have that now, it'll help."

"Of course," Morrison said, and tapped on his phone for a moment. "He called me at 1:11 on Tuesday."

I made a note of the time. I suspected that Fabian had placed this call to Morrison shortly after speaking to this out-of-control former patient—either in person or on the phone—whoever he or she might be.

"Eugene, there was something in Dr. Fabian's notes that I'd like you to take a look at."

"Of course."

I took the legal pad out of my desk drawer and flipped to the page that said:

TR 4/12/91
Patty–Patsy
Greensomething?
Brookhaven 2001

"Any idea what this might mean?" I asked, handing him the pad. "The Brookhaven reference surprised me."

"Well, I don't know about what it says before the mention of Brookhaven," Dr. Morrison said, studying the notes. "But Mark *did* do some counseling for us at Brookhaven in the late nineties and the early 2000s."

"Oh. I see. As far back as '91?" I asked.

"No. I can't remember the exact dates. But starting maybe in '96, '97, '98, thereabouts. I recall he needed medical insurance. So associating himself with Brookhaven for a certain number of hours a week allowed him to get insurance through our arrangement, and then he was able to maintain his private practice later in the day. Before that I believe he was getting insurance through his wife's job. But they divorced. I knew he was in this predicament, so when I had an opening, I made this arrangement with him."

"He wasn't working there at the time of the shooting, was he?"

"Oh, no. No, he stopped counseling at Brookhaven at least ten years ago."

"Okay. And TR? That date in '91? The name Patty or Patsy? Any of that ring a bell?"

Morrison slowly shook his head. "No . . . I'm sorry. I'll think about it, but as I mentioned, we often didn't use names when we talked."

"Well, if you think of anything, give me a call, okay?"

"Sure."

"Oh, and by the way . . . in connection with this difficult former patient, or anyone else, did he mention any sexual assaults that happened in Westford a couple of years ago?"

"Sexual assaults?" Morrison looked tired. "I'm not following."

"There were some sexual assaults in 2013. I don't know if you'd remember."

"Uh . . . no. No, I don't recall. I don't believe he said anything like that about any patients. He never would've been that specific."

"Or any patients who'd been treated at the Carrick Center in Westford?"

"Again, he wouldn't have any reason to be that specific with me. If he thought this particular patient needed treatment for drug addiction, he perhaps might have mentioned that in general terms. But he didn't. That doesn't mean that wasn't the case. But that wasn't really the scope of that conversation. It was more about the harassment specifically."

"Okay. Now, is there anything else that you can tell me about his recent life that you think might be helpful?"

"Well . . . I'm afraid the call was kind of out of the blue. We hadn't talked much in the last year or two. But . . . Henry . . . tell me. Are you running into a lot of difficulty tracking down Fabian's current and former patients?"

I tried to keep my face neutral, so as not to telegraph how poorly this part of the investigation was going. "We're getting there."

"Because . . . I want to offer you a few suggestions."

"Okay?"

"He used a billing company. That might help with some of his current clients."

"We're already on that."

"Good. But I believe he also had an accountant. An accountant might be less tight-fisted with information than a medical billing company. As of a few years ago, I believe he used the same accountant as me. Lorraine Bancroft, on Nutmeg Street. A mutual friend. She might have copies of old checks and financial records that Mark might have filed with them. Maybe a couple of years back, who knows?"

"Okay," I said, trying not to look too hungry for this as I wrote it down. "Now, regarding former patients. What's customary for therapists, when it comes to patient files? How long do you keep them?"

"I can tell you that Mark probably held on to records from seven years back. Or more. But seven years, because that's the cutoff for getting sued. You hold on to the stuff for that long, just in case."

"Would you keep files from further back than seven years, Dr. Morrison?"

"Would *I*? If I was still in private practice, you mean?"

"Yeah."

"Hmm. Probably, for a while longer at least. Once a patient, always a patient, they say. There's always a chance a patient will come back. But after seven years? It's not likely they'll ever come back, and even if they did . . . things would've changed so much that we'd start from scratch. The catching up might be therapeutic."

"Once a patient, always a patient? Is that something they say?"

"Well. There are different schools of thought on this. But the traditional thinking is that once someone is your patient, you cannot and should not ever have any kind of relationship outside of therapy. You can't invite each other to dinner parties after that. You can't go disco dancing together."

Disco dancing. Lest I forget how old Eugene was.

"Because . . . because the therapist knows too much about the patient to ever be friends?"

"Well . . . that, sure. That would perhaps be up to the patient to decide. But the real issue is that the therapist should always be there for the patient *as a therapist* should the need ever arise. So you maintain that distance in case that happens."

"Interesting," I said. "You know, I'll probably have some more therapy questions for you later, but I think I'm going to let you get on with your morning for now. I'm curious, is it Amanda who's picking you up?"

Morrison nodded. I knew he had three or four kids. Amanda Morrison went to high school with me, but I didn't know her well.

"Tell her I said hi, okay?"

"I will."

"Are all your kids still local?" I asked.

"No. Amanda and Scott are. But Justin is in Atlanta."

I helped him up, and as we made our way toward the front entrance, he said, "You know . . . '91. I recall Mark had a patient die in the early nineties. I don't remember what year. But it was a suicide, a young woman, and he was really shaken by it. That was a rough few years for Mark, I think. Around when that happened."

"Okay. Hmm. Maybe that's what he's referring to in the note."

"Possible. Just a thought."

"I wonder . . . could it be that a *relative* of a patient was recently in contact with him? Rather than the patient himself . . . or herself?"

I could imagine a relative of a suicide being angry at the deceased's shrink for not preventing the death somehow. But on the other hand, I couldn't imagine why it would take over twenty years for the grudge to come to a head.

"Uh . . ." Morrison shook his head. "No. That's not the situation he presented to me."

"Maybe in the note . . . he was just going over memorable cases in his mind. Since he was about to retire."

"Yes . . ." Morrison said, and then sighed. "That's entirely possible."

As I opened the door for him, Morrison said, "You needn't wait outside with me. I'd rather have a little time alone on the bench out there. Before Amanda comes and plays mother hen for the rest of the morning."

"I understand," I said. But I helped him down the steps and helped him get settled on the bench.

"It's actually a strangely warm day for December, don't you think?" Eugene squinted up into the sky. "Don't wait with me, Henry. I know you have work to do."

When I went inside, I looked up the accountant Lorraine Bancroft. She was still in town, and still in business. But I had planned to talk to Fabian's son again this morning. I asked Greg to go see Ms. Bancroft, and went to see Brendan Fabian myself.

NADINE

I DON'T SLEEP AT all in the chamber of the roses. I convince myself that it's simply this room that's exhausting me of my good senses, and that I've got to escape it despite this early hour. Not that I have a place to go. I had mentioned Gillette Castle—where my mother and father had occasionally brought me when I was small—to my mother to pad my itinerary. And she'd suggested this inn because of its proximity to the castle. But really, I'd just wanted to get a break from Campion, and to keep from straining my mother's and my tolerance for each other. But of course I won't be going to any damned castle now.

I dress in the dark and leave the old lady innkeeper a big tip on the dresser, to thank her for the scissors and compensate for any confusion my early departure might cause. I tiptoe down the stairs as quietly as I can, and get in my car. My tires crunch over the gravel driveway. I cringe, imagining the innkeeper awakening.

AS A SMALL act of rebellion, I would sometimes linger outside your office building after our session, and smoke a cigarette. I knew that from your side of the building, you couldn't see me. It didn't matter. It turned out I liked cigarettes more than I cared whether you saw me or not. So I'd decided it was a psychologically healthy act.

And then one day in the early spring of 1997—the spring of my alternative high school graduation—that guy in the shirt-sleeves suddenly appeared again. I hadn't seen him in months. But there he was, walking toward the curb as I sat there smoking and reading *The Sandman*.

He definitely recognized me.

"Hey," I said.

"Hello." He stood over me, scrutinizing the cover of my comic book.

"What did you say your name was again?" I asked.

"Johnny," he said. "And you are?"

"Nadine."

"Can I have one of those?"

"What . . . a cigarette?"

"Yeah."

I checked my watch and smiled up at him. "You don't have time, Johnny."

He bit his lip and said, "How about after?"

"After?"

"After. After I put in my fifty minutes."

"More like forty-five minutes now, my friend. How about I leave you one right here on the corner for later?"

"You gonna leave your lighter for me, too?"

"Don't really want to," I said. "Then I'll need to buy a new one."

"Then stay. Looks like you have something to read. Just stay."

His eyes were relaxed, but his mouth was twisted into an expression that was clearly trying to be a smile but couldn't quite manage it. His hair was still so short it was almost military in its appearance.

"I'll think about it," I said. "It *is* a nice day."

"It is," Johnny said, and then went inside.

And I waited, like he asked. In the last few minutes, I almost walked away. But ultimately, I was curious. Because I was so cold and bitter and academic at the alternative school, no one ever flirted with me. Because Johnny seemed a little older and more self-assured than my troubled classmates—never mind his peculiar fashion choices: stiff dark jeans and oversized collared shirt.

"You're still here," he said quietly as I closed my comic book and handed him a cigarette.

I shrugged and stood up. "Bouffant treat you nice today?"

"Bouffant?"

"That's what I call him."

Johnny smiled without opening his mouth. "Nice."

We each smoked a cigarette while we walked around the block. Johnny asked me if I went to Campion High, and I said, simply, "No."

He said, "I didn't, either."

Past tense. He was older than me, as I'd suspected.

He told me he worked at the video store. We talked about movies for a minute, and he asked me if I'd seen *Primal Fear* yet. I said no and he said I really ought to. That he'd see it again if I was looking for someone to watch it with. I told him that I never went to the movies, not anymore.

And he didn't ask for clarification on "not anymore," but said he was thinking of renting *Trainspotting* again soon, and had I seen that? I said no.

"What about *Fargo*? Seen that?"

"Nope."

"*The Cable Guy*?" he growled.

"Uh . . . no."

When we got back to the parking lot, Johnny asked me if I wanted a ride home "or somewhere." I said no thanks.

"Can I have your number?" he asked. "Even if you don't want to see *Primal Fear,* maybe you'd want to see something else."

"Sure," I said, even though I wondered if he'd call me just to keep barking movie titles at me. I wasn't sure I'd like that, but it wasn't like any other guys were calling me. This could still go somewhere interesting, I guessed. Somewhere that might be fun to tell you about later, and see what kind of look might bloom on your face.

HENRY

I'D TOLD FABIAN'S son I'd come and chat with him again at around nine.

Main Street traffic was in its usual snarl, so I went through my old neighborhood to make my way to the east side of town. Passing by my parents' old place, I did my reflexive double take. I can never get used to seeing it painted green instead of white. It's like I've gone color-blind for a moment. It shocked me when my parents announced they were moving to Colorado eight years ago. Turns out they'd only come to this suburban paradise to raise my brother and me—and had little nostalgia for the place once that was over.

I wasn't surprised that Fabian's house was in one of the newer developments further out. By newer, I mean built in the eighties, when our town size doubled. I like to think of myself as a townie because my parents moved here in the late seventies—before it was the popular thing to do. Before the schools started topping the "Best of Connecticut" lists.

I was surprised, though, to find that Fabian's house was

one of the more modest ones on the east side of town. I guess I'd always thought shrinks were rolling in it. When I pulled into the driveway, Brendan was on the brick steps, shivering in sweatpants and a T-shirt. His eyes were red and his cheeks looked streaked and raw.

"You look cold, Brendan," I called as I approached him. "Can we talk inside?"

"I was waiting for you," Brendan said absently. "And I'm not cold."

As Eugene had pointed out, it was a particularly balmy day for December.

"But can we—"

"Yeah," Brendan said. "I have something I want to show you."

Indoors, we sat at the kitchen table and Brendan offered me coffee, which I refused.

"So I thought of something late last night," he said.

"Okay," I replied. "Good."

Brendan put his hands over his temples and started clawing at his hair. "I don't know what my dad would think of this."

I waited for him to go on, glancing around the kitchen. Dishes and a ketchup bottle were in the sink, and on the counter was a cutting board with brown apple slices on it.

"I wanted to tell you about something," Brendan said. "The last night I saw him. I got home late, and I was surprised he was up. And I told you he got out the bourbon, which he had never done before. So we put away a couple of shots together. First time we ever did anything like that. But I actually had the feeling these weren't his first shots that night.

"And he told me he was happy I'm training to do radiology.

He said he was glad I'd settled on something that didn't involve a lot of bullshit. I wasn't sure if that was a compliment or not. But the more he talked, the more I figured what we were really talking about was *his* retirement, not *my* decisions."

Brendan plucked a cloth placemat from the table and began rolling it up very tightly. "And maybe you don't need to know all this. But after everything yesterday, I couldn't sleep. I was wandering around the house, and I saw these files lying on his dresser. Just right there on his dresser, like he'd shoved them up there and gone to bed. And it seems . . . impossible . . . but . . . just wait here."

Brendan unrolled the placemat and got up. I heard him shuffling around in the living room for a minute before he came back with two file folders, tattered and yellowing at the tabs. He tossed them onto the kitchen table.

"I don't know if he'd have wanted me to give these to you . . . but if it helps you figure out who . . . who . . ." He shook his head.

I didn't touch the folders. I was waiting for Brendan to finish.

"I think these must be from his file in the garage. I don't think he would've ever been allowed to give you this, but *I* can, because I'm not a shrink and I don't know the rules. Get it?"

"Got it," I said softly. The clusterfuck of which the DA spoke came to mind. As the kid of a shrink, Brendan apparently knew a little bit about this stuff.

"You know, I never met a single one of his patients. I mean, that I know of. But I always kind of hated them all."

"Yeah?" I said. He'd said as much yesterday.

"I always had a feeling they got something from him that I never got. And now . . . *fuck.* Look what they did now."

I nodded. "I'm sorry. So, just to be clear. He didn't mention *anything* going on related to his work?"

"No." Brendan shook his head, then pushed the files toward me. "When I saw the top one, I almost puked. Right then and there in my dad's bedroom."

I opened it and glanced at the name written at the top of the first sheet.

Streeter, Johnny.

I felt the paper crumple in my grip. My brain couldn't quite string together any words besides *What the fuck?*

"*What?*" I muttered, after a moment.

"That's basically what I said. It was 1997 or so. He was . . . younger then. I mean, obviously."

"Did you read the whole thing?"

"No. I didn't want to. And I didn't think my dad would want me to. But *you* can. Right?"

"Umm . . . right."

I glanced inside the second folder.

Raines, Nadine.

That name was definitely familiar. Oh, shit. I *knew* that name. Not as well as I knew the name Johnny Streeter. But I knew it. The name stirred a memory—deeper, earlier than Johnny Streeter.

I put both files down for a moment, to keep my hands from clutching them too hard.

"These are both old files," Brendan said. "Really old. I'm not sure which one he was looking at. Or both. They might have been filed close together. Same year, same part of the alphabet."

I was trying to listen to Brendan, but the sentiment *What the fuck?* kept getting in the way.

"I was a little kid then, in 1997," Brendan said. "That was around when my parents split up."

I nodded again.

"I'm hoping it'll help you, somehow. I don't know if Johnny Streeter has someone working for him on the outside, or . . . I know that sounds crazy. I just thought you needed to see this."

"I appreciate that, Brendan," I said. "You shouldn't hesitate to come to us if you think of anything else you want us to know. And did you say something about a file cabinet in the garage?"

"Yeah. My dad's had it there for years, under lock and key. He probably brought it home when he switched his files onto a computer in, like, 2000 or so. I'm not sure what his intention was. To eventually enter the stuff onto his laptop, or to shred it, or to go through it and to figure out what needed shredding and what needed keeping. But whatever he meant to do, the thing just collected dust and had old weed killer and lawn fertilizer piled on top of it."

"And you're pretty sure that's where he got these files from?"

"I know it is. I checked it last night. He'd pushed a bunch of stuff out of the way to get to it, and it was unlocked."

"Brendan, I'd like to take that whole file cabinet with me. Does that sound okay to you?"

"That sounds perfect," Brendan said. "Please—get it out of here."

NADINE

I DRIVE TO A rural gas station, buy a coffee, and sip it while parked by a tire air machine. Even as the caffeine washes through me, my brain is stalled in 1997.

Days and weeks passed, and Johnny didn't call me. My hopes for a massive distraction (*I'm dating one of your other patients! What do you think of that, my friend?*) were dashed, and you pressed on. While we mostly talked about school and trying to make new friends and getting along with my mother, you always eventually circled back to what I'd done *in November.* By then the incident was well over a year past, and I was trying to get on with my life. But for you it was like an itch you couldn't help scratching.

"What do you think was different about that day?" you asked me one session. "That day last November. You'd never done anything like that before, and haven't since. So what do you think was different?"

"People at the hospital kept asking me if voices told me to do it," I offered.

You sighed. "You can see why they might have thought that? Because this thing you did . . . it seemed to come out of nowhere."

"Yeah."

"But there was no voice telling you to do it."

I hesitated and smiled. "None but my own."

"Okay. Can you tell me how you felt right before you did it?"

"I felt angry," I said. And you looked surprised, for this was maybe the first time I hadn't answered, *I don't know* or *I felt cold.*

"At whom? Do you know?"

"Well . . . partly at myself."

You looked even more surprised. Or pretended to, for effect. Cocked your head so far to the side that your fluffy hair rested on your shoulder like an affectionate little kitten. "Yourself? Why?"

"Because I had been thinking of cutting *myself* to get his attention. Which seemed stupid and pathetic."

"So you were angry at yourself . . . but you hurt *him*. How did that happen? Was some of the anger at *him* for provoking you, in a way? Provoking you to potentially commit that stupid and pathetic act of cutting yourself?"

There was an element of truth to your suggestion—an element, although not the whole story. But it seemed only an irrevocably small, sad soul could feel that way, and I didn't want to be an irrevocably small, sad soul.

I took a deep breath and stared out the window. A line of trees separated the back of your office building from a bank parking lot. In the spring and early fall there was a wall of leaves to look at. Now, in late fall, you could see through the branches and watch the cars that occasionally drove up to the ATM machine and drive-through teller.

"Maybe I just lost my nerve at the last second. Maybe I was afraid of how it would feel to hurt myself. And there were two arms right there in front of me, and in the final second, I stabbed the one that wouldn't hurt."

You stared at me for a moment, and then looked away. You pushed your hand against your long chin, making a slight scratching noise against your stubble. You maybe hadn't shaved today. The sound distracted me from the pain our conversation had started to drive into my middle.

What did it feel like to be a man? What did it feel like to be a dinosaur?

"Maybe," you repeated.

"Probably," I said softly.

"I don't know," you said, inexplicably examining a perfectly clean fingernail. Why couldn't you look at me, now that I was finally attempting to answer this most difficult question? "I don't know about 'probably.'"

"Why?"

You looked toward the window now. "Nadine, isn't it possible you've been angry for a very long time?"

I thought about this for a couple of minutes, settling into the comfort of its possibility. I was a teenager. Teenagers get angry. My father had died when I was twelve. Children who experienced such losses were "allowed" to be angry. Expected to, even. And while I wasn't sure this explained anything much, I knew it could *appear* to. And I knew that surrendering to this theory could save me. In your eyes, and others' eyes, if not my own.

Forget all the things I really wanted to tell you. Forget that going for Mr. Brewster's arm was far more an act of self-destruction than going for my own. Forget how clear that should have been to any emotionally adept person—because look what had become of my life. For one thing, my only friend in the world was a forty-something dude with bad hair who got paid ninety bucks an hour to half listen to me. I'd have fared far better if I'd just gone ahead and stabbed myself. I'd have recovered from *that* relatively quickly, likely with sympathy and forgiveness.

Tears bubbled into my eyes. You looked blurry and indistinct in your leather chair. It was almost as if I could see you fading away.

"Do you want to try to tell me how you're feeling right now?" you asked. "Is that a difficult question to answer?"

Tears slid off my cheeks, but I didn't grab one of the tissues from the box next to the couch. In your blurred, almost liquid form, I could see our limited future together. You were giving me this gift—this out. A child's grief unexpressed and then transformed into adolescent anger. Despite the insanity of that moment in that social studies classroom, there was apparently a path toward forgiveness and eventually normalcy. It might not be the most sincere path, but you were offering it, and what could I do but take it?

I was crying for what I would never tell you. Crying for its burial. It would sink deeper into me, calcify, and become a part of my adult being. I'd carry it around like an extra bone or organ. I'd never have to show it or explain it unless someone asked.

You were the only one who was ever potentially going to ask. But now you were perhaps offering me something better.

"No," I sobbed.

"It's not?"

"No!" I said, practically screaming, letting tears and snot fall off my face and onto my shirt.

"No because you are angry or because you're not?"

And suddenly I *was* angry. Angry at you. Angry that you couldn't read between the lines of all my notes and cartoons. That you never would.

"Because I am!" I screamed.

I was still weeping when I went to the waiting room to grab my backpack. I barely noticed Johnny sitting there—for the first time since the day he'd taken my number. I didn't look at him or acknowledge him.

And as I walked home that day, I thought about how I'd seen you sigh—with what I guessed was relief—in that moment that I'd exploded. And then I'd seen you settle more comfortably in your chair in the silence that followed. And then smile—just a little—before telling me it was okay to be angry.

Because, I suppose, to you this was what a breakthrough looked like.

HENRY

THE PARKING LOT of the Campion Dental Group is at the top of one of Campion's highest hills. And from the back spaces of that lot, you can see down the hill into the east side of the Edwards Elementary playground and staff parking lot.

Since September, when my girls started kindergarten at Edwards, I occasionally come and park here when I want a moment to think. I'm not spying on the girls or their teachers—the kindergartners use the playground on the other side. I just like to see signs of the school day chugging along as usual. Kids on the swings. Teachers leaning against the brick building, chatting.

There are two files in my passenger seat.

I don't know which one to read first.

I don't want to be angry at you, Fabian.

Whatever is in there, I've made mistakes, too.

I'm not going to be mad at you.

I don't feel convinced. I imagine a mental health professional wouldn't be, either. I push the file aside. Streeter couldn't have killed Fabian—at least with his own two hands—and he wasn't going anywhere. He could come second.

And didn't Fabian's calendar say he'd seen a "Nadine" on Monday? Was that the name that had said "Find old file" next to it on his legal pad notes? I believed it was. And Nadine wasn't a very common name.

I snatched up the file and opened it.

HOSPITAL DISCHARGE SUMMARY

PATIENT NAME: Nadine Raines
PATIENT DOB: 1/13/79
PATIENT ADMISSION DATE: 11/2/95
PATIENT DISCHARGE DATE: 11/20/95
PHYSICIAN: Dr. Robert Bell, Barnes Memorial Hospital Psychiatric Unit

Patient was admitted at four thirty P.M. on 11/2. She was transported to the hospital by an officer from the Campion police department, and accompanied by her mother, who signed for her admission.

REASON FOR ADMISSION: Violent behavior. The patient injured an adult male (her teacher at Campion High School) with a box cutter knife. No previous incidents of violence known. Patient was calm and cooperative at the time of admission.

The patient has been screened for signs of adolescent onset schizophrenia, and results are negative. She has also screened negative for homicidal and suicidal ideation.

The patient has been tearful in evaluative sessions and expressed remorse for her actions as well as a desire to understand why this violent incident occurred. No further violent or erratic behavior has been observed during the patient's hospitalization. This writer recommends outpatient care or multiple individual counseling sessions per week, under careful observation. Lengthier hospitalization at an adolescent facility is recommended if violent behavior occurs again or any homicidal ideation is observed.

No medications administered.

DIAGNOSIS: In progress.

I knew Nadine Raines. Not well. But she was in my high school class. At least, for some of high school. Her friend Julie was my friend Chris's girlfriend sophomore year.

So I remembered her. Most of us probably did.

I remembered her towering over the other girls while playing volleyball, casually slamming the ball over the net when it flew too high for the others to reach. I remembered her sitting in front of me in social studies class. And of course I remembered the other thing. The thing she did. And then no one ever saw her again, as far as I knew.

INITIAL SESSION PROGRESS NOTE

PATIENT NAME: Nadine Raines
INSURANCE: Health Connecticut
INSURANCE NUMBER: 4709916

INSURANCE HOLDER: Susan Gagliardi
DATE OF SERVICE: 11/22/95
TYPE OF SERVICE: Individual Therapy
SERVICE PROVIDER: Mark Fabian, PsyD

The client is a white female, age sixteen. She attended Campion High School before the incident that precipitated her hospitalization. She presents as well-groomed. The client's mother describes her as "an excellent student," in many honors classes and often on the honor roll. No discipline problems in school prior to the violent incident on 11/2. The client is currently being tutored at home as per an agreement with the local school board. She will not return to the public school this year.

The client lives with her mother and stepfather. She has no siblings. Her father is deceased. Mother reports that he died of a drug overdose after a decade of alcoholism and intermittent drug abuse. The client's mother has been the custodial parent since her parents divorced when she was nine, after which she had occasional contact—usually weekend visits—until his death when she was twelve.

The client often hesitated before answering questions, but did answer them. When asked about her time at the hospital, she said it was "sad" and "scary" but says she understands why her parents and the admitting doctor decided to keep her there for observation. "It was kind of a crisis situation."

When asked why she has come to therapy, she answered

> clearly, "Because of what I did to my teacher." When asked if she was angry with her teacher, she said, "I'm not sure." Client agreed to working together to identify the emotions she was feeling leading up to the incident, and to report to this writer or her parents if she feels similar impulses in the near future.
>
> The client conversed casually about her studies and the wish to keep up academically with her classmates despite her expulsion. Client's vocabulary, demeanor, and length of responses improved when discussion moved away from the events of 11/2 and her subsequent weeks in the hospital.
>
> At the end of the session, client said, "Part of me is having trouble believing this really happened."

I paused here for a moment. I was trying to align this information with the vague picture I had of Nadine Raines in my head.

Before the day she became the girl who stabbed the teacher, she was the tall girl who sat in front of me in social studies, who had a long brown ponytail that would sometimes brush my desk when she'd turn and rummage through her backpack, and who'd smile—without really looking at me—when I'd say things like, *Nope, no homework again today.* Walker, Texas Ranger *was on and a man's got priorities.* Once, after a three-day spate of me taking zeroes for homework, she cringed on my behalf and said, *Are you okay? I mean, for real? Is there some reason you haven't been able to do the homework?* I'd said, *No, not really. Taking little risks like this makes me feel—you know—alive.* And she'd countered with, *You think summer school will make you feel alive?*

Returning to Fabian's notes now, I noticed that there was a nine-month gap between the first session notes and the next report.

PROGRESS UPDATE

PATIENT NAME: Nadine Raines
DATE OF SERVICE: 8/30/96

The client has made significant progress developing coping strategies for her new social and academic situation and says that she is "excited" to start school at the alternative program in Hamden. She attended an art class this summer and reports that she made a new female friend there.

She also reports less frequent conflict with her mother. "When she says something that annoys me, I go to my room and draw her as a pelican saying those same words, and it's kind of funny and it calms me down." The client and her mother are looking forward to two trips to visit colleges together in the fall.

Client's mother reports that she spends most of her time alone in her room drawing or preparing for college entrance exams, but hopes she will be more social when school begins in the fall.

Because client's parents' insurance limit on individual therapy fees was reached a month ago, they have asked if her sessions can be reduced to once per week. This writer recommends maintaining the twice a week sessions for the adjustment period of the opening two weeks of her new school, and then reducing to once per week. During this transition, the client has agreed to keep a weekly journal of her progress on the day of her midweek appointment (Tuesdays), and to call this writer if she feels she needs additional support that day/week. The client is aware that she can request a return to more frequent sessions should the need arise.

PROGRESS UPDATE

PATIENT NAME: Nadine Raines
INSURANCE: Health Connecticut
INSURANCE NUMBER: 4709916
INSURANCE HOLDER: Susan Gagliardi
DATE OF SERVICE: 12/22/96
TYPE OF SERVICE: Individual Therapy

The client has been making progress focusing positively on her academic future and developing new relationships. She has completed her college applications and spent some time outside of school with new classmates from her alternative school, meeting at movies and restaurants. The client and her mother have taken several trips to visit potential colleges, and she reports that these trips were "fun" and "surprisingly chill." Client's mother also reports having a positive experience traveling with her daughter, with no significant arguments.

The client continues to express frustration that she will never be able to return to her home high school. Client said she misses friends and classmates.

"Since I don't have siblings, the kids I grew up with and went to school with are like my siblings. I miss them and it makes me sad to think they'll never be in my life anymore. For them, is it like I stabbed *them*? Because I didn't."

This writer discussed with client positive ways to attempt to re-establish old friendships, boundaries and limits in pursuing those relationships, and coping mechanisms if they do not work out as hoped.

Client has expressed some remorse for injuring her teacher in multiple sessions. In more recent sessions, she has expressed an interest in gaining insight into why she acted so violently, and a desire to ensure that "nothing like that happens again."

In the last two sessions, client has brought up the death of her father and her sadness at the circumstances of his death. She recently stated that if she had talked about her grief more at that age, she believes she would not be in her current situation. This writer recommends reinstating biweekly sessions to give the client ample opportunity to discuss this at greater length before her transition to college in six months.

PROGRESS UPDATE

PATIENT NAME: Nadine Raines
INSURANCE: Health Connecticut
INSURANCE NUMBER: 4709916
DATE OF SERVICE: 8/16/97
TYPE OF SERVICE: Individual Therapy

The client is terminating therapy because she is departing for college in two weeks.

Client says she is positive about attending college and studying art and possibly biology. She is eager to begin a new chapter of her life in a new location.

In previous sessions, the client has refused any assistance finding a therapist in her new location. In this final session, she reiterated that she would avail herself of the counseling services at her new school's medical center, should the need arise. We briefly reviewed some signs of need for assistance (e.g., violent fantasies and impulses, obsessive thoughts).

Client has expressed confidence in her ability to cope with anger in nonviolent ways (physical exercise, drawing and writing exercises, breathing techniques) and to recognize when her need for attention is driving her toward negative thoughts and actions.

The client ended appointment with a gift to this writer—an essay collection by Walker Percy.

The patient's mother has expressed doubts about her ending therapy completely upon departure for college.

The patient, however, has not shown any signs of aggressive, impulsive, or destructive behavior since the isolated incident on 11/2/95 that precipitated her parents seeking psychotherapy for her.

The client is now eighteen years old and therefore legally authorized to make decisions about her own medical care.

That was all that Fabian had written about her. But at the end of the file was one other item—another blue exam booklet. This appeared to be the first one—the entries were dated earlier.

September 24, 1996

Hi. This is awkward. Are we going to be honest and admit that a little blue book is going to stand in for a hundred-dollar session?

So, I am supposed to unscatter my thoughts. Well, here's a thought. The new school is easy. There are a couple of nice teachers, two neutral ones, one deadly boring one, and one asshole. I'd have expected more assholes, but in general they just seem like poor saps who couldn't get a teaching job anywhere else. So far I've had a lot of free time to do my drawings and cartoons. Not as much homework. I think I'll be alright, if you're wondering.

October 7, 1996

I doubt there is anyone who tells you everything. Wouldn't that be a form of disorder in itself—a desire or an ability to admit everything? I suppose that's the point and the goal here, but don't you ever find it kind of a gross concept? One of those things we tell ourselves is okay because it's the late twentieth century, but is totally unnatural and wrong? Like flying in an airplane or drinking out of a disposable coffee cup every morning or eating a King Size Snickers bar in one sitting? Do you secretly hate the people who are willing to tell you everything? Of course you won't answer this question, but I would understand if the answer was yes.

October 30, 1996

I'm sorry I haven't done this in a while. I know it's supposed to be every week in place of our Tuesday sessions. But it doesn't feel like much. I'm kind of tired of things the way they are. But I can't rest because I have to work my way out of this shit situation.

November 12, 1996

No, I don't understand Anthony entirely. He tries to be a nice guy. Too hard sometimes. I suppose he is a solid person—like my mother wants to think of herself as a solid person.

I don't think of him as a dinosaur, like I usually do men his age. Maybe because he's married to my mother. So that makes him a different kind of mystery. A mystery I don't want to solve.

This booklet had only one cartoon, on the page opposite the November 5th entry. In this one, the dinosaur was holding a guitar and the doll a tambourine. The doll's eye was still closed.

> ***Doll:*** *If I went back to Breakneck, would I see you there?*
> ***Dinosaur:*** *Probably not.*
> ***Doll:*** *Did you ever finish your song?*
> ***Dinosaur:*** *What do you think, Naddy Baby?*

And opposite the final entry was a pencil drawing of a man's face, taking up nearly the whole page. The man had long straight hair—darkened with thicker pencil strokes—big eyes, big ears, but no nose and no mouth.

Underneath it these words were squeezed in at the bottom:

> *This is the closest I've come to getting my dad's whole face right. But I can never remember his mouth. Maybe it's that I want to draw it as a smile. But the last time I saw that was a long time ago. And maybe a smile doesn't feel right to me now, like it would have then. There are good and bad reasons, why a person might smile.*

I closed the booklet. Between these notes and the other ones, I was fairly certain Nadine was teasing Fabian somehow. Trying to convince him—successfully or unsuccessfully, I couldn't tell—that she wasn't really as disturbed as her behavior toward Mr. Brewster would indicate. Or teasing Fabian with some information she was withholding from him that he was supposed to work very hard to extract.

I watched the Edwards playground. The latest batch of recess kids had just run inside. Probably Nadine went to school here as a little kid. There were only two elementary schools in Campion, and I didn't remember her going to mine, which was on the other side of town.

In any case, Nadine had very likely been in town—and in Fabian's office—in the last few days.

I started my car and head back to the station.

AT MY DESK, I called up Eastern Correctional and put in a request to see Streeter's visitor or phone call records for the last six months. He had none, I was told. No visitors, no phone calls in the past year—which wasn't surprising. Both of his parents were dead now—his mother had died of cancer a couple of years before the shooting, and his father had died in Brookhaven about a year after the shooting. Johnny Streeter had a sister who was eleven years older than him, but who liked to pretend she wasn't related. She lived in Pennsylvania, I think. She went by her married name and didn't even attend his hearing.

I returned my attention to Nadine Raines, checking a couple of our databases for her. There was no Nadine Raines residing in Connecticut, but there was one in Brattleboro, Vermont—with a birthdate of 1/13/79, matching the hospital file.

"I found you, old girl," I muttered. But was she in Vermont *now*?

I eyed the *Insurance holder* line of the old files. *Susan Gagliardi.* Surely a parent or guardian. Maybe divorced, thus the difference in last name. I knew there were Gagliardis in Campion still. In fact one was working at Brookhaven at the time of the shooting.

I found the Campion address of a *Gagliardi, Anthony and Susan.*

Right—Anthony Gagliardi. He'd been working in the administrative building of Brookhaven that March morning in 2010. He'd gotten to work early. Never encountered the shooter because he was in a different building, but had heard the shots and was one of the people who called 911.

He and Susan lived on Durham Hill Road. A little visit was definitely in order.

In the meantime, I wanted someone to start looking at all of the old files from Fabian's garage. I had our rookie Derek help me carry the file cabinet in. Greg came in just as I was parking it by Amy's desk.

"How'd it go with the accountant?" Amy asked him.

"She's consulting a lawyer. Apparently she did sign a confidentiality contract with Fabian. We might need some kind of court order with her just like with the billing company."

"Okay," I said. "I'll work on that. I guess we should've known she wouldn't just hand it over."

"I think she *wanted* to. She clearly liked Fabian a lot. But I think she wants the assurance of a piece of paper that says we made her do it. She said that Fabian hadn't given her this year's paperwork yet, since the year isn't quite over. So the best she can do in any case is information about some of his 2014 patients."

"That might actually be relevant," I said, and told Amy and Greg about my interview with Eugene. Then I showed them the Raines file.

"This Nadine Raines looks very interesting to me right now, and I'm pursuing it," I said. "But given what Eugene Morrison told us this morning about Fabian being harassed by an old patient, I think we should do a cursory look through all the other files we have, just in case. Amy, are you up for that?"

She nodded. I wondered if she thought I was giving her grunt work. In fact, as a fellow townie, I was worried that Greg might enjoy this job too much—sniffing around the shrink files of a couple of decades of Campionites. To Amy, they would just be names.

"Maybe order them by date?" I suggested. "Start looking at which of these people went to him most recently, and who is still in town or nearby. Also . . . I'm waiting for the complete phone records any minute now. So when we get them we can see if any of them has called Dr. Fabian recently. If the phone records come in while I'm out, can you check to see if you find Raines's number in his records first?"

"Sure, Henry," said Amy.

"Greg, you can drive." I grabbed the files from my desk so I could keep looking at them in the car. "We're going to Nadine Raines's parents' house. It looks like she's maybe home for the holidays."

NADINE

OUR SESSIONS WERE gentle after that. Unmemorable. I was polite and mature and sentimental. I told you about all of my father's unfinished songs. The Dance of the Unraked Leaves. The Song of the Pteranodons. (*Caw! Caw! Caw!* He'd have me scream during the refrain, and my mother would often choose that moment to turn on the vacuum cleaner or the blender.) The Ballad of Breakneck Pond. He liked formal titles like that. The Song of the Blank. The Ballad of the Whatever.

We talked matter-of-factly about the loss I'd experienced as a kid, the anger I hadn't had a chance to express. We talked about Mr. Brewster as an innocent bystander of my rage. We did not discuss his gender and age and appearance as somehow symbolic of something I wished to gut or destroy or expose. We didn't discuss yours as the same. We never would.

By then my sessions were only once a week. You had me write little journal entries to stand in for our other sessions. My college acceptances were starting to come in. We talked about where I wanted to go, what I wanted to study, how I'd make new friends. You didn't ever ask me what I'd tell people about high school. I wondered if that meant I didn't need to tell them anything.

Twice, Johnny watched me silently as I went in and out of the waiting room for my backpack at the end of my sessions.

"Hey there," I whispered, the second time. He smiled and said nothing. But the acknowledgment must have meant something to him, because he called me a few days later. He'd apparently held on to my number in the intervening weeks.

It was almost nine o'clock on a Friday night. My parents were out and I was surprised to hear the phone ring. I picked up expecting to hear my mother on the other end, telling me they'd be late.

Instead I heard a deep male hello, followed by, "May I please speak to Nadine?"

"This is Nadine."

"Do you remember a person named Johnny?"

"Yes."

"This is him."

"Oh. Okay. Hi."

I smiled as I pulled myself onto my parents' bed, next to the phone. Despite the odd introduction, this evening was taking on an air of teen movie. An unexpected call from an older guy, at an unexpected hour. So what if he was a little weird? I'd take it.

"What are you doing?" Johnny wanted to know.

"Nothing," I said. "Watching TV and reading a book."

"At the same time?"

"Yeah. I mean the TV's just on because it makes me feel less lonely. I'm reading *A Clockwork Orange*."

"Oh. You seen the movie?"

Oh, Jesus. More movie interrogation.

"No," I admitted.

"I'm not sure if you'd like it."

"Oh."

"You didn't ask me what *I'm* doing."

"What are you doing?" I asked.

"Sewing a button on my shirt. It fell off in the wash but I was lucky I found it."

"Congratulations."

The conversation for the next half hour was surprisingly easy. Casual. He told me about his day at the video rental store. About a woman who rented *When Harry Met Sally* almost every Friday, and about a mother who had to carry out a screaming and red-faced toddler who didn't want to part with a copy of *Aladdin* after having it for a week.

"See, people are very emotional about their movies," Johnny pointed out.

"People are emotional about all sorts of things," I said. "My stepdad is emotional about trains."

"You like your stepdad?"

"He's okay. He's kind of a quiet guy."

"And you like that?"

"Better than having one of those blustery, mean stepdads I'm always hearing about."

"But stepdads have a better reputation than stepmothers,

I think," Johnny said. "Where are all the evil stepdads in the fairy tales?"

"Good question," I said.

And then Johnny went on for a while about how his dad blamed him for everything. And how he couldn't wait to move out of his house. I tried not to sound too excited about the fact that I was going to college, because it might sound like rubbing it in.

After we talked a little while longer, Johnny said, "You know, you kind of remind me of Janeane Garofalo. I mean, except you're a lot taller than her."

"I don't think I know who she is."

"You don't know who anyone is, it seems like."

I've sort of been in a cave since I stabbed my teacher.

"You should watch *The Truth About Cats and Dogs,*" Johnny went on. "It's got her in it. She plays a veterinarian. Actually, you're a little like each of the two main characters in that movie. A little like Janeane Garofalo, a little like Uma Thurman. The movie is kind of mindless, but good. Romantic comedy. There's a little phone sex in it, though. Some people are offended by that part."

"I don't think that would bother me," I said.

"I didn't think it would."

"What's that supposed to mean?"

"Oh, I don't know. You seem like a laid-back kind of person."

"Well . . . sort of."

"*You* ever tried phone sex?"

"*No,*" I said, unsure if I was offended, skeeved, or excited by the question. "Why would I want to do that?"

"You'd rather have the real thing, is what you're saying?"

I hesitated. "Well . . . *probably.* Wouldn't most people?"

"I'm not sure," Johnny said.

"I think I should go."

"Why?"

"I just don't want to talk about this."

"Okay . . . What do you want to talk about?"

I was silent for a while. For more than a year, my life had not been about what I *wanted.* It had been about trying to appear stable, about working hard to get to a college on the other side of the country, about erasing my past and being someone else once this summer was over. What did I want to talk about? I had no idea.

"Rattlesnakes," I offered.

I'd been reading about rattlesnakes since I'd been accepted to a college in the Southwest. It just seemed like something I should know about.

"Rattlesnakes," Johnny repeated. "Is that the kind of thing you and Bouffant talk about?"

I laughed at the unexpected use of your private nickname. It felt weird, having it out in the world, and not just in my head.

"Actually, yes," I admitted. Because by now you let me talk about random, stupid shit during our sessions. We were running out the clock until I went to college. Sunscreen SPF levels. Mike Tyson biting that other guy's ear off. *The X-Files.* The more mundane, the less chance I'd slip up and say something that would worry you.

"Well, on that note maybe *I* should go," said Johnny. "Because I hate reptiles. But do you want to see a movie with me next week? What do you think?"

"Sure," I said.

"What do you want to see?"

"I haven't seen a movie in a theater in almost two years," I said. "Surprise me."

MY COFFEE IS half-gone now, and leaves a funny taste in my mouth. I accidentally bought hazelnut somehow. I think it was mislabeled but naturally I might have been distracted. No matter, because at least I am awake enough now to keep driving.

HENRY

I KNEW THE DURHAM Hill area pretty well—I'd had a friend who'd lived there in high school, and we'd drink beer in his basement. The Gagliardis' place was a light blue raised ranch that clearly had a second floor added at some point—its size seemed awkward for the relatively modest neighborhood.

An older woman answered the door. She was wearing a red sweater that sparkled a little. It sort of matched the unusual shimmer of her silvery-blond hair.

"Susan Gagliardi?" I said.

"Yes?" She looked alarmed. "Is everything alright? Is someone hurt?"

"Uh, no, ma'am. We were actually hoping to chat with your daughter, Nadine. Is she here?"

Susan put a hand to her ear and pinched at it lightly with her thumb and forefinger. "Um. No. No, she's not."

"Now, I know she lives in Vermont. Right? But has she been in town recently?"

"Yes. What is this about?"

"So she's been visiting, but she's not here now?"

"No." She shook her head, which jangled her earrings. I noticed that they stretched her ear holes just a little too much, making her earlobes look painful and just slightly, inexplicably obscene. At the ends of the earrings were little blobs of purple that looked to me like miniature brains.

"Is there some kind of trouble?" she asked.

"No. We're just covering our bases here. I don't know if you heard about the tragedy at the Clement Avenue office building. Dr. Mark Fabian?"

"Oh." Susan drew a long breath in through her nose. "Yes, of course."

"We're just going around talking to all of his patients."

"His patients?" Susan's eyes seemed to relax a bit, but her mouth drew in tight. I wondered if her bullshit antenna was going up. "Nadine was his patient about fifteen . . . no . . . more like twenty years ago. It was still a shock, of course, but I can't imagine she could be very helpful to you."

"Uh-huh. Well, her name came up as a recent patient."

"As a *recent* patient? No, that's not . . ." she stopped talking suddenly. She put her hand to her lower back, as if it ached.

"Not . . . what?" I prompted.

"Well . . . you know she doesn't live here, right?"

"Yes. I know she lives in Vermont. Correct?"

"Well, technically that's her U.S. residence. She often works overseas. She's a traveling nurse. Whenever she can, she works for various organizations that do international medical clinics, things like that."

"I see."

"And she fills in with work in Vermont. There's a phlebotomy certification course she teaches there, part of the year. What I'm saying is that she lives and works too far away to be his patient." I felt like I recognized a little of Nadine in her eyes—in their unusual size, their slight lack of focus. "She has for a *very* long time."

"Okay. Well, we'd just like to touch base with her, like we're doing with all of the patients we can manage to get ahold of. When is the last time you saw your daughter?"

"Yesterday . . . morning."

"Okay. And do you know where she went? Maybe we could grab her cell phone number, if you have it?"

"I know that yesterday she was planning to go to Gillette Castle to do some drawings."

"And you know for sure that's where she went?"

"Yes. I recommended she stay at this one place called the Apple Blossom Inn, which isn't too far from the Gillette Castle area. I believe that was her plan. But she doesn't always necessarily do what I recommend." She smiled stiffly, without opening her mouth.

"Now, why wouldn't she stay here? Gillette Castle is just an hour drive."

"She wanted to have a few nights to herself. With her work. Before spending the actual holiday with us."

I wondered if maybe holiday tensions were high—if Nadine actually left because things hadn't been so pleasant with Mom and Stepdad.

"Okay. Well, do you have that cell number for me?"

"Sure," Susan said. "It's 802-555-7943."

"Anyone else she's been in touch with recently, that you know of? Since she arrived in Campion?"

"Uh . . . well, I know she visited with her old friend Julie."

"Julie . . . ?"

"Julie Olasz."

I wrote that down even though the name was quite familiar. Julie had been my friend Chris's girlfriend for a couple of years, and was in our graduating class. I'd seen her around over the years since. She was always friendly—bordering on flirtatious.

"Do you want to know how to spell that?" Susan asked.

"Uh . . . no. I got it. Anyone else?"

"I don't think so. She's not very connected to Campion these days, so I'd be surprised if there was anyone else. I have no idea who she might've been in touch with in Brattleboro or wherever else. She's not a big social media person."

"Thanks so much," I said. I glanced at Greg and nodded that we could go.

Greg started to reach for the door.

"Officer?" Susan said softly. "Officer Peacher?"

"Yes?" I turned back to her.

"You were in school with my daughter. I'm not sure if you were in the same class or not. But when you were in all the news, I recognized the name."

I was silent. I didn't know where she was going with this. Greg dropped the doorknob and smiled at her gently.

"Did you know her?" Susan wanted to know.

"I had a couple of classes with her, I think. I remember she was tall and had brown hair."

"But you didn't know her well," Susan clarified.

"Right," I said.

Susan studied me. Again I got the vague sense that her eyes couldn't really focus. Her gaze was circling me, I felt. Pulling in different parts of me—hair, feet, shirt, nose—until she constructed her own picture in her brain.

"She's very different now," she said, finally meeting my gaze.

The room was silent for a while. Then, from somewhere in the house, a dryer timer buzzed.

"I guess we all are, Mrs. Gagliardi," I said, all boy-hero. A moment later, I loathed myself for saying it.

"Sure," she said, shrugging. The moment was over, and I couldn't help but feel I'd missed an opportunity. For what, I wasn't certain.

"Well, if I talk to her, I'll tell her to call you," she said. "But probably you'll catch up with her first."

"Bye, now," Greg said.

As we drove away, I tried the number Susan had given us.

"Voice mail," I said. "But it's Nadine's. At least she gave us the right number."

"So you knew Nadine Raines?" Greg asked after I hung up.

"I talked to her a few times. In high school."

"Huh."

Greg had gone to Campion High, too, but was five years younger than me. So—an entirely different era.

"Gillette Castle?" Greg said. "Is this lady serious?"

"Well, I think it goes without saying that her plans probably changed if she bludgeoned that guy to death. But if she *did* do something to him, I don't think her mother knows about it."

Greg grunted in response, and then went quiet as he drove.

I thought about that last day I—or most of us—saw Nadine Raines. The day her mom surely had in mind when she asked if I knew her when we were in high school.

Junior year social studies class. That day, I'd gone to the bathroom to avoid the homework collection. That teacher with the ponytail—I couldn't remember his name now—actually fell for this if you didn't try it too often. He'd get involved in the class and then forget to ask you later.

So I took my time in the boys' room. A good long five minutes or more. And when I came back, the teacher was leaning over his desk with blood on his hands, wrapping his arm with a sweater, muttering "Shit! Ouch!" and Lindsay Banville was on the wall phone behind his desk and there was a puddle of blood on the desk in front of mine. Nadine's desk. But Nadine wasn't at her desk. She was in the corner of the room. Alan Scofield and Cindy Glasser had her cornered. Cindy was talking to her softly. No one noticed that I'd just come in, and I wasn't sure if I should sit at my desk, it was so near the blood.

I almost said "What happened?" to Dan Testa, who was standing nearest to me. But something in the air of the room told me I shouldn't make a sound.

A few seconds later, the vice principal came in and said, "Nadine, come with me," and then told Mr. Ponytail that another teacher was on her way to cover for him so he could go consult with the nurse. He picked up a yellow plastic something from the floor before taking Nadine away.

The teacher who came in put brown paper towels over all of the blood, took us outside, and had us read and do other homework at the picnic tables in the courtyard despite the cold autumn gusts. She seemed to accept that she couldn't keep us from talking about what had just happened—as long as we did it quietly.

It was mostly *I can't believe this!* And *She must be really fucked up! Did he do something first, or did that come out of nowhere?*

Or from sensitive, sincere Cindy Glasser: *You guys. I don't think we should talk like this until we know what really happened. Nadine's really nice.*

But there were a few details. *She had the knife out before he came to her desk. It was like she was planning it the whole time. I thought it was some kind of a toy until I saw that he was bleeding. Lucky it was the top of his arm. Imagine if it was the other side and she cut an artery? There'd be blood, like, shooting everywhere.*

You could tell by the look on her face—she didn't believe what she was doing. She wasn't herself.

Oh my God, is she going crazy? You know her dad died, right?

People don't go crazy because their dad died. Look at Justin Pratt. His *mom died.*

I didn't say they did. I didn't mean it like that.

Do you think she was going to kill him?

No! Don't say that.

I wonder if she had her homework done today. I swear to God, this might be the first day since, like, sixth grade that Nadine hasn't done her homework. You think that has something to do with it?

Shut up. That's not funny.

I didn't say it was funny. They say sometimes it's a small thing that'll make a person snap.

I said nothing. But the more I thought about it, the more it seemed to me I *had* seen something pained in Nadine's face in the moments before I'd gotten up and picked up the bathroom pass and slipped down the hall.

She was turned slightly in my direction as she rummaged through her bag. She'd stopped her rummaging for a moment and glanced at me with an absent but pleading expression. For a moment I wondered if she, too, had forgotten to do her homework. I had thought of saying something like, "You, too, huh? Welcome to the other side." But then there was a severity in her eyes that made me think that maybe Nadine Raines wasn't willing to joke about her *own* missed homework. Plus, if I admitted my predicament to Nadine, I was less likely to get away with my lav trick.

Now that I thought about it, I realized I hadn't joked with her in a few days—maybe a week. That she hadn't initiated any conversation at all herself in that time. She'd been stone-faced and silent and I had figured she didn't feel like talking.

My new girlfriend, Jessica, was practically drooling by the time she caught up with me at my locker after school.

"Oh my God, Henry. You're in that class, right?"

"Yeah."

"Did you see it?"

I sat behind Nadine every day. I was almost friendly with her. It seemed like if anyone should've seen it, it should've been me. But before I answered, Jessica said, "Oh my God. Wow. You were there. Was there a lot of blood?"

"Yeah. Mrs. Nolan kind of cleaned it up. There was some on her desk and some on the floor."

"Do you think she was gonna try to kill him?"

"No . . . I don't think so."

"Why don't you think so?"

"I just . . . I don't think she had a plan. I think it just . . . happened."

"She probably had some kind of a plan if she brought that knife into school."

"Oh . . . yeah, maybe."

"Were you scared?"

I thought for a second before answering, but no longer than a second.

"It happened too fast to really be scared," I said. "It was crazy."

"Did you see she had the knife before she did it?"

"No. I just looked up and she was slamming the blade into his arm."

"Oh my *God*!"

I FELT MYSELF reddening with shame at this twenty-year-old memory, but then my cell phone rang, letting me off the hook. It was Carly Dayton, the DA.

"Henry!" she said. "There's good news and bad news. Caduceus Billing has provided some information on your 'Connor' individual. They're not willing to give out any other information about patients that day. They understand that he's a critical piece for you, but are calling requests for other patients that day 'fishing expeditions.' For each one they're asking for verification of their relationship to the crime. By the way, they've implied that they only bill about two-thirds of his patients."

"But they bill a Connor who sees him on Tuesday evenings?"

"Sure do. Connor Osborne. Here's his address, Henry. Campion resident. Eight-four Highland Road. Okay?"

"Connor Osborne. Eighty-four Highland Road. Okay. Thanks, Carly." I ended the call and turned to Greg. "Did you catch that?"

"Yup," he said, pulled over, and made a U-ey.

NADINE

IT'S JUST OVER an hour from the bottom of the state to the top. There shouldn't be much traffic since I'm just going through the sticks of eastern Connecticut and not through the main highway mess in the middle.

I had not mentioned this destination to my mother. The Nipmuck Forest, where my dad used to take me. Where we'd swim out to the rock in the middle of the lake there. Sometimes he'd strap a fanny pack to the top of his head so we'd arrive with dry snacks to eat. He would meditate while I would unzip the pack and gobble the M&M's from the trail mix. We were far enough from home that I was not embarrassed by his lotus position, or the fanny pack on his head. And he was happier there than anywhere I could think of.

It had not seemed the most important stop till yesterday. When *Not again not again not again* was drowning my judgment and my sense of direction.

IN MY NEXT couple of sessions with you, I had to strangle the impulse to mention my upcoming date with the waiting room dude.

"I've been taking a break on the cartooning stuff," I announced instead. "I've been working on drawing faces from memory."

"Like whose?" you asked, glancing up from your watch.

"Like my friend Julie's. I haven't seen her in a while. The big thing people notice about her is her hair. It's long and wavy and shiny, like a shampoo commercial. But sometimes they don't see her face, I don't think. Her eyes are very unusual, so I started with that. Kind of sad looking, the way they slant down. In a pretty way. But I think it makes people treat her a certain way. Like she's younger than she is. Or more fragile than she is."

"You miss her?"

You knew I did. We talked about it all the time.

"Yeah," I said anyway.

"Have you tried contacting her?"

"We've talked on the phone a couple of times this year. But I haven't seen her in a few months. In the winter you don't see people around the neighborhood. And I leave and get home at different times from everybody else. I mean, everybody who goes to Campion High, anyway."

"Well, it's nice you still talk."

"Yeah. It's nice."

We were quiet for a moment. We both knew it was more pitiful than nice—my oldest friend's occasional awkward acknowledgment.

"I tried drawing my dad once. A week or so ago."

"Really?" Your face elongated with casual interest. "How did that go?"

"I almost finished. Not quite. I couldn't remember his ears very well."

You hesitated. "Well. You could look at a picture."

"I haven't looked at a picture of him in a few years."

"Since he passed?"

"No . . . since maybe two years ago." I hadn't looked at his picture since . . . when? *Since Woodstock '94.* "I got rid of most of the pictures about two years ago."

"Why?"

I shrugged. "I didn't want to look at them anymore, that's all."

You nodded.

"You've never told me what he looked like," you said gently.

"He was kind of tall and he had long dark hair."

"Really long?"

"To his shoulders."

"Ah."

"He was long and skinny on the bottom but strong and bulky in his arms and shoulders," I continued. "Probably because his only regular form of exercise was lifting dumbbells while he watched documentaries about Jimi Hendrix or Led Zeppelin."

You smiled. "Did you watch them with him?"

"Sometimes."

I tried to think of something else to tell you. I'd given a broad bodily description because I genuinely couldn't think of what to say about my father's face. All I could remember now was that you could see a couple of crooked teeth when he smiled really big—which rarely happened. He smiled enough, just not big. I couldn't describe to you how odd his body type seemed to me. I always had this weird sense that his physical presence and demeanor simply didn't fit in this time and space. Or maybe not *always*. Maybe I only remembered it that way? Maybe now it just felt awkward that he had ever physically existed?

"I wonder if you would've liked him," I said.

"What do you think?" you asked. "Would I have?"

"That's an impossible question," I answered. "Because I don't know you."

You blew a long, noisy breath out of your mouth. Like you were snorkeling through all of this adolescent tedium, once again.

"Maybe what you're wondering is generally what other people thought of him."

"Maybe. Maybe I'm just wondering if you would've liked him. Maybe I feel like if I knew whether you would've liked him or not, as a test case, I'd know a little bit more about you as a person."

"A test case. A test case for what?"

"Never mind. I meant just a way of seeing how you really *are*."

"I'm more interested in hearing why you think you've been trying to draw a picture of him lately."

I was quiet for a moment. "He's one of like ten different people I've tried drawing."

"Okay. Him and Julie and who else?"

I rolled my eyes to indicate that it didn't matter, it was stupid, never mind already.

The real answer—that you never insisted upon getting—was this: my other once-close friend Morgan. Mr. Brewster. My grandmother—my father's mother, who had died about two years before. Johnny. And you.

You, I wanted to say. Because each week I forgot what you looked like for a little while.

"No one else worth talking about," I said.

HENRY

Connor Osborne lived at the end of the Highland cul-de-sac. But he was at work, according to his petite blond wife—who answered the door with two small blond children at her feet.

"He works at the Carrick Center in Westford," she told us, pulling the smaller of the two children up to her hip.

I clamped my mouth shut and tried to keep my face neutral. I glanced at Greg, and then remembered I hadn't yet shown him the article from Fabian's laptop. In fact, there were a couple of things I still needed to show him, come to think of it.

"What does your husband do there?" I asked.

"He's the human resources manager," she said.

Before taking off, we asked Connor's wife about the previous night—when her husband had come home, and if they'd spent the evening together.

She said that he'd come home just after seven. Normally he came home earlier, but Tuesday night was his night to stay out an extra hour—to have a little happy hour time with his friends. He got home and had leftover pizza, then helped her give the kids their baths and put them to bed. She had a book club meeting at her neighbor's house down the street. She left after the little one was asleep—while Connor was reading the older one a bedtime story.

The wife—whose name was Andrea—didn't seem at all nervous or disingenuous while she was telling us this. She also didn't seem to be aware that her husband had been seeing a shrink—much less the dead shrink who was all over the local news today.

"What's this about, though?" she asked.

"We believe he may have been a witness in a matter we're investigating," I offered.

On the way to Westford, I told Greg about the article, and we discussed the timeline. If Connor arrived at Fabian's office at six, and had some sort of angry outburst early on in the session, he'd have had about a half hour to clean himself up and get back to his clueless wife and their kids.

"There's the bathroom in the back of Fabian's office suite," I said. "But there were no traces of blood in it."

Greg shrugged. "The guy's got those little kids. He probably keeps baby wipes in his car. Like you do."

I didn't reply to this. Instead, I called Amy. "We're heading to the Carrick Center because it turns out Fabian's last patient on Tuesday is an employee there. So before we get there—I wanted to hear if you made contact with anyone there about Fabian patients? How did that go?"

"Well, look. They said they had no arrangement between Dr. Fabian and their treatment program—no regular referral of patients between the two. I spoke to the director of the center and she hadn't heard of Fabian. She said she couldn't say offhand if any of their patients went to him for any sort of previous or additional treatment. That would require reviewing all of their patient files for references to his name. Now, if we had a particular patient in mind, that would be another story. If we come back to them with a name and a warrant, they seem happy to help."

"Okay," I said. "Thanks."

I ended the call.

"Hmm," said Greg, after a couple of minutes. "I wonder. Now, if this guy committed some kind of an assault and admitted it to his shrink, is the shrink allowed to report it? *Required* to report it?"

"I think this is a gray area. I'm pretty sure they are required to report certain things, like if a kid is being abused, or if someone's life is in danger. And I have no idea what the protocol would be if he *suspected* a patient of something, but wasn't sure. I'm going to have to ask a real shrink about these issues."

Maybe I could ask Eugene. Or a younger therapist. It seemed likely that the specific rules about these things changed over time. Eugene hadn't been a real therapist for years, and seemed generally fuzzy on these issues. He'd thought that accountant would be chomping at the bit to help us, for example. Not quite.

At the Carrick Center front desk, we asked for Connor. Soon a heavyset guy emerged from one of the offices in the back. Round and red-faced, prematurely balding. White dress shirt with a bright tie. As he moved closer to us, I saw that the tie had Donald Ducks on it.

He didn't seem surprised to see us.

"We're from the Campion Police Department," I said, showing him my badge. "Can you talk to us outside for a few minutes?"

He nodded and followed us. When we were outside, he said, "I assume this is about Dr. Fabian? I just heard about him this morning."

"Yes. That's right, Mr. Osborne."

"Okay. Do you mind if we walk a little? This isn't something I need for my coworkers to hear."

"Sure," I said.

"Your wife told us we could find you here," I said, once we'd reached the stone CARRICK CENTER sign. "I'm sorry for your loss. We understand you were a patient of Dr. Fabian's."

Connor stared at me. "My wife doesn't know about Dr. Fabian."

"We didn't tell her, if that's what you're wondering. We just asked where you were."

Connor loosened his Donald Duck tie. "Okay. Alright. I'm going to have an interesting evening."

"Why didn't your wife know about Dr. Fabian?" Greg asked.

"It's a private matter." Connor unbuttoned his top shirt button. I noticed he had a gold chain on under there. I've never connected very well with gold chain guys. "You can understand that, right? Officer Peacher, right?"

"Yeah."

"From Brookhaven." Connor smiled a little.

"Yeah," I admitted.

I saw Greg's gaze shift its focus from Connor to me.

"Mr. Osborne, we'd like to hear about your appointment with Dr. Fabian on Tuesday."

Connor frowned. "You'd like to hear about my appointment?"

"Well, you can start with just . . . if there was anything out of the ordinary . . . if there was anyone waiting for him after your appointment. Anything that might help us."

"Out of the ordinary? Not really."

"Your appointment was at six, correct?"

"Yeah."

"And you stayed for how long?"

Connor hesitated. "Didn't they make you do any therapy after you saw all those people shot? Therapy's an hour."

I ignored Greg's gaze—darting from Connor to me.

"So you left at seven?" I asked.

"Roughly. Yeah. I didn't look at the time, but he usually ended it at five of."

"Was there another patient waiting?"

"Actually . . . yeah. I think so."

I thought back to what Eugene had said—about a former patient's "unexpected office visit."

"What makes you think so?" I asked.

"Well . . . when we were almost done . . . well, like fifteen minutes from done . . . I heard the suite door, and someone moving around in the waiting room."

"And when you left, did you see someone waiting there?"

"No. See, it's set up so you can leave without going by the waiting room again. I think that's on purpose. The waiting room door is further down the hall than the consultation room door."

"Right."

"I mean, you could peek in if you wanted to be obnoxious. But it's set up so you don't naturally see anyone on your way out."

"Right, I saw that."

"You know, I'm pretty sure I'm *usually* his last appointment on Tuesdays."

"How do you know that?"

"I guess he told me once. I used to have a different time, and then he offered to stay late so I could switch to this time."

"Would he usually leave with you? At the same time?"

"No. He'd stay in his office. At least for a little while. He never, like, walked out to the parking lot with me or whatever. If that's what you're asking. I'm pretty sure shrinks don't like to do that stuff. It's all about keeping the discussion in the office. If he walked with me to the parking lot, he might have to listen to me talk about myself for an extra ten minutes, and not get paid for it."

"Okay. So, did you see anyone in the parking lot?" I asked. "Anyone suspicious?"

"No. I mean, his car was there, obviously."

"How do you know it was *his* car?"

"Because occasionally he's parking in the lot right when I'm getting there. I think sometimes he runs out for an early dinner before my appointment."

"Okay. So, it was just a regular appointment. Except that you heard someone coming in for an appointment after you."

"Yeah. Maybe a new patient. Who knows? I wouldn't know. But . . . now that you ask about it, I think Mark looked kind of surprised when we heard the door. Like he wasn't expecting anyone, maybe."

"Hmm," I said. "But you didn't see any other cars in the lot?"

Connor shrugged. "I didn't notice one way or another, I guess. There are other doctors in that building, other buildings that use that big lot."

"And was this the first time that happened? That you heard someone come in for an appointment after your late one, on a Tuesday?"

"Yeah." Connor considered for a moment. "I think so."

"And there was nothing unusual about the appointment itself, for you?"

"Umm . . . not really. He talked about his retirement. He asked me if I'd looked at his list of alternative therapists for once he's gone."

"Was this the first time you had had that discussion?"

"No. I guess he was hoping most of his patients would find someone new before he was officially out. I just haven't looked for someone new because I'm not sure I want to do it anymore."

"Were you upset when you heard he was going to retire?"

"Uh . . . not really. He often seemed kind of . . . tired. Poor guy. It would've been nice for him to have a few years without having to deal with other people's problems."

"Mr. Osborne, did you go straight home after your appointment?"

"Yeah."

"So that would bring you to your house at what, 7:10 or so?"

"I guess, yeah."

"Did you see your wife at that point? Was she home at the time?"

"Uh-huh," Connor said. "She'd already had dinner with the kids, so I had a bite to eat and helped start the kids' baths."

"Did either of you go out after the kids were asleep?"

"My wife had a book club thing—just down the street—she walked. But I didn't go anywhere. I watched some stuff on Netflix."

"Okay. Well, it would really help us if you can remember anything unusual about that evening. You shouldn't hesitate to call us."

"Right . . . absolutely. This is crazy. How'd you know I was going to him, anyway? Did he have a list of patients? Aren't there rules about this kind of thing?"

"There are some. But when there's a homicide . . . anyway, one more thing, Mr. Osborne. We have reason to believe that Dr. Fabian was concerned about a series of sexual assault incidents that occurred close to here. Close to the Carrick Center. Is that something you two discussed recently?"

"What?" Connor puckered his lips, then looked quizzical. "No . . . that's not something we discussed."

"But you know what I'm referring to?"

"I think so." Connor sniffled and then swiped his nostrils with the back of his hand. "A couple of winters ago. The guy who was grabbing women, and they were trying to blame it on Carrick."

"They never caught the guy," I said.

"No. But I don't think it ever happened again after the initial uproar. Whoever the guy was probably decided to move along."

"You and Dr. Fabian never discussed it? Even though this was happening near your place of work?"

Connor shrugged. "It didn't ever come up, that I can remember."

"Okay," I said. "Well, please be in touch if you remember anything else."

"WHAT DO YOU think?" Greg asked me as he started the car.

"I don't know. A mystery patient who wasn't in Fabian's calendar? And all he can give us is the sound of a door and footsteps? And Connor had *time* to do it," I said. "But so far it doesn't look like he had a *reason*. The Carrick Center connection might give us a reason. If we could clarify what that is."

"Right," Greg murmured.

"In the meantime," I said, "I think the next person we really need to find is Nadine Raines. She fits the description of the situation Morrison described, and she was apparently back in his office this week."

"And she has a history of violence," Greg added.

I hesitated. Technically, it was true. But as bloody as it was, it felt strangely clinical to call it that—that perplexing moment in the social studies classroom so many years ago.

"Now, where did she sneak off to?" I said. "I'm going to call the Brattleboro PD, and then I think we should head to this Apple Blossom Inn place that her mother said she's at."

After I'd made the call and set my phone GPS for the Apple Blossom Inn address in East Haddam, Greg said, "But I wonder how this Connor guy would act if you asked for a polygraph."

"I don't want to put him on the defensive. We don't have enough to ask him to do that. For now he's just a guy who went to his regular shrink appointment."

"A guy who is really secretive about it," Greg pointed out.

"Aren't most people?" I said.

"These days? I don't know. Does anybody give a shit these days? Would *you*?"

I didn't answer.

"*Did* they make you go see one after Brookhaven?"

"No. It was optional for me. I don't think it's optional if you actually kill someone, though."

"Seems they ought to have made you go."

"It wouldn't have done anything," I said.

"Well, sure. But still they ought to have made you."

I hesitated. "Yeah. One of many missed opportunities. Story of my life."

Once Greg's eyes were on the road, I opened Fabian's Streeter file and started to read.

INITIAL SESSION PROGRESS NOTE

PATIENT NAME: Jonathan Streeter

INSURANCE: —

INSURANCE NUMBER: —

INSURANCE HOLDER: —

DATE OF SERVICE: 9/20/96

TYPE OF SERVICE: Individual Therapy

Jonathan—prefers the name "Johnny"—is here at the urging of his father, who believes he has a problem controlling his anger. While Johnny says that he does not believe he has a problem, he states that his father has made this treatment a condition of his residence in his parents' home, and has agreed to it. Payment of treatment has been made privately with patient's father. Patient's father describes a recent incident in which Johnny threatened the family cat with a fire iron. Jonathan is aware that this event motivated his father's insistence on this treatment. He denies any thoughts of or plans to harm himself or others at this time, and he willingly discussed the incident in this first session. He said that he was "mildly" angry when he found out that his mother had discarded a set of magazine clippings he'd mistakenly left on the family dining table. He said he pinned the cat to the floor with the fire iron to "demonstrate" to her "what it's like to have something important to you treated so cavalierly." He further noted that "the cat was asleep the whole time and didn't feel threatened" and that "anyone with a brain could see I was joking." His father said that this was the most recent in a series of similar incidents, but this writer thought it best not to press Johnny about other outbursts at this time.

Johnny has agreed to biweekly consultations, Wednesdays and Fridays at two P.M.

Johnny is a recent graduate of St. Joseph's Catholic High School and presents as well-groomed and tidily dressed. He attends classes at SCSU part-time and works at Campion Video. He describes himself as a "film buff" and says he enjoys his job.

NADINE

THERE'S NO ONE manning the rustic shack at the entrance of Bigelow Hollow State Park. It's the same one that was there when I was a kid. I drive down the wooded park road to one of the boating launch areas and park near the pond.

This is Bigelow Pond. The hiking map says Breakneck Pond is about a mile from the picnic area—on a narrow dirt road. Then there are about four miles of trail around it. I don't recall that my father and I ever hiked here in the winter. Every other season, though.

Breakneck Pond. Such an ugly name. I used to wonder why my father liked it so much. I thought the more accessible Bigelow Pond was prettier. But he would make me walk the long trail to the more remote Breakneck Pond. Then, after we arrived, he let me skip rocks and build pteranodon traps while he strummed his guitar and tried to fashion a ballad around the name. *The Ballad of Breakneck Pond.*

When I was six or seven, he tried to write that song. Even at that young age, I suspected he just liked the name. He had no idea what could happen here. But he liked to think something would.

He tried some lyrics about a lonely dude and a deer, and then something about a water snake who enchants an old guy in a rowboat. Then a woman who saves her Labrador mix from drowning in the tangled pond weeds, but then drowns herself. When he switched to a love story, I gave up listening and wandered off to find pteranodons.

It's clear to me what my father loved about these woods. He could lose himself in them. But what did I imagine I would draw here? At the very least maybe I thought there would be snow on the ground. I'd envisioned a desolate beauty that this particular winter stubbornly does not possess.

I gather a few things in my backpack—water, an old protein bar, the boxed bottle of Glenlivet that I bought three days ago for my stepfather's Christmas gift. Then I get out of the car and walk to the edge of the water.

HOW DID WE end up at Johnny's house the night of our third date? I can't remember exactly. He mentioned that his parents were out. And I think I must have said that I wanted to go home with him, and maybe watch a movie "or something." I distinctly remember wanting to see what would happen if I was alone with him in private.

He'd kissed me during the beginning of *Braveheart,* which he had on VHS. His lips felt weird—like touching worms to my mouth. And they were fake buttery from the popcorn we'd been eating. Still, I kissed him back. I didn't want to watch *Braveheart* anyway. He took me by the hand and led me to his room.

After a couple of minutes we were both down to our underwear. He pushed me on his bed and got on top of me.

"I can't," I said reluctantly. "Do you have anything? I don't take pills."

He sighed and rolled his bulgy blue-gray eyes toward the ceiling.

"Right," he said. For a moment I thought he didn't believe me. "I don't."

He took off his plaid shorts and my bra and moved up my stomach. He pushed my breasts together.

"What are we . . ." I started to ask.

It took me a moment to understand, with some relief, that we were still doing this, just in a different sort of way. He was content with that. He'd have to be, because it was over in less than three minutes. Something wet dripped down my chest and pooled in my belly button. And I couldn't figure out why he was laughing.

And then he was still, his bare, skinny chest on mine, heaving up and down. I touched his back for a moment, unsure what was supposed to happen next.

"I'm going to the bathroom for a sec," he said.

I stretched my arms contentedly under his pillows, enjoying the strange freedom of feeling someone else's sheets on my bare skin. One of my hands touched something crisp and papery. I pulled it out. It was a picture, probably from a magazine, glued to a piece of cardboard. A woman with her eyes rolling back and blood coming out of her nose. It took me a second to recognize the image. It was Uma Thurman in *Pulp Fiction,* in the scene when she's overdosing. The mouth of the picture was mangled somewhat, as if a dog had chewed it or someone had rammed a fork through it a few times.

I stared at the picture for a moment. Johnny definitely wasn't expecting to have me in his bed tonight. Otherwise he'd have had condoms and he'd have removed this from my reach.

I heard him coming back down the hall and pushed Uma back under the pillow. But she wouldn't quite go on the first shove, tangling in the opening of the pillowcase so I had to try again just as Johnny walked in.

He put on his boxers and flopped on the bed. He crawled toward me on his elbows, and put his arms around my middle.

After a few moments, the way he held me around the rib cage made me think of a song our music teacher used to have us sing in second grade. "I'm being swallowed by a boa constrictor." Most of the other kids thought it was funny, but I thought it was awful, and that's how I felt now. That this was maybe something I was supposed to like but didn't understand quite how or why.

Johnny's hand was gentle on my back, but his arm was tight over my arm and my chest.

"What's your secret, Nadine?" His voice was low, conspiratorial.

"What do you mean?"

"Why've you gone to Dr. Fabian for so long? I've seen you there for a long time. You must be kind of fucked up."

"Yeah, I must be," I said, trying to laugh.

My arm was starting to hurt.

"You going to answer the question?" Johnny breathed in my ear.

"I don't call him Dr. Fabian, remember? I call him Bouffant."

"Yeah. I like that." He laughed, but the laugh actually sounded like *ha ha*. He did it for at least a minute or two, scaring me. I thought he might never stop.

I'm being swallowed by a boa constrictor.

I couldn't breathe. Stabbing Mr. Brewster wasn't a secret. Everyone knew about it. Well—Johnny didn't know, but that was irrelevant, in a way. Practically everyone else knew, and he had asked for a *secret*. The Mr. Brewster thing wasn't a secret—and never had been. As a scream can't be a secret. And yet Johnny's grip was tightening around me.

I opened my mouth. I was pretty sure I heard words come out of it, but a moment later, I couldn't be absolutely certain. Because in the moments after Johnny let me go, I was too busy trying to catch my breath—without making too many rasping noises, and without looking too relieved—to care.

Johnny was looking through me, at the wall.

"Why do *you* go to Dr. Fabian, Johnny?" I asked, because it seemed to me this had been the point of the conversation all along.

"Because my dad makes me."

"Why does he make you?" I asked softly.

Johnny was silent. He reached under the pillow and pulled out Uma Thurman. He looked at her for a moment, then looked at me.

"Because I scare him," he said.

He stared at me, crumpling Uma Thurman to let me know he'd seen me looking at her.

"Why do you scare him?" I asked, careful not to break his gaze.

"Because I'm bigger than him now. Not like when I was younger, when he could push me around."

"Is that the only reason?" I whispered.

Johnny put his finger on my chin and then ran it all the way down the middle of my chest.

"Nope," he said.

HENRY

PROGRESS UPDATE

PATIENT NAME: Jonathan Streeter
INSURANCE: —
INSURANCE NUMBER: —
INSURANCE HOLDER: —
DATE OF SERVICE: 10/19/96
TYPE OF SERVICE: Individual Therapy

Johnny denies any angry or violent outbursts in the past month since he began consultations. His father has not reported any repeat incidents. When asked by this writer, however, Johnny declines to discuss the precipitating incident—or similar past incidents—any further.

Johnny reports a romantic interest in a young woman who frequents the video store at which he works. Johnny recently reported feeling "pumped" when she stayed for an extra few minutes to engage in conversation about a film they both enjoyed. He then reported feeling angry when she returned a movie and didn't talk to him. He says he had to take his break shortly after the incident, so he could go to his car "and yell all of the things that were in my head, so I wouldn't say them to my boss or the customers."

He said he was "proud" of himself for taking a break and thus not putting himself at risk of offending those around him or putting his job in jeopardy.

When asked if it was possible that the young woman was simply in a hurry, he said, "You'd have known if you were there. It was a diss." When this writer suggested it was not meant as such—as his mother had not meant to hurt or offend him by accidentally throwing away his clippings—he refused to speak for the remainder of the session.

In the following session, this writer suggested that we discuss strategies for separating intended offenses from unintended ones, when it comes to others' behavior. He said he was willing to discuss this, although "it feels all the same." However, he did agree that making this determination might help in strategizing ways to confront these uncomfortable situations.

He has agreed to attempt, for the next few weeks, to observe when he feels most hurt or angry by others' behavior, and to write down exactly what happened.

And then to write down whether or not he believes the offending individual *intended* to hurt him. We will discuss his observations in the next few sessions.

I flipped past Fabian's progress note to find a piece of notebook paper. There a grid was drawn in blue marker. There were four columns, titled: Person, Date, Description, Intentional?

Streeter had reported that someone named Jenny had "rolled eyes when I asked if she liked *Titanic.*" Under "Intentional," he'd written, "Not sure. Maybe was rolling eyes at *Titanic,* not me." He also wrote that his father "called me a degenerate when I took his wet clothes from dryer and put them on a chair so I could dry my work clothes." Intentional? Yes. Someone labeled "name unknown" had "honked and gave the finger when I merged onto Route 5 even though I had no other choice but to merge in that moment or get rammed by a semi." There were about a dozen similarly uninteresting offenses listed, all "intentional." I'm no emotional genius, but I seriously doubted that this exercise had gone as planned.

I'm not going to be angry at you, Fabian. I'm just going to keep reading, for now.

PROGRESS UPDATE

PATIENT NAME: Jonathan Streeter
DATE OF SERVICE: 12/30/96

Johnny has made some progress in exercising his anger management techniques in work situations, as well as confrontations with his mother. By his own admission, he has not made significant progress employing those techniques in confrontations with his father. "It doesn't matter how fast or slow I breathe, he's still an asshole."

Johnny recently describes some sleep difficulty, and occasionally says he feels these problems stem from a traumatic experience at age eleven. His father made reference to this event during our initial phone consultation, but this writer has chosen to wait until Johnny felt comfortable addressing it himself.

Johnny describes a summer night in which he woke up to the smell of smoke in his bedroom. His parents were away on a business-related trip and he was under the care of "Laurie," a nineteen-year-old who was also a family friend. Johnny managed to escape the house fire by climbing out his bedroom window. Laurie, who was sleeping in an upstairs guest room, died of smoke inhalation. Laurie had left a pot of unfinished popcorn on a burner that had not been turned off.

Johnny says his mother believes he has "survivor guilt" from the incident. After several sessions discussing the incident, Johnny admitted that he has "guilt, but not for surviving." He says that his guilt always stemmed from the fact that he had, in the weeks before the tragedy, removed the batteries from the smoke detector in order to power his remote-control Jeep. He believes that Laurie would have survived the incident had there been a working smoke detector in the house.

Johnny says he's "not sure" if it would be appropriate

> or beneficial to confess this detail to his parents at this point—or to Laurie's family. We have agreed to return to this question as he continues to process the incident. He says that his family "never talk about it," and are not aware of his frequent insomnia and occasional nightmares that make him "afraid to go back to sleep."
>
> Johnny has asked me to refer him to a psychiatrist who might prescribe him sleep aids. This writer is concurrently writing a referral to D. Marchese, suggesting that if a prescription is made, it be done on a very limited basis and that a consultation be required for any refills.

So far, I wasn't surprised by any of the family details in Johnny's file. In the days leading up to Johnny's hearing, the papers were filled with background stories about Johnny and his family. Family friends hinted that Johnny's behavior had always troubled his father, though his mother downplayed it. Family members' accounts conflicted as to whether the trouble started before or after the fire. Parents of the deceased babysitter were asked to comment, but didn't. The fire had been in western Massachusetts; the Streeters had moved to Campion after that, and Johnny had been sent to a Catholic school in Meriden. The family kept a low profile in Campion. It felt odd to me, when I first read all of this, that this guy could've been living among us for all these years. He was roughly my age and I'd never encountered him—this tall, skinny dude with a somewhat dopey smile, wearing a Mets cap in nearly every picture of him that the media managed to find. He looked like the kind of guy I probably would've been friends with had he gone to Campion High.

Much was written about Johnny's longtime girlfriend, Jackie. She was eleven years older than him, and he moved in with her when he was twenty-two. They lived together in a little ranch house next to the Exxon station. She worked as an insurance inspector; he worked as a video store clerk and then later at an out-of-town Best Buy. Friends—her friends, because he didn't seem to have many of his own—said that at first Jackie took him in as a roommate, because she sometimes had trouble making her mortgage payment. But over time they somehow developed into a couple. *Sometimes it felt like she was sort of the mom and he was sort of the teenage son,* one of her "friends" said on *Dateline. Sometimes I'd really wonder.* Many speculated that this relationship kept Johnny busy, kept him in check—held off a psychological collapse that might under other circumstances have happened much earlier.

I'd seen Jackie interviewed in various contexts—in person and on TV. Someone had a half-finished amateur "documentary" about Johnny up on YouTube. Jackie was a large, muscular woman who always kept her hair knotted tight on top of her head, like a Sumo wrestler. Johnny started to go off the rails in 2009, when Jackie left him for a guy closer to her age. A few months before the shooting, the Best Buy he worked for closed, and he started getting behind on his rent.

I'd always felt bad for the nurse at Brookhaven on whom he'd tried to blame the whole shooting. Her name was Evie, she'd worked on his father's floor. She'd gone out for coffee with Johnny and then rebuffed him—about three weeks before the shooting. Still, it always seemed like the final straws for his imbalance were isolation and his unaccustomed financial struggle, not so much Evie. But that's just my armchair opinion. In Johnny's interviews with Detective Gagnon, he talked more about Evie than Jackie, his father, or anyone or anything else.

PROGRESS UPDATE

PATIENT NAME: Jonathan Streeter
DATE OF SERVICE: 7/20/97

Johnny reports that he has recently been dating a girl who is "a little younger" than him. He calls her "Uma." Johnny refuses to use her real name. He has previously expressed a sexual attraction to Uma Thurman, and a preoccupation with her romantic life—gleaned from entertainment magazines and gossip programs on television. Johnny has mentioned on multiple occasions that he watched this actress's love scenes in *Dangerous Liaisons* before going to sleep at night. Because of the age and power imbalance, as well as the sexually aggressive nature of the physical relationship featured in this film, and because Johnny has occasionally expressed rage at women who reject him sexually, this writer is concerned that "Uma" may be a minor. When asked by this writer, Johnny said that she is eighteen, but winked after saying so. When this writer repeated the question, Johnny repeated that she is eighteen.

Johnny is aware of statutory rape laws. This writer reminded him that I am legally obligated to report if his new companion is a minor.

NADINE

IT TOOK MY father a while to find me—that time he lost me in these woods when I was six or seven. He'd been screaming my name, but I'd ignored him at first. Then his voice got farther away, and then closer, then farther, and then jagged, like he was almost crying. It was then that I started to call back.

Here! I'm here, Dad! I'm here! Until he found me and pulled me into his chest.

His beer breath felt like home.

I thought I'd lost you. Don't run away on me again, Naddy.

I won't. I didn't mean to. I was just sneaking because I wanted to surprise the pteranodons.

It was maybe not true. I was too old to hunt for winged dinosaurs. But I didn't want to admit that his songs were starting to bore me.

I understand. He was trying to catch his breath. *But I thought I'd lost you.*

You didn't, though. Are there any snacks left?

Only raisins and peanuts, Naddy Baby.

I'm not a baby.

Now my phone *ding-dongs* in my pocket. It's a text from my landlord, asking where I am. I see that my mother also wrote nearly an hour earlier. I'm not sure how long I've been standing here.

Did you end up at the Apple Blossom? She wrote. *Beautiful, isn't it? Please check in by tonight, if you can.*

My poor long-suffering mother, always waiting for some sort of sign that I'm not crazy after all.

I pitch my phone into the water and head up the trail to Breakneck Pond.

HENRY

PROGRESS UPDATE

PATIENT NAME: Jonathan Streeter
DATE OF SERVICE: 11/1/97

Johnny called this office on 10/30 and terminated therapy. He stated that he recently found an apartment with roommates and is therefore no longer bound by his father's conditions for living in his home—which include therapy. Johnny terminated via phone service. This writer called Johnny back and left him a message, and has not heard from him since.

Johnny has exhibited no signs of violent behavior during the course of this treatment. As of his final session, he was continuing his work on strategies for dealing with perceived slights at his workplace and with his family. The situation described in the Progress Note of 7/20

> was previously resolved as the relationship between Johnny and "Uma" ended shortly after the report was written. Before that point, Johnny continued to state that the girl was eighteen and that sexual intercourse never took place.

Well, great, Fabian. He didn't fuck that girl. But he fucked a whole lot more people in the end.

I sucked in a breath and tried to return to my previous mantra. *I'm not going to be angry, Fabian.*

I really was trying. Fabian dealt with Johnny twenty years ago. I dealt with him at the very last possible minute. We both fucked it up some, clearly. But I was still here and poor Fabian wasn't.

I glanced back at Fabian's first appointment note for Nadine and then his first for Johnny. Both started out with multiple days a week. But what was interesting to me was that Nadine had one of her appointments on Fridays at two and Johnny on Fridays at three. Was that why Fabian pulled their files at the same time? Because he filed them by appointment time? Or because they were close alphabetically, and when he grabbed one he pulled out the other? Or because he associated the two together for some additional reason?

"What're you thinking, Peacher?" Greg wanted to know.

I closed the file in my lap.

"Have you ever watched *Rudolph the Red-Nosed Reindeer* as an adult?" I asked Greg. "I mean, the Christmas special from the sixties?"

"No. I watched it every year when I was a kid, though."

"So you remember it pretty well, then?"

"I remember the ice monster. I remember the elf who wanted to be a dentist."

"Well, I was watching it with my girls the night before we found Dr. Fabian, and a lot of it surprised me. Do you remember that Rudolph has a sexy girlfriend named Clarice?"

"I wouldn't have remembered the name, but okay."

"So I was watching it, and there's this moment where the sexy reindeer Clarice randomly breaks into this song called 'There's Always Tomorrow.' The sound quality is pretty bad, like you're hearing it from an old record playing far away, and it's so fucking depressing and full of false Christmas promise, I started wondering how many people in the course of the history of that special have gotten up in the middle of it and walked into a quiet back room of their house and blown their brains out."

"Huh." Greg pulled into a gravel driveway. "Probably one or two. But I don't think there's any way to find those stats."

"I mean, that thing has been playing on TV every year for about fifty years. It's probably happened a couple of times at least."

"I'd think it would be more likely during *Frosty the Snowman,* though." Greg turned off the car. "Frosty melts."

"For me it's not really about the storyline so much as the tone."

"Huh. Well, did the girls like it?"

"Sure. They loved it."

"Well, there you go," Greg said.

Getting out of the car, I tidied the contents of the files and placed them on the passenger seat. As I did it, I thought again of the question I'd been considering before Greg had interrupted—the question of Fabian's association of Streeter and Nadine.

I heard myself hiss with recognition. *Maybe Nadine was "Uma."*

"What is it?" Greg asked.

"Nothing," I said, and slammed the door.

There was only one car at this Apple Blossom place, and it had a Connecticut plate. When we rang the bell, no one answered for a while—until an elderly woman came to the door. She said that she was the "innkeeper," so we asked about a Nadine Raines staying there, and she said no.

I showed her the Vermont DMV picture I'd printed out, just in case.

"Oh," she said. "Yeah, a girl who looked like that stayed last night."

"But she didn't say her name was Nadine Raines?"

"She said her name was Lisa."

"Did she use a credit card?"

"No, sir. She paid in cash."

Greg and I glanced at each other. Nadine Raines was *running*. Nadine Raines was *hiding*.

"When did she leave?" Greg asked.

"Early this morning. *Early*. Before I even got up."

"When do you get up?"

"Six thirty."

"Any chance she's coming back, you think? Did she officially check out or did she leave anything in the room?"

"No. I haven't made up the room yet, but I peeked in to see

if she'd really vacated it. She paid in advance and left her key at the front desk."

"I'd like to check out her room," I said. "If you don't mind?"

"Sure," the lady said.

I went up to the room while Greg went outside and put out a BOLO on her car. Vermont plates, 45SZD.

After unlocking the door for me upstairs, the innkeeper left me in Nadine's room.

I flipped the light on to see an unmade bed and wallpaper splashed with pukey pink roses. The room smelled powerfully of lemony wood cleaner. I tried not to breathe too deeply as I checked the drawers and underneath the bed. She hadn't left anything.

There was a Shaker chair facing the window that overlooked the inn's backyard. It was in an awkward position—pulled unusually close to the window—away from the table where a matching chair stood without a companion.

I stared at that chair, imagining a long, slender back in it, with a brown ponytail hanging down its middle. I didn't move. I waited for her to turn around. I could hear only my breath.

"That's done," Greg said from the doorway. "Anything?"

I turned around. Greg was giving me a funny look.

"Not much. I was just about to check the bathroom."

In the bathroom, there was a plastic water bottle in the wastebasket. Beneath the bottle was a cushion of brown hair—one long swath twisted neatly into a nest.

"*Jesus,*" I said.

"What?" Greg said.

As he came in the bathroom, I saw that he had the Streeter file in his hand.

I swallowed my surprise and pointed to the wastebasket. "Someone was giving herself a makeover in here."

"That's kind of creepy, to put it in the garbage like that."

"Except . . . where else? Leave it lying across a pillow for the old lady to find? Bring it with her?"

"Same length and color as the one they found on Fabian's sweater. Hard to say, though." Greg hesitated. "Peacher, when were you going to tell the rest of us about this Streeter connection?"

"When I finished reading the file," I said. I took it from him. "Look. I'm going to see if this lady will let someone come in here to take the hair and dust for prints on the bottle and around the room. We'll see if we can find some matches with what we've got from Fabian's office."

The innkeeper agreed to keep the door locked and the room unoccupied until we could get someone in there to take prints.

"Seemed like a nice girl," she said as she locked the door. "But you never know."

IN THE CAR, Greg asked me again about the Streeter file.

"Don't let that distract you," I said, and motioned for him to start the car. "Streeter's in jail and Fabian had a brush with him twenty years ago. If I see anything you need to know, I'll tell you. Right now my primary concern is finding this woman. If she took off early this morning, she could be half-way across the country by now. A woman who apparently traveled all around the world? Might be savvy enough to be out of the country, even. When we get back I need you to work on a warrant for her ATM card activity. And her cell phone activity."

"Sure," Greg said, keeping his eyes on the road.

I really wanted to see Nadine Raines again. To see how she'd aged, and how she spoke now, and what kind of look she'd have in her eyes. To see if I felt any sort of instinct about her this time, one way or another. Because I was beginning to wonder about instincts. About Fabian's and mine.

NADINE

AFTER THAT NIGHT with Johnny, I had a lot to report to you. Things hadn't gone as I had anticipated, but that didn't mean I had to throw it all away. I could just tell you the parts you might like.

"I went on a kind of date last week," I said, with a modest little shrug.

"Oh?" You sat up and brightened in that way you did only very occasionally—like it delighted you, for real, to hear I was doing something normal and fun for once.

"Yeah. Me and this guy . . . I mean . . . this guy and I . . . we went to that new pizza place, just around the corner from here."

"Oh . . . I tried that place myself, last week."

"Not bad, right?"

"Right. But . . . how was the . . ." You hesitated, treating the word with delicacy. "Date?"

"Good. Uh, *that* date itself was good. We talked about music a lot. But, uh . . . then we got together again a couple of days later, and that wasn't as good."

You tilted your head just so—as if not sure you should be interested. "Why not?"

"He kissed me," I said, trying to maintain a neutral tone.

From you, an uncomfortable little squint. "And you didn't want him to?"

"Oh . . . I wanted him to. But then it went farther than that and . . . Well, I don't mean to say that I wasn't willing. It was just, afterward I wished maybe it hadn't gone that far."

Your nod was perfectly calm and perfectly understanding. Frustratingly so, even.

"I was a little tipsy," I explained.

Another, similar nod.

"And was he?"

"I think so. He drank the same thing as me. Apple cider mixed with tequila."

Your face changed at the description of the cocktail. You avoided my gaze for a moment.

"Was that his idea or yours?"

I didn't stop to consider the low quality of your voice.

"Would you ask that if I was a guy?" I spat. "I'm eighteen and I wanted to drink as much as he did. It kind of annoys me that whenever there's some kind of vice involved, like drinking or making out, girls supposedly lose their brains or their will somehow. I didn't say I was a victim of someone else's idea here. I just said I wished it hadn't gone that far."

You hesitated. I could tell you were working on constructing some entirely different avenue of discussion for us to explore. It took you nearly a minute to formulate your response.

"Are you sure this relationship is something you want to pursue, given how soon you'll be leaving for Arizona? Are you sure that's intelligent?"

I was silent. You no longer seemed delighted. And your questions were too analytical to feel fatherly or protective. They were simply disapproving.

After a moment, I realized what my error had been. I'd tipped my hand accidentally. I hadn't meant to reveal it was Johnny right away—or ever, perhaps. I'd wanted to milk the incident for your general reaction first, before deciding whether I'd pop out with the identity of the guy involved, and watch you potentially freak out.

But what I'd said about the cider cocktail, or maybe even something else, had probably alerted you to who I was talking about. Maybe Johnny drank that foul mix all the time. Maybe he gave it to all the girls he dated, although I suspected there weren't many of those.

Your initial delight was at my unexpected normalcy—innocently dating a guy in the summer before college. But then I'd betrayed myself. I'd pursued your patient—an extension of you, in a way. For a reaction. To break you, just a little.

I'd not reformed myself—only learned to do the same old twisted things without a box cutter. And you *saw* me. You saw that I was the broken one and always would be. I could tell from the disappointment in your eyes. I wasn't just crazy—I was stupid, which was of course worse.

And to think that I hadn't even told you the half of it. I hadn't told you about his big bony hands pressing against my chest or the jizz I'd mopped up with my lacy pink tank top. All the other little details of that night that I thought might shake your remove. Uncomfortable details I wanted you to gobble up like a cardamom crisp.

I'd wondered since the very beginning, if you had seen this about me. Had you somehow seen, in your infinite psychological professionalism, that this desire danced up and down my veins, redder and more vital even than blood—this wish to expose, and be exposed? This wish to see the shock register in your face, to see you try to hide it, to smile all the way home at the thought of it?

This wish was in my DNA, I was certain. I wanted you to know *why,* but it was starting to look like you never would. We had three sessions left. And maybe it would be best if you just overlooked this thing with Johnny—if you would be willing and lazy enough to pretend I was normal for just a couple more weeks.

The outcome was a 50/50. I had no idea which you would choose.

The next time I came in, you said simply: *We have only three sessions left. What would you like to talk about?*

In such typical fashion, you were making it seem like my choice. You were even going to let me pretend Johnny had never happened. I gripped my hands to keep them from shaking. I wasn't sure if the choice made me relieved or furious.

I looked up at you and smiled as innocently as I knew how.

"Rattlesnakes," I said.

HENRY

AN OFFICER FROM the Brattleboro PD called me on my cell right as we were pulling into the station.

"My partner and I went to her listed address there, and talked to her landlord," he said. "So, she keeps a really small room up there, basically just an attic room that she rents for really cheap to have someplace to live when she's teaching her class, and in between her traveling and volunteer jobs. Like, they have an open arrangement that he can sublet the place whenever he wants as long as it's empty by the time she gets back. The guy said that she teaches some kind of medical class and she does work at a hospital near there sometimes as a float nurse, when she comes home for long enough. He seemed to really like her. Said she'd rented the room for about five years. The guy's apartment reeked of pot, for what that's worth."

"Did he say when the last time he saw her was?" I asked, following Greg into the station.

"Last week. Around the eleventh, he said. Said she told him she was going to visit family in Connecticut for the holidays, and to do some of her artwork down here. He said he was surprised because he never realized she had family so close by."

"Alright." Greg was pouring a cup of coffee, and motioned the pot in my direction. I shook my head. "There someone staying in her place right now?"

"No."

"Okay." I figured we might have reason to search it soon. "Good to know. Thanks a lot. I'll be in touch."

When I hung up, Amy approached me.

"Just got the phone records," she said. "I started to look at them for you. Fabian had calls from that Raines woman's number you wanted me to cross-check."

"Okay. Thanks. What day?"

"Tuesday."

She handed me the records. "There are calls to Fabian's son and his girlfriend, Linda. And that call to Eugene Morrison. Two other numbers this week, that's all. I'm trying to find their identities."

"Next thing I need to do is track Nadine Raines's movement on her cell," I said. "Was on my way to my desk to do a warrant for that."

ONCE THAT WARRANT request was in, I scanned Fabian's files on Johnny Streeter and e-mailed them to Amy, Greg, and Chief Wheeler with the subject line *Fabian treated Streeter, FYI.* I needed to get ahead of this before Greg did. In the text of the e-mail I explained how long ago their interaction had been, and that I'd read the complete file and did not think Streeter's case had a direct connection to Fabian's death. I added that

I was wary of this becoming a distraction—to us, or to the media, should they unfortunately get ahold of this. I suggested we should call Johnny Streeter's sister to see if she had any knowledge of Fabian. And that one of us should go speak to Streeter's old girlfriend Jackie and see if he ever spoke of an old therapist. Meanwhile, I pointed out, it was looking like Nadine Raines was still our main person of interest.

As soon as I hit Send, I said to Amy, "Check out what I just e-mailed you. While you all digest that, I'm going to talk to someone who saw Nadine Raines right before she took off. Shouldn't be long."

IT SEEMED TO me that the only people who spoke to Nadine during her recent visit to town were her parents, her dead shrink, and her old friend and mine, Julie Olasz. Maybe Julie would have something useful to say.

Julie lived in Wallingford now—just a twenty-minute drive away. The Hans Christian Andersen stories were still cued up on my iPod hookup. The somber narrator started in on "The Little Match Girl," and I quickly turned it off.

I was missing the girls. I thought of the time Olivia asked me to read from her storybook the Grimms' tale about the sisters "Snow White and Rose Red."

Near the beginning, there's a part where Snow White and Rose Red spend a night in the woods. When they wake up at daybreak, they catch a glimpse of a boy in white sitting near where they slept. And after he disappeared, they realize they were sleeping right next to a precipice, and that they "would certainly have fallen into the darkness if they had gone only a few paces further." Their mother, upon hearing this, tells them that it was probably the angel who watches over good children.

"Do you really think that there's an angel who watches over good children?" Olivia had interrupted me.

"It's a nice idea," I had replied.

Olivia had sighed. "Okay. But do you think that if the angel wasn't there, Snow White and Rose Red would have fallen into that hole?"

Sophia, who I had not thought was listening because she was playing so intently with her stuffed dogs, had looked up and declared, "I'm like Snow White. Olivia's like Rose Red."

"No, you're not! *I'm* like Snow White!" Olivia had countered.

Sophia had just smiled and said softly, "Nope."

I was glad they didn't ask me to weigh in, because I'd probably have to admit that Sophia was right. It startled me how confident she was of this, and how her confidence enraged Olivia. They *both* knew she was right. Sophia was quieter and more gentle. Olivia was more boisterous. The story said that they were both good and happy girls, but that didn't seem to matter to Olivia or Sophia. They both wanted to be Snow White.

We never finished the story because the girls had started to claw at each other in passionate disagreement. That night Katie and I wondered if we had failed as parents because the girls seemed to put such weird value on whiteness. I'd nonetheless been relieved not to have to answer the question about the bullshit angel who guards good children.

AT JULIE'S ADDRESS was a blue house with two white dormers that someone hadn't yet painted, and a tangle of bikes and Razor scooters on the front lawn. She opened the door after I'd rung the bell twice.

Julie had put on some weight since I saw her last, but still had the long, rippled mermaid hair down past her shoulders, and the same old Bambi eyes.

"Julie?" I said, as I watched her eyes jump with recognition.

"Henry . . . Oh, wow. How *are* you, Peachy?" Her face tightened. "Is everything okay?"

"Yes. Julie, this isn't an emergency. Okay? I'm here to ask you some questions about Nadine Raines, that's all."

"Nadine . . . really?"

"Her mother mentioned that she saw you."

Julie held the door and let me into her kitchen.

"Yeah. We had coffee a few days ago. I hadn't seen her in years."

"What day did you talk to her?"

"Let me see . . . I guess it was Monday. Why, Henry? Has something happened to her?"

"And you haven't heard from her since?"

Julie shook her head, then gestured to a kitchen chair. "My boys are out with their dad right now," she said. "They'll be back in about twenty minutes."

"Okay. Did Nadine say why she was back in town?" I asked, sitting across from Julie. On the table, someone had constructed a small Lego wall around a half-eaten sandwich.

"Well, visiting her parents for the holidays, mainly. I think it was kind of weird for her to be back. Over the years, when her parents have wanted to see her for the holidays, she's always convinced them to come to Vermont, or meet her at 'exotic locales,' as she put it. I seriously think this was the first time she'd set foot in Campion in at least a decade."

"And why do you think that is?" I asked.

Julie clicked her long fingernails noisily, then sighed. "What's this about?"

"Did she mention anything about Dr. Fabian? Dr. Mark Fabian?"

"No. The therapist who they just found? No, she didn't. Why?"

"So . . . just . . . no mention of him?"

Julie just shook her head. "Henry . . . tell me there's not some chance . . ."

"We're talking to *lots* of his patients, current and former."

Julie stared at me. "She was his *patient*?"

"And everyone he could've seen or come in contact with that day," I added.

"And that would've included Nadine?"

"We believe so."

"Oh, for fuck's sake." Julie closed her eyes for a moment. "You guys have proof she was there, or you just heard she was in town the same time this happened, and decided to go after her because of her reputation?"

"Is that how you think we do things? What do you take me for? Boss Hog?"

Julie plunked her elbow on the table and leaned her chin into her palm. "You didn't answer the question."

"I didn't know she was in town. I'd pretty much forgotten

about her at least a decade ago until we found some indication, in Dr. Fabian's office, that she'd been to see him recently. Okay? So if you're willing, I want you to talk to me a little bit more about your old friend."

"Fine." Julie picked up a couple of Legos and began to press them into the wall around the sandwich. "What do you want to know?"

"I guess you didn't know that Dr. Fabian was Nadine's therapist at one time."

Julie shook her head. "I knew they made her go to a shrink. After the thing happened. Since we weren't good friends after that, I didn't know the details. Just that she went."

"Okay. So just to clarify the history here, you were best friends all growing up. And then not so much after the thing . . . the thing with that teacher."

"Mr. Brewster . . . yeah, for sure. But it wasn't like we were great friends the day before that happened and then I never spoke to her again. She'd actually distanced herself from me quite a bit by the time that happened. For about a year, I'd say. Frankly, I *still* like to think that if we were closer that year, I could've stopped it somehow."

"Why do you think she was distant for that year before?"

"Well . . . I had a boyfriend, which was a new thing. Chris. Well, you remember. So maybe she felt like I was neglecting her. But . . . I think it wasn't just that."

"What else do you think it was?" I asked.

"I think she was still grieving about her dad, on some level. Her dad had died a few years earlier, you know? And I think it would come back to haunt her every so often, over the years when we were in junior high . . . high school. I think she'd have dark periods sometimes. That's why I always felt bad that it ended the way it did. Because she was troubled enough, I think, that someone should've noticed before the thing happened with the teacher."

"Wait. How old were we when her dad died?" I asked.

I knew this information was mentioned in Fabian's file, but I hadn't paid much attention to the exact age.

"Uh . . . eleven or twelve. No. Twelve. The end of sixth grade."

"So what year would that have been?"

"Mmm . . . '91, then."

Ninety-one. *TR 4/12/91.*

"Julie. What was Nadine's dad's first name?"

"Umm . . . Jim?"

"You sure of that?"

"No. Maybe it was Tim."

"Okay," I said. I was trying not to look too excited. Maybe Jim, maybe Tim. If it was Tim, we were getting somewhere.

"So after it happened . . . I mean, the thing with the teacher, were you two ever close enough again to talk about *why* she had done it?"

Julie shook her head. "We got together occasionally for a piece of pizza or whatever. Just me letting her know I hadn't *totally* dumped her. But we had different lives after that. Me finishing high school with everyone else, her at the alternative school and doing this weird art zine and constantly cramming for SATs and all kinds of things that I guess were supposed to make up for being in an alternative school when it came time to apply for college."

"I wonder if she had to disclose to colleges why she was at that school?"

My phone buzzed and I glanced at it. Chief Wheeler had replied to my e-mail. *In my office ASAP when you return.*

"I doubt it," Julie said. "That teacher never pressed charges. If there was any legal record of it, I assume it was sealed because she was a minor. I think the general thinking was that this was more of a mental health situation than a legal situation, given how random it was. There was some agreement that if she got serious help and didn't come back to the school, no one was going to make a legal issue of it."

"I wonder if that was the right thing. Looking back."

My phone buzzed again. A text from Wheeler—the exact same words as the e-mail.

"It was a hard situation. But it was before school shootings were, like, a thing. So maybe it was easier to just bury the incident—and the kid, in a way—without having to cover all of the legal bases."

Then Julie was quiet for a while, tapping two Legos together.

"I wonder if that shrink ever figured out why she did it," she said. "Because I sure never did. I mean, if I had to guess, I think it had something to do with her dad. You know, they were never sure if it was an overdose or suicide."

"That must have been really rough for her. As a kid."

"That would be an understatement. Can you imagine? I mean, now that we both have kids. Can you *imagine*?"

I didn't really want to, so I said, "But how does that translate into violence . . . in your opinion?"

"I think something was happening with her in that year

before . . . that year when she was so often aloof, and I wasn't paying attention because I was too busy smooching Chris."

She wasn't kidding. I remembered Chris always pinning her to her locker, their faces smushed together. I remembered being insanely jealous. I hadn't had a girlfriend yet, at the time.

"You know what I think started us on different paths, though? Even before Chris? When she and Amanda and I stopped hanging out as, like, a threesome."

"Amanda . . . Morrison?" I said.

"Yeah. Back when she and Nadine and I were all kind of in the same neighborhood, we were all friends. Nadine didn't have as much patience for us after her dad died, you know? But what sealed the deal was when Amanda and I started working as candy stripers at Brookhaven. Such righteous little Girl Scout types we were, then."

"When was this?"

"The end of freshman year, I think. We were doing that, but Nadine refused. She said she didn't want to go in that place. I didn't particularly want to do it either, but Amanda's dad was encouraging her to do it and she didn't want to do it alone. You know, he had all of his kids volunteering there, building their college resumes and whatnot. That was kind of a perk—hanging with Amanda's hot older brothers, because they worked there in the summers. They were in a punk band and one of them had that sexy hair like the guy in the Red Hot Chili Peppers. Amanda didn't have to twist my arm too much, and then I tried to twist Nadine's arm, but she wouldn't do it."

"Maybe she didn't want to have to hang out where her stepfather worked," I suggested.

Julie shrugged. "She said everyone there probably hated her."

"What did that mean?"

Julie pressed a blue Lego into the wall. "I don't know how much you know about Nadine's dad. But she told me once that her dad had been stealing some kind of drugs from the Brookhaven pharmacy supply, and that's why he was fired."

"Nadine's dad . . . her real dad . . . worked at Brookhaven?"

"Yeah. You didn't know that?"

"No," I admitted.

"It was brief, but yeah. As a janitor or something. I want to say her stepdad kind of helped him get the job, if you can believe that. So he could be near Nadine. Anyway, they think that's where he got the drugs he OD'ed on. So . . . yeah. You can see how Brookhaven wouldn't be her favorite place."

"So she was embarrassed to be there, you think? Or mad at the people who fired him?"

"Maybe both. Maybe neither. Maybe it was just painful. But . . . in any case, Amanda and I volunteered a couple of times a week, and ended up hanging out a lot *without* Nadine because of it."

"And she got mad at you for it?"

"Probably. But what I'm saying is, whatever the story was with her dad, she internalized it. This was a teenage kid feeling so troubled over her dad that she didn't want to show her face at Brookhaven. And isolated herself. There was probably a lot going on in her brain, and without friends or family to talk to, it had no outlet."

"Okay. But how do you go from 'no outlet' to stabbing a teacher?"

"Well, I don't *know*. I didn't say I had *all* the answers. And that's not really the answer you're looking for right *now*, is it?"

Julie blinked at me. She had so much mascara on that it made me think of spiders. Then she sighed, got up, and took a wineglass down from the cabinet.

"I need some shiraz," she said.

"Because of me? Because of Nadine?"

"Because I have to make dinner. Because I hate cooking and the wine helps me forget that I'll be doing it almost every night for the next twelve years at least."

"Order a pizza," I suggested.

She smiled at me. "We had pizza last night, Henry, but thanks for the life hack there, old friend."

"One more question, Julie. Later in high school, after that thing happened with the teacher, and she was kicked out of school . . . did she ever mention knowing someone named Johnny?"

"Johnny?" She looked up, and her spidery eyes seemed to pop. "*No.*"

"Never?"

"Never."

"You just answered so quick, I wonder if—"

"*No,*" she said again.

"Okay. I'll let you get to your cooking, then." I said. "I should go."

Julie pulled a half-empty bottle of wine from the corner of her counter. "I wonder . . . What do you think draws people back to Campion when they are perfectly free to leave and never come back? Does it have some kind of magnetic pull? Or is that just how *all* hometowns feel?"

"I don't know," I admitted.

"It doesn't feel like much of anything special from an objective point of view. Population twenty-five thousand. Three Dunkin' Donuts, no bookstore. State champs in boys' soccer and girls' softball."

"I'm not sure the soccer thing is true anymore—it's not like when Chris and I were varsity."

"Alright, who gives a shit, Peachy?" Julie poured red wine into her glass. "I just don't know why Nadine would come back around here, when she's got the whole world to go to. I hope you can be fair to her."

"Of course I will."

Julie considered her glass and then dumped in one more slug before jamming the cork back into the bottle. "It might not be so easy. You saw her *stab* someone once. You have that image in your head forever. But that's not the only image of her there is."

"I actually didn't see her do it. I was in her class, but I was in the bathroom when it happened."

"I thought I remembered you telling about it."

"Yeah. You probably *do* remember that. But I was in the bathroom."

"What're you trying to tell me now, exactly?"

"Not much. Just that I could sometimes be an ass, back then."

She raised her eyebrows and took a sip of wine. "Well. You're not an ass *now,* right?"

"You're too kind."

"I mean, all things considered, Peachy. I hear you've done some pretty un-assy things in the last few years."

That wine of hers looked pretty good right about now. I wished I could spend the evening at this messy table, drinking and confessing inconsequential sins to old friends.

"I still have work to do," I said.

Julie tilted her glass toward me, as if toasting to me. "Don't we all."

NADINE

OUR SECOND TO last session.

You were letting me talk about small refrigerators. The kind everybody gets for their dorm room. My mom and I had gone shopping for one and it felt like the most normal thing we'd done in years. She'd also insisted on getting me some fluffy teal towels and a cute desk lamp with a twisty adjustable neck. This was really happening. For her and for me.

You asked me how big the fridge was. I showed you with my hands.

"Just big enough for a six pack and a few containers of yogurt," I said.

"That's probably all you need," you admitted. "In college."

"Yeah," I agreed.

In the silence that followed, I thought of my dad. What would *he* say I needed? He'd have laughed at my little refrigerator, probably. He'd have given me some kind of music, and some kind of simple utilitarian object, like a pencil or a comb or a pair of old shoes.

Which music, and which object? I shook off the questions, because it all would've been an affectation anyway. And then I looked at my watch. We had only fifteen minutes left. You seemed to notice that, too.

Time to talk about Something Significant.

"You didn't mention last time if you saw that young man again," you said quietly.

"Oh. No. I didn't. I meant to write about it in the notebook, but I forgot. There wouldn't have been much to write, anyway."

You hesitated. "So it's over."

I shrugged. "Yeah. Probably that's the smartest thing."

Normally you might have told me to set aside what was smart for a moment, and consider how I *felt*. But we both knew that that wasn't the most important thing in this situation.

Ten minutes left. There was something else I needed to say about Johnny, I decided. I *could* wait till next week. But next week was our last session and I didn't want this to be the last thing I told you.

I opened my mouth and just let it fall out:

"There's something you ought to know."

"What's that, Nadine?"

"I just want to say it and I don't want to talk about it. I just want to say it as a favor to you, and then we don't really *talk* about it."

You tried not to look amused. "A favor?"

"I'm pretty sure he started the fire," I said—loudly, so I wouldn't need to say it again.

"He. Who?"

"When he was eleven. Because he had a crush on the babysitter and he tried to kiss her and she laughed and made him feel stupid. He might have thought he wanted to rescue her, or he might have wanted to kill her, but either way, he started it."

"You . . ." You folded your arms. "I—"

"Maybe you're not allowed to say much," I interrupted. "And that's okay. I just wanted to mention that to you before I move to the other side of the country and never see you again."

Those last words nearly made my voice break. One more session and you'd be dead to me. Dead as a dinosaur.

You were silent, but couldn't hide the surprise in your eyes. I was pretty sure they didn't cover situations like this in Shrink School.

And then I was too sad to look at you. I'd so wanted to break you, months and months ago. And now I had, just a little bit. Now that I didn't really want to anymore. But now I didn't feel I had a choice.

I glanced at my watch again.

"We're out of time," I said. "We have to stop now."

There were a couple of minutes left, actually. But close enough. I didn't want to sit here and feel tempted to enjoy the look on your face.

Because although I had great affection for you, you hadn't changed me at all.

HENRY

BACK AT THE station, Amy was hard at work at her desk, sifting through Fabian's old files while she nibbled on a piece of pizza. Greg was off somewhere trying to get some more dirt on Connor Osbourne, she said.

Wheeler's office door was closed. I quickly checked the vital records database for a Tim Raines in the early nineties.

Raines, Timothy Michael. He had died on April 12, 1991.

Score. I wasn't sure what kind of score, but it made me feel better about having to knock on Wheeler's door.

WHEELER LOOKED UP from his computer but didn't say hello.

"That was a heck of an e-mail bomb to drop right before walking out the door, Henry."

"Sorry. I wanted you all to see it ASAP but I had someone to go talk to. This Nadine Raines lead we've got—an old friend of hers saw her just two days before Fabian's death, and I wanted to see what she had to say."

As I sat down, I noticed that there was a blood-red spot in

one of the whites of Wheeler's eyes. It was about the size of the head of a pin—tiny but gruesome in its brightness.

"Anything useful?" he asked.

"Um . . . Sort of."

I described for him Fabian's scribbled notes, and their possible connection to Nadine and her father's death. I tried to make eye contact without appearing to look directly at the red spot.

"Henry." Wheeler sighed and folded his meaty hands on the desk. "I'm sure that Dr. Fabian was thinking about a *lot* of things on the day he was killed. None of them are necessarily related to how he *died*. What's relevant is what the perp was thinking, no?"

"Nadine Raines is our main suspect. And Fabian was privy to what she was thinking. So what he was writing about that *is* relevant, I'd say."

"Of course, that's one way of looking it," Wheeler said. "You know, I'm wondering why Fabian never came forward before, after the shooting. It seems like he could've provided some insight about Streeter, about his family?"

"Maybe not useful insight, by that point. The thing had already happened. Fabian treated him years and years before. I don't know if you noticed, but Streeter's dad paid him kind of under the table, so there was no insurance record or anything for anybody to access after the shooting."

"Fabian himself would've had to have come forward saying Streeter was once his patient. Just seems like he could've . . ."

"Maybe he wanted to keep it a secret," I interrupted. "Probably that's most likely."

"Because . . ."

I looked at my hands for a second. I was beginning to wonder if Wheeler's blood spot was real or something my brain had conjured up to make this moment especially uncomfortable. Maybe the more I looked at it, the bigger it would get.

"Because he was ashamed," I said. "Because he didn't do enough."

"Henry." I looked up but tried to focus on Wheeler's chin.

Wheeler sighed and placed his palm gently over his eye. "It's a broken blood vessel, apparently. It's harmless and it'll go away in a few days. But not before I scare the shit out of my grandkids on Christmas."

I nodded.

"Henry, should I be worried about you?"

I hesitated. "Why do you ask?"

"Greg mentioned you were talking about Rudolph the Red-Nosed Reindeer shooting himself, or something."

"That's a bit of a misquote. Greg and I have very different senses of humor."

"Right. I guess I've noticed that lately. Look. I think I'm going to ask you to have Amy do the legwork on talking to anyone directly related to Streeter. At least to start. Just so there are no questions later, things that might make things difficult for the prosecutor and whatnot. Just to keep things on the up and up."

"Sure. Okay."

Wheeler looked like he'd expected to have to say more.

"Well . . . good," he said slowly.

I hesitated, realizing that Nadine might very likely have had direct contact with Streeter. But I didn't have any intention of handing her off to anyone else.

"Great," I said. "If that's settled, I'm going to get back to work."

Back at my desk, I managed to get Michelle Zimmerman—the current director of Brookhaven—on the phone. She was friendly, but she had started working at Brookhaven in 2006. So when I read her Fabian's legal pad scribble that mentioned Brookhaven, she didn't know what to make of it.

"I had no idea Dr. Fabian even worked here," she told me. "It's so sad, what's happened. Have you spoken to Eugene about it?"

"Yes, I have. But I'm wondering if you could put me in touch with some of the other longtime employees who might know what this means? Particularly anyone who would've worked with Fabian? In the late nineties–early 2000s range?"

"Sure, I can try to get a list together for you. But someone who comes to mind right away who you should talk to is Bev Hatfield. Do you know her? I think she went to all of the memorials."

"I'm not sure if I met her."

"She worked there from the beginning. From 1988. Retired in 2009."

I took Bev's number once Michelle found it.

"She lives in the Milbridge apartment complex in Southington," Michelle continued. "She was a good, dedicated worker, knew the place inside and out. Not to mention all the gossip."

"Thanks. That sounds great—I'll check in with her. Now, Anthony Gagliardi's been there since the very beginning, too, right?"

"Yes." Michelle hesitated. "But he often isn't directly involved with the residents. He might not know as much about Dr. Fabian's involvement with that."

"Okay," I said. "Thanks, Michelle."

BEV HATFIELD STUDIED Fabian's "Brookhaven" note carefully, crunching on a butter cookie from a tin and then flicking the crumbs from her pearly pink fingernails.

I was sitting—at Bev's insistence—in a fat beige recliner by her small fake Christmas tree with an impressive supply of gifts beneath it. They were wrapped in green with winking Santas and red with silver angels, stacked in alternating layers that had to have been deliberate. From somewhere in the kitchen, Bing Crosby was softly insisting that it was beginning to look a lot like Christmas.

"Patricia Greenblatt," Bev said, handing me the note. "I'll bet that's who he means. I remember her, of course. She was a patient at Brookhaven a good long time. About seven or eight years, I think. See, that's an argument for not shipping folks out to a home too early. Someone's going to end up paying through the nose if you live too long. Her son was a sweetheart, but I think that's the situation he got himself in. Even with the family money she had. Brookhaven. Luxury retirement. Not cheap."

"This was a local family?"

"I'm not sure what you mean by that. I don't think he lived in Campion, but somewhere close."

Bev offered me the cookie tin, and I took a second one. I hadn't had dinner.

"You remember this son's name?"

"Mmm . . . no. I want to say Daniel or David. He was an orthodontist, so you could look him up. How many Greenblatt orthodontists could there be around here?"

"Right. Well, yeah. We'll do that, I'm sure. Now, Dr. Fabian wrote this note shortly before he was killed. Can you think of any reason he'd have done that?"

"Hmm." Bev put down the tin and fluffed her hair, which was platinum blond but had the shape of a colonial era wig. "It was years ago, when Mrs. Greenblatt was a patient there. I don't remember exactly when she died. But . . . a few years before I retired, at least."

"Was she living at Brookhaven in 2001?"

"Sounds about right."

"Was she one of the patients who Dr. Fabian counseled? That you recall?"

Bev's eyes jumped with a sort of momentary recognition.

"Uh . . . *yes.* Yes, in fact. Now, he was usually counseling new folks getting adjusted to life at Brookhaven. Or sometimes did grief counseling if a married couple was there together, and a spouse died. But with Mrs. Greenblatt it was a different kind of a situation."

She was silent for a moment. Bing Crosby sang about toys in every store, and then I had a moment of blind panic. *Toys.* Had Katie bought any Santa gifts yet? Olivia wanted some sort of monstrous pink plastic dollhouse castle she'd seen in a catalog. Sophia wanted an alarm clock and a Saint Bernard.

"I'd forgotten about this," Bev said. "There were a tense few days there at Brookhaven. There was a brand new nurse. Pretty young. And she reported some kind of problem with Mrs. Greenblatt. Now, I think she was showing some early signs of dementia and that may have been getting worse. I'm not sure what the details were. But Fabian was called in and then her son was called in. Then there was some meeting between the family and a few of the staff members. I'm not quite sure what happened. But by the end of it the new nurse was gone. And Mrs. Greenblatt was moved to a different floor. I think there was an issue with her medication, maybe among other things."

"Huh. You think there was some misconduct on the part of the nurse?"

"Possible. We all thought so. It was kind of . . . hush hush."

"Was Dr. Morrison involved?"

"Sure. Well, probably. I mean, there were more hands-on doctors on staff . . . he was there more overseeing things generally, at that point. But that far back, I think he was."

"Do you remember the nurse's name? Where she went from there?"

Bev shook her head. "Sorry. She was a young thing. I didn't really get to know her, and then she was gone."

"I wonder if someone else would remember."

"Maybe Morrison might," Bev put in. "Although I hear he's not really himself anymore, all the time."

"Do you know of anyone else who was at Brookhaven in 2001? Who I could get her name from?"

"Mmm. My friend Nancy Little. She's in Florida now, but

she might remember. We were there about ten years together. And there's a couple of people in the administrative office, too, who've been there for quite a while. That Gagliardi guy, for example."

"Right. That guy," I said. Nadine's stepfather. He was next on my list.

After I took down the name and cell number for Bev's friend, I said, "Listen, Bev. Tell me about Fabian at that time. Do you think the patients liked him?"

Bev thought for a moment. From the kitchen, some lady was singing about muddling through somehow.

"Yes, from what I remember. He seemed like a gentle person. Laid-back. He didn't force himself on the patients. What I mean is, like if a new patient was having trouble, and a doctor set him or her up with Dr. Fabian, he would go in there and chat with them once. And if they seemed to want to chat more, he'd set up another appointment. If they didn't, he would be very clear about that. He'd just say, *you know, I don't think I'm what this person needs. You're going to have to try something else.* He knew that a lot of old folks weren't into therapy, and he respected that."

"Okay," I said. "Thanks, Bev. That's interesting."

I sat back in the recliner for a moment. I didn't want to leave yet. Bev reminded me of my late grandma—her tidy apartment and her workmanlike, almost automated attention to Christmas.

My cell started ringing. I stepped out of Bev's apartment to answer, hoping there was some word about Nadine Raines' location. But Amy was just letting me know that she had gotten ahold of Streeter's sister. She'd never heard of Dr. Fabian.

Her parents never talked to her about their "strategies" for dealing with Johnny's problems. They tried something new every few months, she said. Especially when he was a teenager. And anyway, she hadn't spoken to Johnny since before the shooting. She never visited him in prison.

"By the way, Amy," I said, after the update. "How's it going with Fabian's old files?"

"It's going. No phone number matches on any other old patients besides Nadine Raines. They're pretty old files—not many of those patients seem to be around anymore, but the ones who are I'm keeping as a separate list for you."

"Great. Thanks. Now, have you come across a file of anyone with the last name Greenblatt, by any chance?"

"Greenblatt. I don't remember that name."

"Well, if you do, can you give it to me?"

"Sure."

"It would be from the time when he was counseling at Brookhaven."

"I don't think he marked Brookhaven patients separately. But sure. I'll let you know. For the moment, though, I was headed out to pay a visit to Streeter's old girlfriend Jackie Greer, like we said. See if he ever mentioned Fabian to her. See if there's any sign of recent involvement or secondhand contact."

"Sounds good."

I stepped back into Bev's apartment to thank her once more.

She offered me a parting cookie. "You were there that day, weren't you? That day all those people were shot? You were one of the officers who came?"

"Yeah," I said.

"I wasn't," Bev said. "I retired the year before."

"I'm glad you weren't there," I offered.

"I don't know," She put down her cookie tin. "I just don't know."

She lowered herself into her recliner and closed her eyes. She only nodded when I said goodbye.

NADINE

AND THEN IT was our final session before I left for college—August 1997.

I gave you that dumb book and you acted surprised. Like a patient never gave you a gift before?

You said, "Well, thank you. I read a bit of Walker Percy years ago. And I've liked what I've read."

I said I'd bought it because I would miss you. You didn't reply.

The reason for the selection was that I'd read *The Moviegoer* a couple of weeks before and liked it; it seemed as good a gift as any, and there was the added hint of Johnny in the title. When I went to a used bookstore to find a copy, all I could find was Percy's essay collection called *The Message in a Bottle*. I liked that title even better, and it helped me refine my idea. I brought it home and tried to read the opening essay. I liked the first two pages, but then got lost in the intricacy of the words and closed the book. No matter. It would still make a good gift.

"Thank you," you said again, after an awkward silence. "I

wish you all the best in Arizona. I have a feeling you'll do quite well."

You shook my hand when the time was up. I cried all the way home.

And then, for a week, I jumped whenever the phone rang. It was never you. I watched *Days of Our Lives* and sweated in the summer heat as I packed up my last bags, packed up the family car for the trip across the country with my mother and stepfather.

And for the first week or two at school in Flagstaff, my heart would thump a little bit harder as I'd open my mailbox. You didn't have my address, but I thought that if you'd figured me out you'd have tracked me down.

But classes picked up and I went to a party or two and then there was an unmistakable autumn chill in the air. It felt like a different sort of chill in the mountains of Arizona, and I felt breathlessly, nakedly far from home.

I comforted myself that this was exactly what was supposed to happen—what you would've wanted for me. I knew you hadn't read between the lines, or perhaps even opened that gift book at all.

It mattered. But not as much as it could have.

I'VE BEEN WALKING for a while and I can just see Breakneck now. Although the weather is mild, there aren't many people out hiking. Only seven shopping days till Christmas. All I'd had to buy was Glenlivet and a boxed set of *Call the Midwife* DVDs, and now I'm not sure if I'll have a chance to give either of them anyway.

I lower myself onto the bank of the Breakneck, pull the Glenlivet out of its box, and unscrew the top. I take a sip and relish the warmth in my throat. I've always loved that feeling too much, but I suppose that's one of the more normal things I could confess to you at this point in our relationship, Bouffant.

I gaze at the wall of trees across the pond, wondering how many people have gotten lost here. It's not a huge place, but it's still a forest and somehow people manage.

In 1994, a girl got lost in these woods. Her name was Suri, and she was around my age at the time—fourteen or so. She was a Hasidic Jewish girl who'd come here on a bus full of her classmates. They were on a field trip to Old Sturbridge Village, and stopped here for a picnic lunch. A few of the kids wandered off for a hike; Suri got lost somehow and didn't come back. When park rangers couldn't find her after the first day of searching, busloads of Brooklyn Hasidic Jews came at the following dawn to scour the woods along with the authorities. There were helicopters and sniffer dogs.

I'm not sure it's a good idea for them to use dogs, my mother had remarked as we watched the local news together. *I don't think strict Jews like dogs.*

Anthony only grunted in response—by then even he was used to the dumb shit my mom would say—and we both were captivated by the search in a way that she wasn't—checking the local channels for news every couple of hours. I'm not sure what the draw was for Anthony. But I'd thought to myself that this was probably the ballad my father had been trying to think up for all of those hours by the pond. It had happened two years too late for him to write it. *The Ballad of Breakneck*

Pond. Would he ever have guessed it was supposed to be about a much-loved Hasidic Jewish girl from Brooklyn, the same age as the solitary daughter he had abandoned for a deep and painless sleep?

I take another small sip of scotch and watch the ripples on the pond.

HENRY

I DIDN'T HURRY INSIDE because I knew the girls were asleep.

I could tell from the shifting blue light against the shades that Katie was watching TV in the dark. Probably that Netflix series she'd recently discovered—about the British lady cop who keeps going into fugue states.

I closed my eyes.

You were there that day, weren't you?

What was most startling about Bev saying this was that she didn't qualify my presence the way other people always seemed to want to. She didn't say anything about courage or heroics. All she wanted to know was if I was there.

Yes. In the broadest sense, we can at least say I was there.

BY THE TIME I got to Brookhaven, Johnny had shot up the dining room.

I never saw the carnage there because I never entered that room. People always assume I saw it. I didn't. I only saw upstairs.

Eugene was on the floor of the hall outside of the dining room, bleeding and whimpering, "Stairs. Stairs. He's going for the stairs."

He looked like he was holding in his insides. A man in a blue shirt and baseball cap was opening the door to the stairwell and the hall. He had something black in his hand but I didn't really see it as he disappeared behind the door.

When I got into the stairwell, I heard his footsteps above me, and then the *ker-CHUNK* of the heavy stairwell door. I raced up to the second floor, my heart sounding like an ocean in my ears, my gun drawn. When I opened the door, there was a startling silence all along the cream-colored corridor. A wizened woman in a soft pink sweater scooched her walker into a doorway, head down, toilet flushing somewhere behind her. The floor seemed abandoned but for her.

And then shooting. Once, twice. Muffled. From one of the rooms down the hall. No. From above me. He'd gone two flights up, not one.

Back in the stairwell, I raced up the next flight. Until the last step, when I felt something warm my face, my arms, my legs. My foot seemed to be melting into that warmth.

Pop.

I needed to pull the foot out of its own puddle. I stared at my foot, which strangely did not appear liquid at all.

Pop.

Those were shots. There was no time to figure out this biological anomaly—my melting foot. I dragged it behind me and bolted out of the stairwell. As I charged down the hall, I saw the blue-shirted gunman aim into a room and fire.

I aimed and shot and missed. Because my index finger was melting.

A few feet from me, a food cart wailed.

A woman in purple scrubs was crouched behind the cart, arms wrapped around a bald person with skinny limbs. That's where the wailing was coming from.

"Shhh," said the woman, pressing herself against the tiny man, and then lifting her head. Her gaze found me. In it was sadness—no—horror—that I was melting, one extremity at a time.

Pop.

No. *Fuck you, Henry,* I heard my brain say. *This is you freezing. You're not melting. You're freezing. Like an animal. Unfreeze. Unfreeze. Un—*

"Shoot him," she said softly.

And then the baseball-capped gunman turned around and saw me. He shot. My left shoulder exploded with pain but my legs remained frozen in place. My gun was still in my right hand.

"Shoot him!" she screamed at me.

The man in the baseball cap stared for a moment, then began to lift his gun again.

Then I fired. Twice. And he fell.

NADINE

I KEEP WALKING AND I keep drinking.

I thought I'd lost you, Naddy Baby.

And the sorry truth is that he *did* lose me. For so long, and it makes me sad. And angry. But it was never *all* his fault—I don't care what anyone says.

I'm moving away from the pond now, into the trees. Weaving in and out of the marked trail.

I believed in things like ghosts and ESP. I believed in left-over pteranodons. Ultimately, I'd have believed anything.

I'm trying to keep walking, but my legs feel like noodles. When I see a fallen tree a few feet from the trail, I sit on it.

"I'm here," I whisper.

I want to see him here, coming through the trees. I want to see his too-tight Led Zeppelin T-shirt and smell the beer on his breath.

The *I'm here* is for him but still all I can picture is *you*.

You, about whom I know almost nothing. Except that you were kind, but maybe not competent. *Just like him.* You were the right size and age and general shape. But you could not understand me, and you certainly could never forgive me. Because your blood was nothing like mine.

I slide off the fallen tree and into the wet oak leaves beneath it. After a couple of long sips of Glenlivet, I pull my furry hood over my head and lie back in the leaves. A sharp stick nudges my shoulder, and I wriggle out of its reach.

I stare up at the jumble of dark branches veining the white sky. They appear to twist before my eyes, forming a crosshatch so thick I'm afraid no pteranodon could get through it, if it was gliding from higher up.

So what am I supposed to do now? Pretend I am Suri from Brooklyn? Lie here in the woods and wait for my busloads of bearded saviors?

The thicket above me sways, creaks gently, and then goes black.

HENRY

S*O YOU SEE, Fabian. I think you and I have some things in common.*

You maybe could have stopped Johnny twenty years ago. Or at least, I bet you think you could have. How could you not?

I think the same way. Not about twenty years ago. But about those last possible minutes. No, I couldn't have stopped him in the cafeteria. I wasn't even there yet. But I could've stopped him on the third floor, if I had been faster and sharper. Three people died on the third floor. Would you like to know their names? Florence Rattel. Paula Fischer. William Dotson.

Three people that might not have died on March 7, 2010. Three families that have to live with that fucked-up reality every day for the rest of their lives. But maybe it was worse for you. Because maybe you took on the whole ten.

Your son said you hadn't been the same in the last few years. Was it because of Streeter? Was it worrying how much you could've done? What was it like for you, to have Johnny

Streeter in your files and your memory, and not share it with anyone?

I've been wondering lately if you were kind of a shitty therapist. And that shouldn't matter. I get it, Fabian. I understand half-assed more than almost anything. It's how I lived a fair amount of my life. And even if you were the same way, you didn't deserve to die like that.

NADINE

I SURRENDER TO THE cold and wet of the leaves, and I drift off.

It's the day they found Suri here. They found her praying by a tree. Anthony and I were watching the news report. We were both relieved, but he seemed uncharacteristically delighted. When he saw a glimpse of her on the screen, he gripped my shoulder and pulled me into his side for a moment.

"Great job!" he shouted. "They found her!"

We were both caught up in this joyous, though voyeuristic, moment. I leaned against his shoulder, welcoming its warmth in the initial seconds, but then pulling away quickly, feeling it as a jarring sensation of something forbidden.

Anthony didn't seem to notice when I stepped away from him. He was still glued to the television. He was nodding and smiling as the news reporter explained that Suri had rationed the food from her packed lunch.

I went to my room, where I could privately pretend, for a few minutes outside of Anthony's presence, that *I* was the one who'd been lost and then found.

WHEN I OPEN my eyes, the air is cold and the woods are dark.

What time is it? I fumble for my phone and then remember that it's at the bottom of Bigelow Pond.

I get up and make my way in the direction that I think that I came from. I *thrash thrash thrash* in the leaves and the sticks for four or five minutes, until the wide trail-road back to the boat launch opens up before me.

There is enough moonlight to see my way down the road. Whenever I hear a creak or a snap, I comfort myself that it's him. He's still here. Still enjoying the solitude, still trying to figure out how to finish his song.

HENRY

KATIE WAS ASLEEP on the couch when I went inside. Unusual, but not unheard of. There was a bowl of popcorn on the side table, with an open Sprite can behind it.

There were doll clothes and kid clothes all over the carpet—and at her feet, a naked doll with a napkin ring around her neck, and one of Katie's red cloth Christmas napkins fastened over her face. I could surmise what happened here. Frustration over the treatment of this doll—or the difficulty of removing the napkin ring from her neck—led to tantruming and then a hasty and dramatic bedtime, followed by some short-lived Mommy time that Katie was too exhausted to actually enjoy.

They didn't make me detective for nothing, Fabian.

I started to pick up the clothes, and put them in the blue and purple bins next to the couch. Blue was Olivia's and purple was Sophia's. But I had no idea which doll clothes belonged to which kid. Put them away anyway to show Katie I wasn't as lazy as she liked to think? Or leave them out and save her the grief of the girls fighting out my mistakes in the morning?

I left the stuff where it was and climbed the stairs. I tiptoed past the girls' room and flipped on the bathroom light. A blue-eyed something grinned at me from behind the toothbrush holder.

"Aahh!" I hollered, before I could stop myself.

Elf on the Shelf, the self-satisfied little fucker. He had been a gift from my parents, and Katie and I both hated him. We only took him out when we were feeling desperate—which seemed more often lately.

I grabbed the toothpaste and turned the elf's back to me while I brushed.

"Daddy?"

I turned around to see Olivia standing in the hallway, wearing candy cane pajamas.

"What are you doing up, honey?"

"I heard you yelling. I thought you were having another nightmare."

"Oh. No. And you need to get back in bed."

"Can you read me 'The Snow Queen'?"

I wished both kids were up. And I imagined Olivia telling Sophia tomorrow—after I left early—that I'd treated her to a late-night story. But then, Sophia hated the Snow Queen. I could leave her a note promising her I'd read her one of those books she liked—we both liked—about the talking dog named Martha. Maybe that would help. Help lessen this sinking feeling that somehow Olivia was becoming mine, and Sophia Katie's.

"Umm . . . okay," I said. "And then back to bed."

"Yay!" Olivia said in a stage whisper.

I let her get on our bed. Mostly I read it very quickly, thinking that Katie would come up any minute and get mad at me for priming the kid to be grumpy in the morning. But I slowed down as we neared the end, after Gerda finds Kay at the Snow Queen's palace and they finally make their way home to their old neighborhood, where they grew up together.

Olivia, who had begun to doze in the middle, probably sensed the change in my voice, and perked up as I read my favorite part—some of the very last sentences—

> Very soon they recognized the large town where they lived, and the tall steeples of the churches, in which the sweet bells were ringing a merry peal as they entered it, and found their way to their grandmother's door. They went upstairs into the little room, where all looked just as it used to do. The old clock was going "tick, tick," and the hands pointed to the time of day, but as they passed through the door into the room, they perceived that they were both grown up, and become a man and woman. The roses out on the roof were in full bloom, and peered in at the window; and there stood the little chairs, on which they had sat when children; and Kay and Gerda seated themselves each on their own chair, and held each other by the hand, while the cold empty grandeur of the Snow Queen's palace vanished from their memories like a painful dream.

Olivia and I were both quiet after the end. Olivia stared at the blue-white woman on the back of the book.

"Do you think they'll ever remember it again? Being with the Snow Queen? Do you think they'll talk about it?"

"It makes it sound like they won't. Since they're back home now and they're happy."

"But *you* remembered. *You* talked about it."

"What?"

"That time in the snow."

I hesitated. I knew what she was talking about, and it shouldn't have surprised me that she remembered. When Katie was pregnant, she read somewhere that there's something in egg yolks that helps the baby's memory develop. Since this was the closest thing she could find to a direct correlation between pregnancy diet and smart kids, she ate an obscene number of omelets every week. I think it worked, although now I wonder if we had truly considered the daily reality of having twin girls who will never forget a single fucking thing we ever say or do. Forgetful children might've been easier.

"Remember?" Olivia prompted.

Olivia was thinking of a January evening nearly a year ago, when I had gone outside to do some snowblowing after dinner. After I'd cleared our walk, I'd started in on our elderly neighbor's walk as well. The neighbor, Lois, had heard my snowblower, pushed a curtain aside, and pressed her face against the glass to look.

Her face was distorted through the glass, her white hair askew.

She was Florence Rattel. From the third floor. She was so

thoroughly Florence Rattel from the third floor that I couldn't move for a minute or two. Then I dropped the handle of the snowblower.

It spit and sputtered once, but its engine continued to rumble. I heard it, but as a muffled hum. For a moment I felt not just cold but bloodless. I had nothing left. I was all fear and skin and bones. *We all were.*

The face disappeared from the window. After a couple of minutes, I grabbed the snowblower handle and started to move again.

I cleared our driveway, widened our sidewalks, made a path to our trash cans, and then went back to Lois's house and finished her walk. After that I went to our next neighbor Bill's house and cleared his walk. When I started on his driveway, he came outside and reminded me that he had his own snowblower. So I snowblew a thin path in the sidewalk all along our block, and then went home.

"Where've you been?" Katie had asked when I stepped inside. "The girls were waiting to give you hot chocolate."

Sophia had a hot chocolate mustache. Olivia was spooning her hot chocolate from a mug to a bowl, making a big mess.

We'd just read "The Snow Queen" for the first time a couple of days before, so I'd said, "No big deal. The Snow Queen picked me up and pulled me around the block a couple of times."

Olivia, who used to fall for this stuff more back when she was four, put down her spoon and ran to the window to look.

"Where? *Where,* Daddy?"

"She's gone now, though," I'd said.

"Good," Sophia had replied, patiently handing me a Swiss Miss packet.

Now Olivia studied me carefully.

"Yes," I said. "I remember."

"I wonder if you'll see her again."

"Maybe."

Olivia traced her finger around the Snow Queen's face, letting it linger at her delicate chin. "Don't let her take you with her."

"I won't," I said. "I'm going to bring you back to bed now. Okay?"

"Okay." Olivia picked up her book and followed me down the hall. "Did she look like she does in the picture?"

"Not exactly. Her hair was whiter and shinier. Her eyes were weirder."

I opened her door and pointed silently at her bed, putting my finger to my lips to remind her not to wake up her sister.

"Everything looks weirder in real life," Olivia whispered, and then climbed into bed.

NADINE

I SEE THE BOAT launch. My car is still here. I don't know why I thought it might not be.

I fall into the driver's seat and close my eyes. The dark spins. I'm not sure if I'm still drunk, but I know that I am exhausted. Even if I felt like driving, where would I go? I heat up my car and turn on the interior light. Once the car is warm, I turn the ignition off again, crawl over the console, and curl up in the backseat.

DECEMBER 18, 2015

NADINE

I OPEN MY EYES and uncurl myself from the corner of the back-seat. I am stunned not so much by the daylight but the possibility that I must have slept through some of the tail end of the dark. I climb into the front seat and turn on the engine and the heat for a few minutes.

As I rummage through my bag for some water, my hand touches a glass bottle. I pull out the Glenlivet. I've drunk a third of my stepfather's scotch. My mother would never get him Glenlivet because she didn't like to indulge him with that sort of thing. But I know him just well enough—and just differently enough from my mother—to get him what I know he actually wants.

Anthony.

Last night comes rushing back to me. Passed out, I'd dreamed about the time he and I watched the news about that girl Suri.

I rotate the Glenlivet bottle in my hand and try to place that moment in a specific time frame. Suri was around the same age as me. Fourteen or fifteen. That was one reason her story had so captivated me.

Nineteen ninety-four. So yes, it was the same year. I was still in school, so Anthony and I would watch the news in the evenings. It wasn't summer yet.

The summer of Woodstock '94. That was a couple of months later. And so it hadn't happened yet. If it had, I wouldn't have considered hugging him, even for a second.

The Glenlivet label is warped and gummy from the moisture in the woods.

Anthony.

I think of another time I was alone with him—this one a couple of years later. *After* Mr. Brewster.

Anthony and I were standing in the kitchen. He was fiddling with a package of Fig Newtons, struggling to get the sleeve of cookies back in the box.

Do you understand why we're sending you to Dr. Fabian?

Yeah. Because that's the deal you made so I wouldn't have to go to another hospital, or have criminal charges.

Okay. Well, on the face of it, of course. But it's also because your mother and I care about you.

Uh-huh.

It stands to reason that you'd have things you'd want to talk about . . . but maybe not with us.

I had felt my cheeks burn a little. Of course *things you want to talk about* meant sex and drugs, and for me especially, violence. Funny that my cheeks could burn at that implication, knowing what my stepfather knew about me. How could I still be embarrassed?

And if this was all for me, for my precious girl-secrets, why did I not get to pick the person to whom I told them? It felt too strangely intimate for Anthony to get to be the one to make that choice. And yet—he'd chosen me a perfect dinosaur, so how could I complain?

I shove the Glenlivet bottle back in my bag.

A tired, familiar anger rises in my throat. I want to call Anthony now. But I've sunk my phone in Bigelow Pond.

I take a breath and close my eyes. The anger is still there, but I realize that it is, at long last, no longer mixed with shame.

Forget calling. I'll drive back to Campion. I'll find him there.

I don't have an X-Acto, but I think I'm more resourceful now.

HENRY

I DROVE BY BROOKHAVEN practically every day, but this was the first time I'd actually entered the place in a couple of years. It was a relief to head straight into the administrative building, which had an anonymous corporate feel. I was greeted by a lipsticked receptionist at a formidably tall curved metal desk that made her look like she was emerging from a soup pot. I felt like I could be at any office; the secretary was young and didn't seem to notice my name. I asked for Anthony Gagliardi, and she brought me to his office.

One side of his office was all glass, overlooking Brookhaven's main residential building. It was from here that Gagliardi had heard the gunshots, called 911, gathered everyone on this floor, led them out through the Japanese tea garden at the south side of the property, and out to the main road. His assistant had broken away and run toward the gunshots, hoping to help the residents. By the time he'd arrived, Streeter was already down.

Anthony was a familiar face from all of the various memorials after the shooting. I recalled him at a podium reading a few lines of Ralph Waldo Emerson, scratching his bald head nervously but speaking with great passion and exaggerated enunciation. He was short but had a big voice.

Now Anthony didn't look surprised to see me. His wife had obviously talked to him about our visit to their home.

"How can I help you, Officer Peacher?" he asked, anyway. "My wife told me you've been chatting with some of Dr. Fabian's patients. Present and former."

"Ah. Well, yes."

Anthony nodded and bobbed his shiny head back and forth, as if weighing the wisdom of this endeavor.

"But that's not my main concern here at the moment," I said. "I wanted to ask you a couple of questions more in your capacity as a longtime administrator at Brookhaven."

"Oh?" Anthony pulled a chair from the corner of the room to a spot close to his desk, then nodded for me to sit.

"Yes. A couple of things. First of all, I'm going to show you a note Dr. Fabian wrote shortly before his death and see if it means anything to you. Your name has come up a few times as one of the people who's been at Brookhaven the longest."

"One of the lifers, yes," Anthony said, smiling a little.

I showed him a copy I'd made of Fabian's legal pad notes:

TR 4/12/91
Patty–Patsy
Greensomething?
Brookhaven 2001

"Huh," Anthony said.

"I've had a couple of other folks chime in about this, but I want to see if it rings any bells for you before I tell you what they thought."

"Hmm. Well, now. I don't recall when exactly Dr. Fabian did counseling here."

"Eugene Morrison says roughly the late nineties till about 2004, but I'm not sure how accurate his memory is."

"Nineteen ninety-one. . . That was . . ." Anthony glanced at me, then back at the paper. "That was quite a few years before Mark worked here at all."

"But in 2001 he worked here. And . . . Patsy or Patty Green-something?"

"I believe there was a longtime patient named Greenblatt. Yes. Her son helped fund one of the picnic areas along the garden walk. There's a little stone bench with her name on it."

"So the son . . . he's been a big benefactor to this place?"

"Well. No. Just, after she died, he gave some money in her name."

"A nurse we spoke to said the same name. She believes Fabian counseled this Greenblatt patient at one point."

"It's absolutely possible. I think he was definitely working here for some of the time she was a resident."

"This nurse also said there was some trouble with this Greenblatt lady in 2001, and that a young nurse—a new nurse—was fired over it."

Anthony's gaze still fixed on the notes. "Fired? Really?"

"Yes. You don't recall this?"

"Well." He sighed and slowly handed back the paper. "I'm

not always kept abreast of all the nitty-gritty of the patients and the personnel."

"Is that a no?"

"Right. That's a no."

"How far back do your employment records go?"

"Um, I'm not sure. That's not really my area. You ought to talk to Yvonne in HR before you leave, though. You never know. I wonder if you'd be able to access that far back, though."

"I was told seven years is the magic number, because of possible malpractice suits."

"Well, yes. For patient records. I'm sure you're finding that with . . ." Anthony hesitated a moment. "Fabian."

Anthony eased away from me a few inches, turning his swivel chair slightly toward his desk.

"We've had *some* luck, though," I said, purposefully vague.

Was Anthony turning red? He was a naturally rosy-complected guy. But was he embarrassed that I might have read his stepdaughter's records? Could he have any inkling that they still existed?

I sighed. "Poor Dr. Fabian," I said.

"Yes. I feel terrible. I'd heard he was about to retire."

"How did you know that?"

Anthony shrugged. "Susan heard from someone. Susan, my wife. I don't know. My wife hears everything."

Anthony picked up the phone on his desk and tapped two buttons. "Yvonne? Yeah. It's me. In a few minutes, I'm going to be sending you a gentleman from the Campion police department. Fellow by the name of Officer Peacher—you may know him by reputation already. Yup. He is looking for some information about a nurse who was apparently employed by Brookhaven briefly in 2001. Let go after some difficulty with a patient named Greenblatt. I'm not sure how far back your records go for employees. Thought I'd give you a heads-up so he won't have to sit around waiting. Okay? Yeah, 2001. No. We don't have a name. Right. Yeah. See what you can do. Thanks."

He hung up. "I'm intrigued about this myself."

I nodded. "Can I ask . . . were you satisfied with Dr. Fabian's treatment of Nadine? Did that work out for you all?"

Anthony gazed out the window.

"Yes. Yes, I would say it did."

"Do you think Nadine would agree with you?"

Anthony cocked his head but continued to stare out the window. "That's a harder call."

"What makes you say that?"

"She didn't talk to us much at the time." He turned back to me, meeting my gaze again. His expression was disarmingly neutral. "She was a teenager then, after all."

I nodded. "We believe Nadine may have checked in with Dr. Fabian on this visit, so we were looking to chat with her."

Anthony raised his eyebrows in what looked to me like fake surprise. "That so?"

His wife had to have already told him this.

"Do you have any idea why Nadine would've gone to this therapist after so long? Is it possible she was in communication with him over the years?"

"I guess I wouldn't be surprised."

Well, this was different. A different sort of response from what we'd heard from Nadine's mother. "Why do you say that?"

"Nothing about her has ever been predictable." His lips twitched up as he said this, and there seemed to be a little pride in his eyes. Proud of Nadine, or proud of his own willingness to say this so freely?

"Was she having any difficulties on this visit that would lead her to feel she needed the services of a therapist?"

"Like, were we driving her crazy, you asking?" Anthony tried to smile.

"That or any other difficulties?"

"Not any obvious difficulties." Anthony leaned back in his chair and folded his arms. "We were all getting along, if that's what you're getting at."

"Any recent trouble in her life at home? Relationships?"

"Not that I know of. But Nadine was never really one to tell us her troubles."

"So I wonder, then. If she ever had difficulty with Dr. Fabian . . . if that wasn't working out for her. When she was a kid, I mean. You think she would have told you that?"

Anthony sighed. "Probably not."

"Did you know Dr. Fabian outside of his being Nadine's therapist?"

"No. I didn't. That wouldn't have worked . . . you know?"

"But he worked at Brookhaven for a time, didn't he?"

"Yes, a few years. But that was *after* he was her therapist."

"But you both worked at Brookhaven at the same time."

"Briefly, and years ago. He was here part-time, and my understanding was that he maintained his private practice at that time."

"You two didn't know each other well?"

Anthony shrugged and then shook his head. "I'm in financial management, and he counseled the occasional patient. We didn't get to know each other."

"But Eugene Morrison is a mutual friend."

"Ah. Yes. Certainly, Eugene was a good friend at one time. Eugene is friends with everyone, really. I suppose he's been a little distant since the shooting, since retiring, and with all of his injuries that he has to deal with. But we've been friends over the years, yes. We went to Eugene's daughter's wedding years back. And his son—I took his son on for an internship one year. We'd had Eugene and his wife over for the occasional dinner, back before she passed."

He was talking fast—as if trying to convince himself of the strength of this now-bloodless friendship. Or to move the conversation away from the topic of Nadine's treatment. I couldn't tell which.

"Was it awkward at all, having your stepdaughter go to therapy with someone who was a good friend of a friend?" I asked.

"Well . . . uh . . . I didn't think of it that way at the time. Eugene was a friend. I asked him if he had any colleagues he trusted, who he recommended, when we were looking for someone to help Nadine. I preferred that to just reaching for the phone book. So did my wife. We wanted someone good, and Eugene assured me that Fabian was good."

"Okay. That makes sense." It didn't entirely, but I wasn't going to say so. There were a couple of things that bothered me about this arrangement, but for now it seemed best to keep them to myself.

"You have any idea why Nadine's not responding to any phone calls from her mother?" I asked.

Amy and I had tried Nadine's number a couple of times as well. But of course we hadn't gotten an answer.

Anthony shrugged. "That's nothing new. She calls Susan and me when she's good and ready to talk. Which isn't often."

"Any idea where she is?"

"I know she was planning to go off and draw some pictures before Christmas."

"Your wife mentioned Gillette Castle."

"Oh. Yeah, I guess that would've been on her list. You know, Nadine is pretty independent and one of those people who needs a lot of time to herself, I think. She told her mother she'd be back by the morning of Christmas Eve, and I'm pretty sure she'll keep her word on that. She does what she says. She's that kind of a person."

Anthony's lips formed a tight smile, as if for a photo he was being forced to take.

"Mr. Gagliardi, I want to ask you something."

"What?"

"Did you know that Nadine had a relationship with Johnny Streeter at one point?"

"*What?*" The smile fell from Anthony's face.

"She never mentioned that to you?"

"Are you serious?" Anthony put his hands on his desk. He seemed to be contemplating standing, but then sighed and let his hands fall back to his lap. "No. I think you're probably mistaken about that."

"Well . . . Starting in 1997 from what I understand. How

long the relationship lasted, I'm still unclear. Was hoping you could maybe clarify."

"I didn't know anything about that. Quite frankly, that sounds like the sort of thing somebody around here would *say* about Nadine. But you know, Nadine hasn't lived close to here for about twenty years. She didn't really have any friends here."

"Where was she when the shooting happened? You remember?"

"South Africa. She was there almost three years."

"Starting when?"

"Starting in 2009."

"Huh. What was she doing there?"

"Helping train rural nurses who were working with AIDS patients who were starting antiretroviral treatment."

"I see." That sounded like pretty serious work. Before things got scary in social studies class, Nadine had indeed seemed like a serious person.

"She was there with her boyfriend Daryl. We liked him a lot. He's a doctor."

"She still in this relationship?"

"No. Too bad."

"Is she in a relationship now?"

Anthony shook his head. "Not that she's shared with us."

I got up.

"Um, Officer Peacher?"

"Yeah?"

"She may have mentioned Gillette Castle to her mother. But to me she mentioned a place called Bigelow Hollow."

"Where's that?"

"Northeast corner. It's in a state forest there near some of those teeny tiny towns. She said her dad used to take her there when she was small."

I wrote down *Bigelow Hollow.* "Her dad?"

"Her real dad."

"So that was going to be one of her sentimental stops."

"She said so, yeah. And I don't know how good the phone reception is up there. So that might be why you're having trouble reaching her."

I nodded. "I'm sure it's something like that. Well, if Nadine contacts you, please be in touch."

"Don't forget to stop in and talk to Yvonne," Anthony reminded me.

I didn't forget. And I wasn't surprised when Yvonne reported to me that she hadn't found anything likely to help me. Employee files were alphabetical. Without a name, it would be difficult to find what I was looking for—if such a record existed at all. But she'd ask around for hints on a name, keep looking, and get back to me.

I decided I needed to read over Nadine's files again. I would look at them when I got back to the station. I'd told Anthony that his choice of Nadine's shrink "made sense." But it didn't. Not really. Sure, if one of my girls ever needed a shrink—if I let them listen to "The Red Shoes" one too many times, for example—I wouldn't want to send them just anywhere. I'd want some pretty confident recommendations.

But was I the only one who thought a man in his forties was a weird choice for a teenage girl who had just stabbed her male teacher—also roughly forty, if my recollection was correct? Was I old-fashioned or new-fangled to think this? Or did I just not know enough about therapy? Wouldn't you worry that she'd eventually end up wanting to stab *that* guy, too? Maybe if I'd read more than Freud Cliffs Notes, I'd see it differently. Maybe to the educated mind it was actually a really stellar idea.

And what did Nadine think? Wouldn't it be difficult to talk to someone whom you thought might be in your stepfather's pocket? Did she think that? Did she, then, take the therapy at all seriously? Or did it make her angrier? Could she possibly be angry about something, still, after all these years?

NADINE

THERE'S LOTS OF traffic on 84 West through Hartford. Maybe everybody who's not working today is going to the mall for Christmas presents.

It'll take me a little longer to get to Campion than I thought.

Since we didn't have time the other day, Bouffant, I can tell you a little more about how I got here. When I waltzed into your office a few days ago, we didn't have the time or the inclination to cover all that much ground. If you'll indulge me, I'd like to fill in some of the details. To explain to you who I've been since that last session in which you "wished me all the best." You said you had a feeling I'd do quite well. I wonder not only if you meant it, but if you would think it turned out to be true.

NORTHERN ARIZONA UNIVERSITY. I really was a regular girl for a couple of years. I had a few friends with whom to party and study and everything in between.

Sophomore year I had a friend who wouldn't shut up

about some test she'd cheated on, and how bad she felt about it. For breaking the student honor code. She kept saying she wanted to do something to make up for it. Tell the professor and potentially flunk the course? Deliberately flunk the next exam? Nothing I suggested satisfied her. It seemed to me she just wanted to keep talking about it until I said, "Look, forget about it. Everyone cheats." Or something like that. Which I almost did, while we were walking through the student union. But just before I said it, I saw a poster on the wall advertising a blood drive on the following day.

"Give blood," I said.

"What?"

"Go give blood tomorrow. And while you're lying there having a pint taken out of you, think about your cheating the whole time."

"I'm afraid of needles," she said.

"Even better."

"What does the one thing have to do with the other?" she protested. "Shouldn't the punishment fit the crime?"

"You've already considered and rejected punishments that fit the crime, that won't do anyone any good. This at least would."

Before she could say anything else, I offered, "I'll go with you. I'll give, too."

"But you didn't do anything bad."

I hesitated. I remember thinking something like, *Bless your heart.*

"I'm sure I can think of something I've done to deserve it.

Anyway, who cares. I'll match you. If you say no now, you're denying the blood bank *two* pints."

For good measure, I told her boyfriend the plan as soon as we got back to our dorm. So then there were three pints of blood on the line.

We all went. My friend turned green but fulfilled her obligation. Her boyfriend passed out. I almost looked away when the young male technician was about to stick the needle in my arm, but then decided I needed to watch. I held my breath and didn't flinch. And then as the blood ran into the line, I started asking the guy about his job—how long he'd been doing it, how much training it required. He said he loved it but he was training to be an EMT next.

This young man wasn't much older than me, and already a contributing member of society. And I wondered if I could have the intestinal fortitude to do what he did. The question distracted me for days, and then weeks. I started feeling the veins in my arms, and those of friends, when they were too drunk to care what I was doing.

I was studying art and political science—both rather aimlessly, and because they seemed easy and noncompetitive enough not to lead me needlessly into any nervous breakdowns or stress-rage incidents. My friends thought I had a vague and halfhearted goal to attend law school. In truth, I had no goals, except to feel and appear relatively normal.

The young man—and the conversation I had with him—both stayed with me. I graduated a semester early because I had taken classes in the summer, and often taken an extra course load. I told my mother and Anthony that I wasn't sure about applying to grad school just yet. And rather than pound the pavement looking for a nonexistent job for an art and poli-sci major, I was planning to use the following months taking a phlebotomy program so I would have a useful skill for the interim.

My mother had difficulty putting aside her obvious hesitation—her recently troubled daughter sticking needles in people? Surely not a good idea.

My stepfather Anthony may have thought he was calling my bluff when he offered an alternative plan—take an accelerated postdoc RN program, and he would pay for it. If I was *really* interested in this sort of a career.

No, I said. Just phlebotomy for me, for now. Just tubes and veins and blue rubber tourniquets.

Shall we get Freudian for a minute here? Yes, I got the certification. And yes, I spent the subsequent two years sticking a sharp thing into people's arms. Maybe I was exercising an unhealthy impulse that whole time? However you might feel about that, I believe I was good at it. I had several regulars who requested me. And although I might not seem like the kindliest person to you, it's easy to sustain a sweet and patient demeanor for ten minutes.

But let's go back to the topic of unhealthy impulses. Let's consider that for a moment or two more. After a couple of years on a bloodmobile, I landed a night shift hospital job in Phoenix. Forty plus draws a night, in time for the doctors who came in in the morning, expecting to see patient results before the start of the day. People are usually simple and resigned at three in the morning when they are awoken for a blood draw. Learning how to deal with such a person is a limited and specialized anthropological skill. You do not need to understand people generally to do this—just people in that particular moment. Soft small talk, quick stick. Anyway, I slept in the afternoons and had my free time in the mornings while my roommate was at work. I'd read graphic novels and occasionally make my own sketches as well. I briefly toyed with a fairylike character shaped like a butterfly needle, but it just didn't feel right. I was a regular person for a while—or close enough. I paid taxes. I watched *The Sopranos*. I had a cat.

One night, when I was twenty-six, something happened. It was on a weekend—when I sometimes slept very little, for fear of reversing my body's nocturnal development. I hiked a lot then—on Camelback Mountain, or outside the city, near Cave Creek. I never saw a rattlesnake but I think I heard one once. I'd learned to love the desert—and long hikes in which you could get lost in sweat and heat and sand and forget who you were. Forget almost that you were a person, then come home and shower and live the rest of the day in an air-conditioned half-self haze.

I was in such a haze when I pulled into a parking space of a pizza and sub shop for my dinner. I was listening to a news story so didn't go inside right away.

When I got into the shop to order my dinner, a guy with a thick gray beard was ahead of me. After he finished ordering his pizza slices, he turned to me.

"You're not too bright, are you?" he said, and stared at me, waiting for me to answer. He had jolly sparkling eyes, and pinkish cheeks. Like a young Santa Claus, if Santa Claus was an asshole who smelled like cigarette smoke and not quite enough Speed Stick.

"You didn't see that I was waiting for that spot?" he demanded.

"I didn't," I said. "I'm sorry."

"You need to pay attention to what's going on around you."

I looked him up and down. He had on a dark blue suit, which felt somehow incompatible with his Hells Angels beard and demeanor.

"Well, it looks like you found another spot pretty fast?" I said, as he paid for his pizza. I wanted to add, *Shit like this happens in parking lots. I'm sure you'll get over it.* But my job had taught me to be momentarily perky, and avoid confrontations.

"Not the point," he mumbled, but didn't seem to want to let me out of his frustrated gaze.

"Have a nice dinner, sir," I said, because I was hungry and I wanted this to end.

He harrumphed and left with his pizza. I watched his retreating blue back. What exactly was this guy playing at, with his fancy suit and overgrown beard? What was he hiding?

After I got my sandwich, I sat in my car and considered our exchange. I was angry at this stranger for making a judgment on my brain over a meaningless moment in a parking lot. And yet—something about his smell or his eyes or his disposition made me wonder how it would feel inside the grip of his thick, probably hairy arms. My stomach revolted at the thought. I couldn't imagine simply going home and eating my turkey club.

As I started out of the parking lot in my car, I noticed the man was driving the shiny red pickup truck in front of me. I recognized the arm of his blue suit hanging casually out the window, and the overgrown gray of the back of his head. I followed the truck. I cannot say exactly what I was curious about, except to understand how such a person moves through the world. I had noticed, at my job, that older men often scolded younger women as a matter of course, as a matter of everyday habit. But it didn't particularly bother me at the lab or the hospital, because I understood that people were vulnerable and socially careless in the moments before a blood draw.

But this was different. This man who came out of nowhere and needed for a female—preferably a young one, and presumably a dumb one—to share the pain of his bad day—to absorb some of it for him, in fact. He assumed I would do so—because, frankly, I didn't have a choice, did I? He was entitled to it.

Maybe this was the knowledge that I had been seeking all of those confused younger years. I had imagined a collective men's heart and I wished to unlock it. The secret, it turned out, was maybe merely this entitlement. And this entitlement was something I granted with that very wish itself. Their ability to do this attracted and repulsed me. They did it because they could, and they could because I let them. And I let them because I was mesmerized with the fundamental cause of this transaction. But could it be just that—a snake eating its own tail? There had to be something real in there somewhere.

What was the real secret, then? Perhaps only that you seek it like a cat seeks the end of a string. You can't resist. You don't care that there's actually nothing really there but the chase itself.

Young Santa didn't live all that far away from the pizza shop—in a modest apartment complex about five minutes away. I kept driving so I wouldn't have to follow him into the parking lot, in which case he'd know he was being followed.

I drove a half mile down the road and turned around at a gas station. When I came back, I parked at the opposite side of the apartment lot from his red truck. He was parked at an apartment 4B, from which a light popped on, and in which he was likely now eating his pizza slices.

I held my small Swiss Army key chain in my hands. I pulled out the blade and gripped the handle tight. How would I feel if I ended up finding this man in one of the hospital beds at three A.M.—a week from now, or even a year from now—needing his blood drawn? Surely I'd remember his face. Would I let him doze off after I slipped the needle in, and take vial after vial until he was drained down to some fundamental essence that I could observe and then finally understand?

What would he say to me then, and what would I say back?

I sucked in a breath, because this scenario made me feel warm all over—a vile response that I could not let stand. Because maybe he *would* show up in one of those hospital beds one day—him or someone too much like him for me to resist.

I held the knife there for a second, but the cold of it on my fingers made my heart pound with a familiar anger. I tried to steady my breathing. I tried to remember if I screamed something on that day with Mr. Brewster.

But I couldn't. All I could remember was that there was

something freeing, something rapturous, even, about that moment when my hand came down and broke through his skin. *There. See? No secret there. Nothing to hold me in your thrall.*

The light went out in 4B. It seemed early for this man to be going to bed, but maybe he was just turning out a kitchen light as he retired to his couch.

Relaxed was a quarter of the way to broken. Or something like that.

Did I really think that once?

Not again. I exhaled. No, I didn't want to do this again. But something needed to happen.

I got out of my car and slashed the right back tire of the pickup. The feel of the knife in the tough rubber was surprisingly satisfying. It was enough.

I got back in my car, closed my door as quietly as I could, and started to drive home.

Maybe inside of that apartment he was caring for a Mrs. Claus—a Mrs. Claus with breast cancer or something. *Oh shit.* And what if tomorrow morning he needed to bring her to her chemo treatment and he found his tire flat?

Why hadn't I thought of that before I got out of the car?

But then, I had all kinds of extenuating circumstances that he might not have thought of, either.

I didn't sleep at all the rest of that Saturday, but collapsed on Sunday afternoon, and slept well enough to keep my hands steady that night. And to make small talk while I found veins and capped vials.

HENRY

BEFORE TAKING OUT Nadine's old file, I got online, typed in "Bigelow Hollow," and found a site about "Bigelow Hollow State Park & Nipmuck State Forest." The place was in a town called Union. I made a quick call to Connecticut State Troop D. Several of the tiny towns around the state forest there—which contained this Bigelow Hollow that Gagliardi mentioned—didn't have their own individual police departments.

I asked the trooper to put officers in the area on alert for a silver Toyota with Vermont plates. They said they'd send someone to circle around the state park's roads.

When I got off the phone, I clicked on the map the site provided. I'd lived in Connecticut all my life and never heard of this place. It was a few miles wide, and had three bodies of water: Bigelow Pond, Mashapaug Pond, and Breakneck Pond.

The third pond name gave me pause. Hadn't Nadine mentioned the word "Breakneck" somewhere in her notes to Fabian?

"Henry!"

Greg was standing over me now. "What?"

"Some kid just waltzed in the front door. Says he's one of Fabian's patients."

"A kid? How old?"

"Like a teenager. He says he cut school to come talk to us because his parents wouldn't let him come yesterday."

I stood up. "Well, this should be interesting."

THE KID'S NAME was Liam. He was tall and pale with blond-red Little Orphan Annie curls.

While he spoke, he nursed the Coke Greg had supplied for him. He said he'd been going to Dr. Fabian for about a year.

"My parents made me go when they decided to get a divorce," he said.

"Ah," I said. "Well, did you like Dr. Fabian?"

"He was a nice guy. I feel bad about what happened to him."

"And you went and saw him Tuesday, at five," I offered.

Liam stared at me. "How'd you know that?"

"We have his schedule."

"Then why didn't you come interrogate me yet?"

"Because we didn't have your last name. So if you had a five o'clock session, you left by . . . what? Six?"

"Yup."

"Did anything unusual happen in the session?"

"No." Liam sipped his Coke. "Not really."

"Did anyone come into the office or the waiting room while you were talking?"

"No."

"Did you see anything out of the ordinary in the office, waiting room, or parking lot that day?"

"Nope." Liam burped softly behind his hand.

"Now, you cut school to come talk to us. Was there anything in particular you felt we should know about Dr. Fabian, or anything you saw?"

"Nope. But I thought if you came to me it would be worse than me coming to you."

"Worse in what sense?"

"I dunno. You might think I was hiding something."

"Are you?"

"No." Liam shrugged. "That's what I'm saying."

"Okay. Now, I have a question for you. Do you ever see the patient who comes in after you on Tuesdays?"

"Usually I just hear him. But I've seen him a couple of times. He's a big guy, dark hair. But I don't know his name."

Connor Osborne. Fabian's next scheduled appointment.

"Did you see him or hear him on Tuesday?"

"Tuesday? No. Not that time. But . . ."

Liam paused, clearly for dramatic effect.

"Yes, Liam? Is there something you want us to know?"

"He was kind of . . . loud. Kind of . . . weird."

"Can you explain what you mean by that? Weird how?"

"Well, one time I came back into the waiting room because I thought I'd left my phone in there. And he was just sitting there, watching me look under the chairs and by the magazines and stuff, and he said to me, 'WHAT'RE YOU DOING HERE?' And I was like, 'What? Why are you asking me that?' And he's like, 'You should be out playing baseball, and sneaking beers with your friends.' And I didn't know what to say. I was like, 'I do all that stuff, but I still have time to come here, too.' And I left before he could saying anything back."

"Uh-huh," I said.

"And one other time, he walked right in on Dr. Fabian and me."

"Really?" I said. This sounded a little more relevant. A little more highly *inappropriate.* A possible sign of impulse control issues for Connor Osborne.

"Yeah. Well, we went overtime, because I was . . . upset about something."

Liam folded the tab of his soda can back and forth until it came off in his hand. "It was kind of a messed-up situation, so Fabian let me stay a whole extra ten minutes, at least."

A whole extra ten minutes, I thought. *Knock yourself out, Fabian.*

"What was so messed up?" I asked. "Is that part of the story?"

"Fabian had told me something. He told me that my dad was getting married again. He thought *I* had told him that. But I hadn't. My *dad* had. My dad hadn't told me yet, and *Fabian* told me by mistake."

"Oh." I hesitated. "Wow."

"Yeah. So, we're just sitting there. And he's giving me extra time to, like, respond to that, because he feels bad that he fucked up. And I wasn't mad at him at all for telling me. Really, he was an old guy and he probably had a lot of different people to keep track of. Anyway, the guy from the waiting room comes right in and when he sees us there, he's like,

'Oh, geez. I'm *so* sorry. When you didn't come out like you usually do, and it was so quiet, I figured I'd just go home if you weren't here. Sorry. Sorry!'"

"He didn't knock?"

"Uh, I think he knocked, but didn't wait. Just stuck his big head in. And he was *loud*. Like he was maybe a little drunk or something. Didn't know how loud he was talking."

"And what did Fabian say?"

"He told the guy we'd just be a minute. And he apologized to me for the interruption. Not that it was his fault."

"When was that?"

"Um . . . three months ago, maybe?"

"Okay. Any other encounters with that patient?"

"Nope. None where we talked. I might've seen him once or twice. But the fact that both times I heard him speak, something seemed a little off . . . I thought that was notable."

Notable. I wondered what Fabian thought of this kid.

"Thanks for your time, Liam," I said. "I'm going to have an officer drive you back to school."

"WHAT DO YOU think?" I asked Greg and Amy, after Liam had gone.

"It explains the thing his girlfriend was saying," Amy said. "About the fuck-up with a patient. Unfortunate, but mild, considering."

"I wonder if Connor occasionally *does* do happy hour like his wife thinks," Greg said. "Squeezes both in after work on Tuesday. Bar and then therapy."

"Happy hour followed by a sobering hour," I said.

"Even if Liam *isn't* dramatizing the situation—which seems like a big if to me—I doubt that the therapist would let him come to therapy *drunk,*" I said. "So he had a drink sometimes to loosen him up. I don't think it means much."

"I'm still not convinced we know the whole story on this guy," Greg said. "What with that article on Fabian's computer and everything. I'm still chatting with some of his friends and neighbors. Unless you had something else you wanted me to do today."

"Not at the moment. You stay on that. I'm still working on some stuff related to Nadine Raines, so we can be ready for her when we find her."

NADINE

ALMOST IN CAMPION now. When I see the familiar exit along 391, my heart jumps and I have to look away even though I'll be taking it. To the place where I was crazy. To the place where I always will be.

But we're not there yet. And still there's more I want you to know.

SO, THERE I was, age twenty-six, still sucking blood out of half-conscious patients in the wee hours. But the otherness of the night shift—it wasn't enough. Nor was the ego-bleaching heat of the desert sun. That girl with the X-Acto would always catch up. Unless I kept moving.

There was a nurse I'd met and become friendly with, who worked for a nursing agency that sent her to a different city every few months. No sooner had we had coffee together a few times than she had flown off to Miami. I was envious—there was no travel-work agency for phlebotomists—and I wondered if she kept running for a reason, or ran just for the fun of it.

So in 2005, I took up Anthony's still-standing offer to send me to nursing school. An accelerated postbac program that would take just under eighteen months. Something that would keep my brain and body so busy that I'd not find myself in any parking lots with Swiss Army knives anytime soon. I still did some phlebotomy part-time, just to keep myself running on automatic.

Was I cut out to be a nurse? You might be surprised. I'm careful and efficient and I've found self-loathing, in the right form and dosage, to be a decent safeguard against sloppy mistakes. Also, I've found—and maybe you're not allowed to agree with this, Bouffant—that understanding oneself is not a prerequisite for being useful. And while I don't necessarily have a remarkable bedside manner, I believe I have sufficient sympathy for people's worst moments.

In any case, you need two solid years in one place before any agency will take you, and I did those in Phoenix. Specializing in ICU. Then I signed with an agency that sent me to Atlanta, then Kansas City.

After that was Minneapolis, where I met Daryl. He was a doctor not much older than me. Skinny and short, sharp-chinned and scruffy-haired, I barely noticed him at first. But one day we nearly ran into each other as I'd turned abruptly from an awkwardly positioned computer cart while he was making his way down the hall behind me. "Excuse me," he said, and held my gaze for a second longer than usual. He had, since I'd last seen him the previous week, grown a dark stubble around his mouth and chin. Just enough to make him seem slightly masculine now—rather than boyish. Along with it, I now noticed the depth and shine of his eyes—a regular brown, but thoughtful, watchful.

I asked him to grab lunch with me a couple of days later. We had fried chicken together in the cafeteria. I noticed his unusually prominent canine teeth and tried not to wonder what he noticed about me. We discovered that we were both graphic novel enthusiasts. And we were both Wilco fans—or at least, I pretended to be one.

We were an item after a month, residing mostly at his place. We did outdoorsy stuff together when we had the time, and otherwise got lots of Indian takeout and watched Comedy Central. We both liked to drink wine and laugh a lot. Neither of us liked to talk about work. Neither of us cared much that coworkers quietly found our height difference amusing. I liked that he would never really feel older than me.

And he wasn't much for talk of the past. He didn't ask a lot of questions. His parents were both doctors. It was always a given that he would be one, too. He didn't ever say this with any sort of resentment. He knew a doctor was a lucky enough fate to be funneled into. He'd seen enough tragedy at his job to know what kind of circumstances one could reasonably resent.

What did he know about me? That I was a phlebotomist before I was a nurse, that I had a BA in art and poli-sci and that I grew up in a Connecticut suburb, the only child of a divorced woman who'd remarried a good provider. That I liked the desert and I liked to draw. He knew as much about me as I did about him.

He convinced me to extend my time at this hospital. Not permanently, but for another six months. He was a Minnesota native, but he wasn't long for Minneapolis, either. He was planning to go to South Africa with an organization that was helping with PEPFAR—President's Emergency Plan for AIDS Relief. He'd always wanted to combine being a doctor with traveling. At least, while he was young.

And so it was clear, then, that this relationship would not last forever. That was fine with me. I knew that my capacity for normalcy was limited; all it had to do was sustain itself until its prescribed end date.

IT DIDN'T SUSTAIN itself that long. Three months before Daryl was supposed to leave for South Africa, along came Robert.

Robert was my patient for three days. Triple bypass with an extra couple of days in the ICU because of some inconsistent test results that made the surgeon nervous. He was about sixty, with a gentle Bryan Cranston sort of look. A bit craggy around the mouth, with thoughtful wrinkles up the forehead.

About an hour after we took out his breathing tube, he murmured to me, "I'm glad you're here."

It certainly wasn't the first time a patient had said something like that to me. After the haze of anesthesia, some patients are combative. Some are magnanimous. Some both in the span of ten minutes. It barely registered as I started to check his blood pressure.

When I glanced up at him, his gaze was surprisingly alert.

He expected me to respond. Usually I had comforting, if canned, replies ready for patients who spoke this way. *Well, we're glad* you're *here, Mr. So and So!*

But the warmth in his gaze made me shy.

"No problem. Of course," I said quietly.

"Of course. Of course. Of course," he repeated softly, almost singing the words. I couldn't tell if he was mocking me or simply too out of it to come up with words of his own. The repetition was disarming.

An hour later I came in to check everything again. I did so silently because his eyes were closed, but as I was walking out of the room, he said, "Your mother probably never told you—"

I turned around. "What?"

"I'm not sure if your mother ever told you."

"Told me what?"

He smiled weakly. I stepped closer to his bed. He reached for my hand, and I let him take it. He stared into my eyes.

"Oh," he said, dropping my hand. "I'm sorry, dear. I'm sorry to bother you."

He recognized now that I was not the person he meant to speak to.

"You're not bothering me," I whispered.

He smiled. "Thank you, dear. I'm sorry."

I hesitated. "My mother never told me what?"

"I'm sorry," he said. "I was dreaming."

He closed his eyes again to verify this. He slept most of the rest of my shift.

I came in the next day hoping that he'd have been moved

down to Med-Surg. I'd thought about him all night in spite of myself.

He was still there.

"Hello there, Mr. Chandler," I said as I entered his room.

"You can call me Robert."

"Okay."

I'd checked his pain meds. They had him off morphine now and onto relatively light Percocet. The moony fellow I'd met last shift was gone, and he'd taken his secret with him.

"My brother won't be coming in today," he told me. "He's working."

I was under the impression Robert was divorced.

"Do you have kids, did you say?" I asked.

"Yes. But one's doing a year abroad in Munich. The other one just started a new job in New York. I told them both not to come."

And were they both supposed to listen to you? I wondered.

"Daughters? Sons?" I asked.

"My son's in Munich. My daughter is in New York."

So if someone should've or could've been there, it particularly should've been her.

"They've both called today," he said.

"Excellent," I replied.

What was it her mother never told her? I desperately wanted to know. But I had to focus on checking Robert's vitals. When I was done, I checked his incision. I paused, my rubber-gloved hand lingering on his chest.

"Is it okay?" he asked. He'd seen that I'd frozen. "Is everything okay?"

"Absolutely," I said, mustering a smile as I turned away.

I stepped out of the room for a deep breath and a glass of water. It had unsettled me, how much I liked looking at the staggered red-brown line down his chest.

This was my last shift with him. I didn't check the incision again.

By the time I had another shift later that week, he was gone. I felt relieved, but I missed him. At my lunch break, I wasn't very hungry. I looked up which Med-Surg floor he'd gone to, and then went to the gift shop. Everything there was so floral and feminine, except for a few paperback thrillers and news magazines. But when I wandered by the glass case in the back, near the Precious Moments figurines, I spotted a couple of starfish nestled in wooden boxes.

I selected one. Maybe starfish could represent healing, since they had the power to regrow severed limbs? Whatever. An element of randomness in a gift is never a bad thing; it motivates the recipient to interpret meaning where you never intended, but would if you could.

I took the elevator up to his floor, and knocked gently.

"Come in?" he called.

He looked so dignified there, with a hooded sweatshirt pulled over his hospital gown. His incision was inaccessible to me now. With other patients the wounds and the dressings were separate from their selves. Something to be treated delicately, but technically. But with him, it had been different. I felt like I'd started to see a glimpse inside of him, and wanted to see more.

"I just wanted to say hi, and to see how you're doing," I said.

"I'm doing quite well," he said, picking up a cup of water and drinking from it. "Thank you."

"I brought you a starfish," I said.

"Oh." His gaze fixed on the gift box for a moment, and then on me. "How thoughtful."

"Hey Robbie," someone said from the doorway. "Is this a bad time? Are you working him up right now, dear?"

I turned to see a man roughly Robert's age standing there. His dark eyes and the perfect egg shape of his face were the same as Robert's, and his hair a similar color, but thinner. He had a laptop case slung over his arm, a coffee in one hand.

For a moment I thought Robert was multiplying against my offensive neediness. But then I remembered him mentioning his brother when he was in the ICU. This man looked like he could even be his twin.

"Uh. No. I was just leaving," I said.

I stared at the starfish. What had gotten into me? And yet—this was a familiar moment. When your weirdness decides to come to Jesus without your express and conscious permission.

"It's from everyone in the ICU," I said, putting it on the table next to his bed. *Shit.* What if he sent us all a thank-you note?

"That's so nice, miss. Miss . . ." He struggled for my last name, which he had never known.

If he sent a thank-you note, no one would really have time to give it much thought. They'd skip over the part about the starfish and perhaps assume it was general gratitude, or eccentricity on the part of the patient.

"I've got to get back to the ICU," I mumbled.

WHEN DARYL GOT home, he found me weeping in the dark.

"What's wrong, Nadine? What's wrong?"

The concern in his voice saddened me. He had no idea that there was no urgency here at all. Nothing acute. Only a dull ache I could never make him understand. *Once you've been crazy, can you ever really be anything else?*

I did attempt, however, to convey part of the problem.

"I don't think I can do this job anymore."

"What happened?"

"I just don't think I'm cut out for it."

"Well . . . nobody is."

"You are, aren't you?"

"Not *all* the time."

He stroked my hair for a couple of minutes.

"Take me with you," I said.

"What?"

"To South Africa. Can you take me with you?"

"The job there won't be easier than here."

"I know that. But it'll be different."

He paused. "Are you saying you want to stay together?"

The feeling was something like that time I cried in your office and told you I was angry. The moment opened up, and I saw how normal it could look from a different perspective.

My tears *could* have a conventional emotional purpose: I wanted to be with Daryl. I didn't want him to go off to the other side of the world and leave me alone. It was possible I felt that way. It could even be true.

"Yeah," I said, after a while.

HENRY

BACK AT MY desk, I looked at Nadine's files again.

Where was that mention of *Breakneck*?

I scanned through until I found it—in one of those creepy dinosaur cartoons:

> ***Doll:*** *If I went back to Breakneck, would I see you there?*
> ***Dinosaur:*** *Probably not.*
> ***Doll:*** *Did you ever finish your song?*
> ***Dinosaur:*** *What do you think, Naddy Baby?*

As I went through Fabian's notes again, I realized something didn't sit well with me. Now that I'd talked to Nadine's stepfather.

Anthony Gagliardi. I read again through all of Fabian's notes and verified that Anthony was not really mentioned at all. Sure, Nadine may have had more pressing concerns. Violent behavior. Dead dad. Troubled relationship with mom. Maybe the stepfather didn't rate.

And Fabian didn't seem to have much to say in general. He only wrote formal notes when Nadine started sessions, dropped a weekly session, added one, and when she left. It wasn't totally clear to me why he had her add a session after a year in therapy, when it seemed she was getting better. The insurance money had kicked back in, so he figured he'd exhaust her insurance allotment before she shipped off to college? Was that in her best interest? Or was he concerned she wasn't actually improving at all? It wasn't clear.

Fabian's notes didn't satisfy me, so I opened the first of Nadine's blue books. I found the part I'd wanted to see again.

> *No, I don't understand Anthony entirely. He tries to be a nice guy. Too hard sometimes. I suppose he is a solid person—like my mother wants to think of herself as a solid person.*
>
> *I don't think of him as a dinosaur, like I usually do men his age. Maybe because he's married to my mother. So that makes him a different kind of mystery. A mystery I don't want to solve.*

That's as much airplay as Anthony got in *any* of the notes. Was Nadine trying to be provocative here? That seemed to be a theme for her. Some of the time, anyway. What did she want Fabian to believe, or not believe?

I read both blue books, from September 1996 to August 1997. Until I reached the second-to-last line of the very last entry: *If you listened to about every other word, you'd be close to the truth.*

Now, what was this about? Was she telling Fabian she'd been lying the whole time? Or telling him she'd left something out? Was she trying to telegraph something she couldn't say directly? About whom? Herself, or someone else? Or was this just a way for her to feel some sort of power over Fabian in the final moments, after submitting to nearly two years of his authority as her "doctor"?

I flipped to the beginning of the book and tried reading every other word.

Hi is are going be and that little book going stand . . .

This awkward we to realistic admit a blue is going . . .

It was worth a shot. Apparently Nadine wasn't as diabolical as all of that. Just in case, I tried the beginning of the second notebook, too.

The has back but grown to these entries asked if was at father

Insurance kicked in I've used writing little you me I mad my

Nope.

I spread out Fabian's notes and the two blue notebooks on my desk. My gaze kept bouncing back to the same few sentences.

In the dinosaur cartoons: *There is part of your story that you've never told me. Are you ever going to tell me?*

And in her regular notes:

So that makes him a different kind of mystery. A mystery I don't want to solve.

Do you secretly hate the people who are willing to tell you everything?

If you listened to about every other word, you'd be close to the truth.

She *was* trying to provoke Fabian. Did he know it then? Or did he figure it out on the day he died?

I closed the little book and got up. I couldn't stay here wondering at my desk when there were people to talk to. There was this Greenblatt incident to dig up. I could try to track down sonny-boy Greenblatt, orthodontist. Or I could try and pick Morrison's declining brain one more time. I decided I'd start with that. I took the Nadine file with me.

EUGENE MORRISON LIVED in the McMansion part of town, but in one of the older, subtler houses on its outskirts that seemed to have inspired the later ones.

There were a few cars in the driveway, so I wondered if I was interrupting some kind of afternoon social gathering. Not that I could imagine the increasingly doddering Dr. Morrison hosting one.

I was greeted at the door by a kid with a missing front tooth.

"Is that your car?" he demanded. "Are you a cop?"

"Yeah," I said. "Is Dr. Morrison here?"

"He's my grandpa, yeah. He's watching TV. Is he in trouble?"

"No," I said.

A woman gently pushed the boy aside and stepped into the doorway. "Can I help you? Oh. Henry? Am I right? *Henry?*"

Amanda Morrison. I recognized her right away. She hadn't seemed to have aged much except for some knowing little lines at the outer corners of her eyes. She was wearing a lot of makeup, a snug black skirt, and a pink blouse.

"Yeah. Amanda. Long time no see. You don't live in Campion anymore, do you?"

"No. Wolcott. But I'm down here all the time lately. For my dad."

"That's your kid?"

"That's my kid, yup." She hesitated, apparently weighing whether we needed to catch up any more than that. "You . . . you wanted to talk to my dad?"

"Yeah. Is he okay? I just wanted to chat with him one more time about Dr. Fabian. I'm sure you've heard . . ."

"Of course." She opened the door to let me in. "He's in the basement with my daughter. They're watching a cooking show, I guess. You can send her up here."

"You spend a lot of time here in Campion with your dad?"

Amanda nodded. "Since he was hurt, yes. More and more."

"Is someone with him all the time?"

"Not *all* the time, no. But we worry."

"Is his memory okay, you think?"

"Yeah. Memory's not the issue. He's just having trouble getting around. And sometimes he seems to stop . . . caring."

"Caring about . . ."

"Oh . . . things like . . . eating, for example. It's been a problem before. It comes and goes. We usually all go out for pizza on Tuesday nights."

"He didn't want to go this week?"

"Well, he went along." Amanda smiled a little. She seemed grateful to have a chance to talk about it. "He just didn't eat. The leftover pizza is still in his fridge."

"Oh. You know, I don't want to upset him. You think he'll be okay if I talk to him? About Dr. Fabian?"

"Oh. Well, yes. What's happened is another shock to his system, of course. But I think it helps him to talk. To feel like he's being helpful."

I nodded. Amanda led me to the basement door and called her daughter up the stairs.

EUGENE MUTED HIS cooking show after we'd exchanged a little small talk. A pretty older lady continued to braise baby artichokes on the giant flat screen.

"Eugene, earlier today I spoke to a nurse who used to work at Brookhaven." Eugene dragged his gaze off the brunette and her skillet. "Bev Hatfield."

"Oh!" Eugene's face lit up. "I miss her. Really great lady. Excellent at her job."

"Well, she had some insights about those notes I showed you yesterday, that Fabian had written down. She felt they were probably connected to a woman who Fabian treated at Brookhaven, named Patricia Greenblatt."

"Ah," Eugene said, taking off his glasses. "Greenblatt. She lived at Brookhaven for quite some time."

"So you *do* remember her."

"Yes, I remember the name now."

"Bev seemed to think there was in incident with her in 2001, that led to a new nurse being fired. A young nurse."

"Hmm . . ." Eugene squinted at me. "I don't remember that. You say Fabian was her counselor? The way I remember it, she had a female counselor. While Fabian was our go-to therapist who worked with patients in the morning, we had a couple of counselors we'd work with on a case-by-case basis if for whatever reason it didn't work out with Fabian."

"Why would it not work out with Fabian?"

Eugene picked up a remote and snapped off the television. "Well. Sometimes it was a scheduling issue. Or if a female counselor was more appropriate for whatever reason, or if there was some medical reason why a psychiatrist like myself might be a better fit, because of the patient's diagnosis or prescription medication needs. We would have Lori Regnary come in sometimes, or Melissa Troyer. Both practiced in Campion. Melissa still does, I think. Anyway, I believe Mrs. Greenblatt worked with Regnary, if memory serves. I could be wrong about that."

"So the situation with the fired nurse?"

"Is it possible that a nurse left right around the same time that Mrs. Greenblatt had her little crisis? And Bev is just remembering it that way?"

"Well . . . Eugene . . . what exactly *was* Mrs. Greenblatt's crisis?" I asked.

Eugene reached for a glass that had been sitting on the small table next to him. It was half filled with orange juice. Slowly, shakily, he brought it to his lips and took a small sip.

"From what I remember, she was suddenly very frightened to be on the first floor of the facility. She felt that made her vulnerable to intruders. I believe that Fabian felt that she was experiencing some dementia, and that she was possibly reliving some memories of an assault or some sort of sensitive situation in her younger years. Ultimately, he thought it was better for her to work with one of the female counselors."

"Okay. I see. Hmm. That's interesting."

Eugene returned the glass to the table. "Is it?"

"Well, it just brings to mind a separate issue." I hesitated. "Do you remember Anthony Gagliardi's stepdaughter, Nadine Raines?"

Eugene squinted at me again, thinking about this.

"She was my age, Amanda's age," I added. "All in the same graduating class. I mean, technically."

"Of course. Yes, I recall she had some trouble, back when you were all kids."

Amanda was right. Eugene's memory was actually mostly intact. It was his spirit that seemed a little deficient.

"She did, yeah." I hesitated. "I understand that you recommended Dr. Fabian to her parents for her treatment, in the aftermath of that . . . trouble."

"Did I?"

"Anthony Gagliardi says you did."

Eugene sighed. "Well, then probably I did. So many years ago . . . you know, I've recommended Dr. Fabian and several other colleagues to so many people over the years. It's the nature of the business . . . people want a personal recommendation when they're looking for therapy. You don't want to go to just anyone."

"Right," I said. "But I kind of wonder why they didn't send her to a female therapist."

Morrison frowned. "That's a good question. I wonder that, too, now that you mention it. Considering . . ."

He didn't finish his thought. Instead he picked up the juice glass again. His grip was so shaky, I was tempted to hold the glass for him.

"But you recommended Fabian," I reminded him.

"I probably recommended him and several others, male and female. That's what I usually did, when people asked. I always recommended my friend Sarah Hoffman, too, for example. She's retired now. But anyway, I'd have left it to the person asking to decide if they wanted a male or a female, a social worker or a PhD psychologist, or whatever."

"So you didn't know that they ultimately went with Fabian."

Morrison smiled weakly. "If I did, I forgot a long time ago, my friend."

I nodded. "Eugene, while we're on this subject . . . I was thinking about something we talked about yesterday. I'm curious now. As a therapist who used to be in private practice, what would you do if an old patient came back *many* years later, like over a decade, and wanted to start up again like before? What would be normal procedure in that instance?"

"Well. There is no normal procedure, exactly. I'd listen to this individual. Try to understand what brought him or her back. Is it an unresolved issue from the time when we were working together? Is it that they haven't established a trust relationship with any other therapists since we worked together?"

"Would you let them come back?"

"If I thought it would benefit the patient, sure. But I would probably challenge them on it a bit first."

"Has that ever happened to you?"

"I think I had one come back after about three years."

"But, like . . . over ten years?"

"No. That's fairly unusual. I'd think. Peculiar. Interesting, perhaps, though. You see, we *do* wonder about our patients later. How they're doing. How life has treated them."

"Yeah. I can imagine. Well, it's been helpful talking to you, Eugene. Thank you."

I headed up the basement stairs. When I got to the top, Amanda seemed to be waiting for me. She was perched on the couch there, her black-hosed feet pulled up while she stared at her phone. I could hear her kids in the kitchen.

"How long have you been a cop, Henry?" Amanda asked without looking up.

"About thirteen years," I said.

"Are there other cops in your family?"

"Nope. Just me."

Amanda put her phone down.

"My dad wanted me to be a therapist like him. This whole thing reminds me that I'm glad I said no."

"Yeah?" I wondered if she'd been listening in on our conversation downstairs. Or if she was sick of the tedium of staying with the kids and the old man—and reluctant to let me leave.

"I mean, not a psychiatrist. He always knew I wasn't smart enough to get through medical school. But he wanted us all to do something medical. Like if it's not in the medical field, it doesn't count."

"Are your brothers doctors?"

"Just the older one. Justin's a pediatrician. Hey. Do you want to sit down? Can I get you something to drink?"

"No, thanks. I'm going to have to get going back to the station."

"Scott was smart," she continued. "His way out was medical administration. Like, he can go to work at a medical clinic but not have to wear a white coat or get involved in anyone's body."

"Or mind," I added.

"Or mind. Exactly."

"What is it you do again?" I asked.

"I'm an event coordinator."

"Oh. Like a wedding planner?"

"Kind of like that. But more corporate stuff."

"I see."

I almost said *Sounds like fun,* but I didn't want to lie.

"I was recently chatting with Julie," I offered. "Julie Olasz."

"Oh!" Amanda brightened. "How is she? I see her on Facebook, but we haven't seen each other in a few years."

"Well, we were talking about Nadine Raines."

"Nadine Raines. Oh."

"She was apparently in town recently."

"Really." Amanda frowned. "Wow, that's a name I haven't heard in years."

"Right. Me neither. So, you didn't know she was around lately?"

"No. I was never really close to her, like Julie was. We all played in that neighborhood together, when we were kids. But when I was about twelve or thirteen, we moved to this house."

Amanda studied me for a moment. "Should I be afraid to ask? How'd she turn out? Do you know what she's been up to?"

"She's a nurse, actually."

"Oh, *Jesus.*"

"Why Jesus?"

"Well. You know. Would you want her to be *your* nurse? Knowing what you know?"

"Huh. Yeah. Probably not," I admitted.

Amanda sighed. "You were in that class, too, weren't you?"

I checked the time on my phone. "Hmm?"

"I will *never* forget that."

"Yeah," I said again. I'd forgotten Amanda was in that class, too.

"A nurse. Can you imagine?"

"Well, twenty years is a long time."

"Remember that movie *Misery,* based on the Stephen King book?"

"Parts of it. I remember parts of it."

"Didn't Kathy Bates turn out to be some kind of a sick nurse who killed babies or something?"

"Yeah, I don't remember," I said. I officially wanted to leave now, but decided I should let Amanda finish her point.

"I wonder how many sadistic nurses there are out there. If they let Nadine Raines be a nurse, you really have to wonder."

I thought about Nadine's reluctance to volunteer at Brookhaven, back when it was somehow the cool thing to do.

"Amanda," I said. "It's been a pleasure. But I have to get back to work."

In the car, I called Greg to check in.

"You coming back here?"

"I was thinking about it. Why, what's up?"

"Well, I just dug this up. That Connor guy. I was asking

around, chatting with a couple of his friends and neighbors, trying to see if I could poke any holes in his story. Now, lady up the street confirms that his wife went to her book club meeting just like they both say. But she mentioned something I found interesting."

"What's that?"

"His sister was Dawn Koenig. You remember that name?"

Yes. I did. And it knocked the breath out of me for a second. I was able to recover quickly, though. It was the upstairs names that made me nauseous sometimes.

"One of the Brookhaven victims," I said.

"Yeah. She was working in the cafeteria. Different last name from Connor because she was married."

"That kind of explains why he'd be in therapy."

"Yeah. And it explains why he was looking at you kinda funny. But I'm just putting a couple of things together here. His sister was killed by Streeter. Streeter was a former patient of Fabian's. Now, that's an unfortunate coincidence, don't you think? Should Connor have been crying on the shoulder of the guy who used to headshrink his sister's murderer?"

"No," I said slowly.

What the fuck, Fabian?

"But I think it might be slim pickings for shrinks in this town?" I said.

"Maybe *this* was the screw-up his girlfriend mentioned—the memory slip? Not the Liam thing?"

"Or maybe the poor guy had started messing up left and right. If his memory was getting bad enough."

"Well." Greg sniffled. "This definitely seems like something he shouldn't have told Connor."

"Maybe he did, and maybe he didn't. But I'd think it would've been quite a scene if he did." I paused. "I think I'd like to talk to Connor again. How about you?"

"Yeah. I would, too. Should I try to get him to come down here, then?"

"Sure. I'll be there in a few minutes."

BUT FIRST I needed more coffee. There were a few cars tying up the Dunkin' Donuts drive-thru, but I got into line anyway. While I waited, I pulled Fabian's old notes into my lap.

I looked at all the cartoons of the doll and the dinosaur. The doll was obviously her: *Naddy Baby.* Was the dinosaur Fabian? Or maybe just a tool to confound Fabian? The conversations between the doll and the dinosaur made significantly less sense than the notes written directly to Fabian.

> ***Doll:*** *Are you going to break my heart, Talmadge?*
> ***Dinosaur:*** *How would I do that?*
> ***Doll:*** *There is part of your story that you've never told me. Are you ever going to tell me?*
> ***Dinosaur:*** *How can I now, Baby Doll? I'm dead. Not just dead. Meteor dead. Volcano dead. Earthquake dead.*

The dinosaur was long dead. Like her father. The dinosaur was her father?

Anthony wasn't dead. So he wasn't a dinosaur? No, it wasn't that simple.

> ***Dinosaur:*** *How many more dinosaurs do you think you'll know in your life?*
> ***Doll:*** *Maybe many. Maybe none.*
> ***Dinosaur:*** *Will you know a dinosaur when you see one?*
> ***Doll:*** *How could I not?*
> ***Dinosaur:*** *Because one of your eyes is broken, Baby Doll.*

What were dinosaurs, then? Drug addicts? Toxic men?

And then the final doll and dinosaur cartoon, with the gift between them.

> ***Doll:*** *Please, look, look, Talmadge! At last, page last! One good-bye! Oh, good-bye! Two good-byes!*

She'd drawn this the same day she'd written her final entry—on the opposite page, in the same blue ink. The same day she'd written *If you listened to about every other word, you'd be close to the truth.*

Same day. I looked back at the cartoon and read every other word.

Please look at page one oh two.

"Oh," I said aloud. They were drawn looking at a wrapped gift. And hadn't Fabian's old notes said she'd given him a book?

I looked at her final progress note, before she went away to college. *Client ended appointment with a gift to this writer—an essay collection by Walker Percy.*

"Oh!" I said aloud.

I took a breath. Reality check. I hadn't found a confession

or a smoking gun. I'd just found a second layer of provocation, written by a fucked-up teenager nearly two decades ago.

And yet.

The car ahead of me pulled forward. So did I. I was one car away from ordering my large coffee, four sugars.

I remembered that fucked-up teenager—in that final moment before she went off the deep end. I remembered the way her eyes looked—so hurt it seemed like they might just bleed.

I pulled out of the coffee line and drove to Fabian's office.

NADINE

CAMPION. I DECIDE to head back to Mom and Anthony's place first, before I try Brookhaven.

And now I'm on Durham Hill, staring up at our weird blue house, top-heavy from all of my mom's bizarre addition ideas. I'm not sure why they stayed in this house after I went to college. When they got married when I was ten, they stayed here because my mother didn't want my life to change too much. I would think after I'd gone they'd want something new. Maybe even to move out of town, and not the be the Parents of That Girl. But I guess not everybody thinks the way I do. There are people who get over things.

Anthony's car isn't in the driveway, and I doubt it's in the garage.

I go inside the house.

"Anthony?" I say quietly.

I walk through each of the rooms even though I know he's not here. The kitchen where my father used to strum his guitar—though long since remodeled, so I can't really identify exactly where our little breakfast table used to stand. My mother and Anthony's room, where I smiled self-consciously into the phone as I took my first call from a guy, such as he was. *Johnny.* The dining room, where I can see out to the patio where we ate pasta salad and talked about why I couldn't go to Woodstock '94.

And then I was back in the kitchen, where there was still a utility drawer. I wondered if Anthony had ever gotten a new X-Acto knife. It appeared to me that he and my mother were addicted to online shopping, so surely they needed something with which to open all of those packages.

The kitchen wall has, since I was a teenager, been painted a cheerful peach. Back then it was a strange lilac blue that my mother liked—that didn't quite work but we all pretended.

I touch the peach wall. I stare at my hand for a moment and try to remember all of the things it has done since I was sixteen.

Above my hand is the nail with the extra keys—Anthony's among them. I grab them and bring them with me to my car.

HENRY

THE OFFICE WAS quiet. The lab folks had of course finished packing up everything they needed, and left Wednesday evening. No one had touched it since. It would probably be Fabian's son's responsibility to pack up everything else and end the lease; it would probably be on someone else to have a carpet cleaner come and shampoo out the bloodstains.

And what does one do with a dead therapist's couch? I sat on it and stared into Fabian's empty leather chair.

If I could tell you one thing, what would it be, Fabian?

I imagined him sitting there—thick white hair framing his face, head wound healed. Eyes open.

It would not be about those three souls on the third floor. It should be, but it wouldn't be. It would be about Sophia and Olivia. It would be that every day I think about odds. I sit in that Campion Dental Group parking lot and watch their school and think about the odds of evil, the odds of random violence. The odds of it finding the same town—the same family—twice. I think the odds are with us. I think of them like sitting ducks at school or when we go to a mall or a

McDonald's, but then steady my breath and quietly thank the odds. I do this almost every day—which, sick as it sounds, feels sometimes like thanking the odds for Brookhaven. And that's not how I mean it at all. It's simply what allows me to look them in the face and take the risk of loving them.

I've said before that I think maybe you weren't the hottest therapist. And that makes it easier to tell you this, Fabian.

I stood up and approached the bookshelf wall. It was sectioned off into twelve shelves—three columns of four down to the floor. I began with the shelf that had been in disarray. A book with the title *Chronic Pain*. Some medical journals. Elisabeth Kübler-Ross. Could someone possibly have been rummaging for something? Or just grabbed the bookend in a blind rage?

Next shelf up.

The Body in Pain by Elaine Scarry. A couple of Jung books and *The Hero With a Thousand Faces.* Did Fabian read all of this stuff? I wondered.

Parenting from the Inside Out. Maybe I should borrow that one. Or maybe I didn't want my insides to be involved in my parenting. It was hard to say.

My cell rang. It was Katie, so I picked up.

"Olivia wants to talk to you. Do you have a minute?"

"A minute, yeah."

There was a pause, and then Olivia was on.

"Dad," she said.

The word stunned me for a moment. Lately, Olivia occasionally didn't say *Daddy.* Katie thought it was because her kindergarten teacher referred to *your mom and dad* all the time. But that didn't explain why she hadn't dropped the *Mommy* yet.

"Yeah?" I said.

"There's something about the story I want to ask you about."

"Okay. I only have a minute, but—"

"Mommy read me 'Hansel and Gretel' from the book. And there's a couple things I don't get."

I shifted my gaze one shelf up, focusing just on the author names. Burns. Herman. Silver. Chapman.

"What, you're off 'The Snow Queen' now?"

"I don't understand why the dad leaves the kids in the woods. Why doesn't he just leave the stepmother in the woods instead, if she's so mean?"

"Well, that's a good question. I'm not sure."

"She probably eats as much food as the kids, anyway, since grown-ups eat more food."

I kicked off my shoes and stood on Fabian's leather chair to get a better look at the higher shelves.

"Well, she probably has a lot more experience making her way through the woods by herself," I pointed out. "She'd probably always find her way back. The kids, though, are probably going to stay lost."

Olivia started crunching on something—an apple or a carrot. "Well. Then do something else to her."

The top shelf was dusty. The selection of books seemed more random, less shrinklike. Something about John Lennon. A couple of books of photography.

"I mean, how about they just poison her?" Olivia said.

William Styron. Irvin Yalom. Walker Percy.

My heart jumped and I pulled down the Walker Percy. It was a faded orange hardcover, with lettering that was probably once gold. Now it looked yellow-tan. *The Message in the Bottle* was the title.

"I'm sorry, sweetheart. But I have to go now."

"Why?"

"I'm actually working. You should ask your mom about it. And I'll give it some thought."

"When will you get home?"

"I don't know, honey."

"We'll forget to talk about it by then."

"Okay," I said absently. "Bye-bye."

I put my cell in my pocket and opened the front cover. It smelled old, but the binding was still tight. The title page said *How Queer Man Is, How Queer Language Is, and What One Has to Do with the Other.*

I flipped to page 102. There, squeezed into the bottom margin, was a note written in blue pen.

> *So. There is something I've meant to tell you. About him. I meant to tell you but I told that guy Johnny instead. You could ask him if you're ever wondering, and maybe he'd tell you. And then you'd know for sure what you probably always suspected: Perversion is in my blood. Anyway, wish me luck! And same to you.*

I took a breath. Nadine, you little brat. Those wounded eyes were still staring me down, twenty years later.

Do your homework, they said.

NADINE

In Taung, South Africa, I would sometimes walk all the long way across town after work to buy sausages or a few pieces of Kentucky Fried Chicken, and then take a kombi taxi back. Only very occasionally would I get the chicken, because it was exorbitantly priced. And the whole endeavor would take a couple of hours. But Daryl and I liked the novelty of "take-out" in such a remote place.

Between the hospital and the main part of town, there were stretches of road that were relatively uninhabited but for the occasional lone brick house. I loved the red dirt, the heat, the sparse desert plants, the gospel music often wafting from the last house before the AME church.

Along the way, I'd always get at least three shouts of the Setswana "Lekgoa!" And I'd smile at the anonymity of it. White person! With no distinct identity or history.

Perfect. Because very little of what I used to be was relevant here. From which faraway country or state I came. Where I went to college, the fact that I'd drawn pictures, or what I wanted to be before I became a nurse. Even the fact that I'd stabbed a guy once, potentially. The setting and circumstances of that incident were so distant from those of most of the people I knew here. If I'd attempted to share it, they'd likely have forgotten and dismissed it by now—like an insufferable American movie that never should have made its way onto South African television.

When my cell rang, I was hanging one arm out the kombi window, using the other to hold an iced guava juice I'd been sucking on. I fumbled with the phone and saw the familiar number.

Normally, my mother called once a month. Always on a predetermined Sunday at five P.M. my time. I'd go outside and stand on the brick wall near the front entrance of the clinic, where the cell reception was slightly better than the rest of the hospital.

This call was different—three P.M. on a Monday. I was surprised to hear her voice on the other end—usually international calls didn't come through that well when I tried to answer them in a car.

"Nadine? Nadine? Can you hear me?"

"Yeah?" The guava juice spilled on my hand. "Mom?"

"I'm so glad I got you. I wanted to tell you that Anthony is okay."

"What?"

"I didn't know if you'd hear anything, from your friends, about what's been happening in Campion."

Funny that my mother would think I'd still have friends in Campion.

"There was a shooting at Brookhaven. Really bad." Then she sputtered and sobbed.

"Mom? A shooting at the nursing home?"

"Yeah. It was early in the morning. Anthony was there, but it wasn't in the administrative building. It was in the first residential building next to his building. A lot of patients were killed. They don't know the exact number yet. And a nurse and some cafeteria workers."

"Jesus, Mom. Oh my God."

"I don't know how I thought you'd know but I wanted to talk to you first."

"Okay."

"It's a shock."

And then, over the miles and the static, I could hear my mother breathing. Did she want me to say something comforting? Did she want me to cry? Even in the most extreme of situations, it felt like she was testing me—making sure I contained the regular, expected emotions.

"How is Anthony?" I asked.

"He's okay. Glued to the news at the moment."

It felt like I should ask to speak to Anthony myself. To ask to hear his voice and offer my condolences directly. And yet, there was an unpredictability in dealing with Anthony. My mother—despite her always-obvious anxieties about me—was easier. My mother was happy for me to pretend the right emotions. Anthony seemed to want something else from me entirely—something I'd never gotten right.

"Waiting to see who made it and who didn't," my mother continued. "Dr. Morrison was rushed away in an ambulance. I don't know if you remember him, but he's still the director."

"Oh, no," I murmured.

How could she think I'd forget Dr. Morrison? He'd lived on our street before Brookhaven made him Richie Rich. He'd introduced her to Anthony. He had a kind face and a patient way with his daughter Amanda, who I'd always found to be a bit of a sourpuss.

"Do they know who the shooter is? Did they kill him?"

"He was shot but he's still alive. His name is Johnny Streeter."

"His name is what?" I felt something liquid run down between my legs. I thought I was peeing my pants until my eyes focused on the iced guava package, tilted over in my hands so all of the melted contents had dripped out onto my lap.

"Johnny Streeter. He's supposedly local but no one seems to have known him."

"Oh."

I was silent. The kombie was coming to a stop. Not the hospital stop, but still I stood slightly to indicate that I wanted to get off.

"Nadine? Nadine?" I could hear my mother saying as I shoved my phone in my bra.

I stepped over the bags of the lady next to me, and off the van.

"What's happening?" my mother was saying, when I took the phone out again.

"Mom?"

"Mma, you forgot your delicious food!" someone yelled from the kombie, and waved the KFC bag out the window.

I took it and thanked the man who'd found it.

"Nadine?" my mother was repeating.

"Mom?" I said, putting the phone up to my ear.

"Nadine?"

"Mom?" I could hear her now but I realized I didn't want to.

Johnny Streeter. Surely the same one. There couldn't be many Johnny Streeters.

"Yeah? Nadine?"

"I'm losing you," I said, waited a few seconds, and hung up.

It was true. Not because of the phone reception, which was mercilessly clear. But because hearing that name made me feel I was sinking into this red dirt. I stood motionless for a couple of minutes, guava juice soaking the front of my skirt, overpriced American fast food slipping out of my sweaty hand.

"Lekgoa!" someone yelled at me, passing on a bicycle.

My legs lurched back into action, moving me in the direction of the hospital.

THAT EVENING, WHEN Daryl got off his shift, he found me sitting at our kitchen table, staring at our cold bag of chicken.

"What's wrong?"

"Something happened. My mom called me."

"Is she okay?"

"Yeah. She's okay. My stepfather is okay. But there was a shooting where he works. That fancy old folks home where he works."

"What? What the fuck?"

Daryl turned the light on.

"Turn it back off, please," I said. I had stopped crying an hour ago, but I didn't want him to see how raw my face was.

He did as I asked.

"Anyone killed?"

"Lots, they think. I'll bet it'll even be on BBC tomorrow if you look for it."

"Jesus. Did he see the shooter? Was he near the shooter?"

"He's okay. The shooter wasn't in his building. That's all I know."

"Seems like these guys are always trying to think of sicker and sicker places to do this. What's next? An NICU?"

"Don't even say that. Don't *say* that."

"Why not? If you're sick enough for an Amish elementary school, if you're sick enough for an old folks home, why not? I'm sure there's someone out there thinking about it."

I was silent. I wanted to tell him to shut up. But I knew from experience that he just needed to say a few outrageous things whenever he heard news like this. It was a symptom of his more general decency.

"There's no end to it. There's no outer limit."

"No," I whispered. "I guess there's not."

Daryl was silent now. He'd said his one angry thing and now he was ready to sit quietly in the dark.

He reached for my hand and I pulled it away.

"What?" he said. "What is it?"

"I need to get up," I said. "I need to take a walk."

"At this hour? You know you can't. It's getting dark."

"I'll stay inside the hospital walls."

"I can't take a walk right now. I'm too exhausted."

"I know. I'm not asking you to."

"Stay here with me," he said.

But to stay would mean telling him all the things he should have known years ago.

"I can't," was all I said.

I went outside, walked to the hospital entrance, and sat on a wall. I sat there until I could look up and see the Southern Hemisphere stars. I had rarely ever noticed them up there, until Daryl had started to school me on them. I tried to look for the Vela—the "false cross," because some people mistook it for the Southern Cross. It was my favorite because I liked both of its names.

But without Daryl there, I couldn't make out any constellations. They were all just stars. Beautiful, but to me, impossible to separate into the pictures I was supposed to see.

Johnny Streeter.

I'd forgotten that name for so long. I'd forgotten he ever existed. My brush with crazy had never left me—not really. But that name and that night had, over the years. As had the starchy feel of his dark blue sheets, the panic in my throat at his surprisingly strong grip, and the cleansing breath I took when he released it.

And his monotone on the phone the next morning.

I was drunk. I shouldn't have said those things. If you tell anyone what I said, I'll tell them what you *said.*

And the uneasy, but slightly exhilarated, feeling it gave me to hear him say that. Because I didn't care who else he told, as long as he told *you,* Bouffant. And even *dared* him to tell, by telling you exactly what I wasn't supposed to. To me, Johnny's words weren't so much a threat as a promise. And I was naïve enough to think a promise like that would mean something to someone like Johnny a day or a week—even an hour—after he said it.

The exchange itself was insignificant now. Now that Johnny had gone and done this inhuman thing. But still I was the girl who'd been in his bed. On top of everything else, I would always be that girl, too—no matter how many oceans or years away I got.

When I returned to our apartment, I watched Daryl sleep for a while. I kissed him on the head. I knew we wouldn't be together for much longer. He was planning to return to Minnesota in a couple of months. He'd assumed I'd go with him. I hadn't yet said for sure.

Daryl wanted children someday and I'd never explicitly said I would never have them. But I never would. I was only willing to go so far in the endeavor to prove I wasn't crazy. Because imagine those poor kids, if I turned out to be wrong?

And Daryl would be forty someday. And forty-five. And older. I couldn't imagine him growing into a dinosaur. How could we exist together then? I might just want to take out a corkscrew or pair of scissors and find out a little bit more about him.

I kissed him again.

"I love you as you are," I whispered.

"You too," he murmured, startling me as I'd thought he was sleeping.

I didn't reply. I waited about ten minutes. He was snoring by then.

"You don't know what I am," I whispered, and then lay down next to him.

HENRY

THE OFFICER AT the front gate of Eastern Correctional drank from a Styrofoam cup as I explained to him I'd just called ahead about speaking to an inmate.

"You talked to the warden?"

"I spoke to the shift commander. A Captain Baird."

"Just a second." He got on the phone for a moment. "Alright. You can park right over there and go in the white double doors."

In the building, the officers had me waiting in a windowless room with a smudged white table. While I sat there, I bit off a couple of overgrown fingernails and thought about what Olivia had called to ask me. *I mean, how about they just poison her?*

Now, how and when had she learned to think that way? Crunching so casually on an apple like a cynical old lady sucking on a cigarette?

Before I'd had time to really start worrying about this in earnest, a young officer brought in Streeter and parked him in a chair. The officer nodded to me and retreated out of the room—but I could see through the little rectangle of glass on the door that he was going to stay nearby until Johnny and I were done.

Johnny Streeter was wearing an orange jumpsuit. He looked a little less athletic than he had five years ago, a little more wan. And his bald spot was larger. Or the short prison haircut just made it look more prominent.

"Henry Peacher?" he said. He seemed to wrestle with himself for a moment—trying to get his arms into a comfortable position even though they were still handcuffed. "That really you? When they told me it was you, I thought it was a joke."

"I just have a few questions for you," I said.

"What took you so long?"

"It's not about Brookhaven. Not really."

"No?" He stared at me. I'd forgotten that thing about his eyes—their slight bulge, and the feeling that you were seeing just a bit more of the whites than you were supposed to.

"I know this is a little unexpected. But can you tell me about someone named Dr. Mark Fabian?"

"Who?" Streeter said, then snuffled and then nuzzled the shoulder of his jumpsuit to wipe his nose.

"He's someone I believe you knew at one time."

"A doctor?" Streeter shook his head. "I don't know many doctors."

"He was your therapist," I reminded him.

"My therapist? When they arrested me? That shrink was a lady."

"No. Not your shrink after the shooting. Your shrink before."

"I didn't have a . . ." Streeter hesitated. "A shrink."

"His records say you did. Starting in 1996, and then stopping in 1997."

"Ninety-six? Oh. Well, yeah. When I was nineteen or twenty or so, I did go to a guy for a while—on again, off again. I forgot about that. So what's up with that guy? Has he been talking about me to the press? Cashing in? Don't tell me he's written a book or something."

"No," I said quietly. "No book."

I was pretty sure Streeter didn't have access to television, but I'd forgotten to ask. So it was hard to tell if this was an act.

"When was the last time you had any contact with Dr. Fabian?" I asked.

"I told you." Streeter leaned back in his chair. "I was about twenty."

"So almost twenty years ago, then."

"Yes." Streeter looked bored. "Correct."

"What about any of your family or friends? Any of them go to him, ever?"

"Nobody else I know went to him. That I know of. When I was his patient, my dad would call him and try to sniff around about what I said or didn't, or whatever."

"Okay. But recently?"

"No. I don't think so, anyway. My parents were the only ones who knew about that. And they're both dead." Streeter shrugged. "My sister hates me. And my uncle only came here once, to tell me when my dad died. Now, what is this, *really*?"

"Did you ever know someone named Nadine Raines?"

"Nadine Raines." Streeter puckered his lips and made a long sucking noise. "That sounds familiar, actually."

"She went to the same therapist as you. Dr. Fabian."

"Oh! That girl." His lips twitched into a smirk, and then went flat again. "Yeah."

"You been in any kind of contact with her recently?"

"No." Streeter looked quizzical for a moment. "I barely remember her."

"Well, what do you remember?"

Streeter hesitated, and then said, "We fucked once."

"Okay. Anything else?"

"That's all that was memorable."

"Yeah?" I said softly.

When Streeter's face relaxed, his eyes still had that glassy bulginess. "Yeah."

"Okay. Well, when's the last time you talked to her or had any contact with her?"

"Back then. When I was about twenty or so. Ninety-six, ninety-seven, like you said."

"You didn't keep in touch? Like when she went to college, or after that?"

"*No.* It was just like a fling, like kids have. Right?"

"Did she ever talk about Dr. Fabian?" I asked.

"Sometimes, I guess."

"Did she have any problems with him, any issues?"

"This is a girl I was with one or two nights twenty years

ago. What're you asking me? I don't know. She didn't say anything one way or another about that shrink dude. We had other things on our mind, right?"

"I don't know. It feels like you're leaving something out. Now, I have reason to believe that Nadine told you some information. Some sensitive information. And I'd like your clarification on that."

"Some sensitive information? Can you be a little more specific there, Henry?"

I cleared my throat. "I believe she told you some kind of a secret, maybe about a male person in her life. Does that ring a bell?"

"Well, let's see. As I told you, it was a long time ago. I'd have to really think about this."

"Fine," I said. "Take your time."

"Okay," Streeter said, and closed his eyes.

I watched his eyelids, which flinched a little. He had long, dark lashes that made him look almost childlike when you couldn't see those weird eyes.

Everything looks weirder in real life, I heard a little voice say. Is that what I'd say back to Olivia when she asked me, someday, why I didn't kill Streeter at Brookhaven? Would it be easier to explain *why not* than it would've been to explain *why*?

But maybe Olivia would never ask why or why not. Olivia never asked the questions I expected her to. In fact, she asked even harder ones. She'd probably want to know, quite simply, how someone like Johnny Streeter *happens*. How something like him exists and why I can't do much about it.

"Now, why don't you ask her yourself?" Streeter said, opening his eyes. "Or did she tell you something and you're looking for people to confirm it?"

"Maybe you could just tell me what you know about Nadine," I said. "Just anything you remember."

Streeter shrugged his skinny orange shoulders. "Nadine was a little fucked-up."

"Well . . . what did she tell you, specifically?"

"Well. Look. I don't know if this is what you're looking for, but she said her dad was, like, a perv."

"Her dad?" I asked. "Or her stepdad? This is important."

"Her . . . wait, she had a stepdad?"

"Yes. Her dad died when she was younger. When you knew her, she lived with her stepdad."

"Well, I guess that's who she meant, then."

"Did he do something to her? Abuse her in some way?"

"I don't know. She said he liked to show his dick to people."

I tried to keep my face expressionless. This wasn't what I was expecting, and I wasn't sure I should believe it.

"To her?" I asked.

"I don't know. I don't remember. I just remember her saying he liked to show it around."

I hesitated, thinking of Nadine's words in her final, hidden note to Fabian: *Perversion is in my blood.* Wouldn't that most likely refer to her father?

"Okay," I said. "But is this something he did to *her*?"

"You know, I assumed that. But I didn't ask questions. We talked a lot about a lot of things . . ." Johnny looked at me pointedly. "*Did* a lot of things . . . that night."

He was so *proud* of that.

"And she didn't say anything else about it?"

"She said she hated herself."

Watching Streeter smile, I was starting to feel like some part of my brain was burning—slowly, like something accidentally left in the oven.

"Herself or him?"

Streeter was still smiling, like this was a punch line of some kind. "Herself."

Poor Nadine. Nadine with the brown ponytail and the sad eyes. Whatever she was now, when she had known Johnny, she was still just a kid.

"Did you tell anyone this?" I asked.

"No. Why would I?"

"We all know you didn't think much of Brookhaven."

Streeter's smile disappeared. "What?"

"Her father worked at Brookhaven," I said. It was true either way—whether she had been talking about Anthony or her real father.

"He *did*? Huh."

"So none of this had anything to do with what you did."

"No. What, like when she was a kid told she me to go shoot people there? Is that what you're getting at?"

"Is it something I *should* be getting at?" I asked, hearing my voice drop off at the end of the question. I already knew the answer. Brookhaven would make more sense if it had another layer. But it didn't have one. Johnny was the only layer.

"Fuck, no," Johnny said. "Is she trying to take *credit*?"

NADINE

I PARK ABOUT A mile from Brookhaven's main lot and walk down through their sprawling gardens. I wonder if Brookhaven has a regular police presence now, because of what happened in 2010. Copycats seem unlikely, but nonetheless maybe it makes everybody feel better to have the cops checking in.

As one approaches the main building, the brick path opens up into a charming little courtyard. On one of its iron benches is an elderly woman with a walker, and a younger woman, probably a visiting relative, unwinding an endless pink knitted scarf from her neck.

"Whew," she is saying. "I didn't even need this."

"I told you you wouldn't," her older companion replies.

From here I can see Anthony's office. He's been in the same one since I was a kid. The second wide window on the third floor. The first, next to it—the corner office—was Dr. Morrison's.

I stare up at those windows and wonder if Anthony can see

me. I imagine I don't look so hot after spending a night in my car and drinking his Glenlivet in the woods.

After a couple of minutes, I hear a cough behind me.

"Are you alright?" one of the women asks me. I can't tell which one because I'm not looking at them.

"Yeah," I say. "Thanks."

I check my pocket for Anthony's keys and head for the parking lot to find his car.

HENRY

"DETECTIVE. DETECTIVE!"

The burning sensation was subsiding a little now.

Streeter and I were both standing. Me right by the table, him in the corner of the room. The officer who'd been waiting outside the room was now between us. Streeter was trying to wipe his bloody nose with the shoulder of his jumpsuit.

"What the fuck?" he was screaming. "I have nothing else to say to you!"

"What happened?" the officer asked. He pulled me out of the room just as another officer arrived and stepped inside with Streeter.

I couldn't actually say what happened. I couldn't quite remember. But my right hand hurt.

"I've got to go," I said. "I think I have someone to arrest in Campion."

I wasn't sure it was true yet, but I didn't want to stick around here. This was turning out to be an *apologize later* kind of moment. I needed to get back to Campion.

"Did he give you what you need?" the officer wanted to know.

"Enough," I said.

I PASSED A pickup truck on the road back to Campion. Then a Lexus. Everyone was going demonstrably slow because of my vehicular presence. This was how it always was, of course, but it felt particularly frustrating in this moment.

I picked up my cell and called Julie Olasz.

"Hey there," she said. "How's it going?"

"I just remembered something else I wanted to ask you about Nadine."

I heard her sigh. "What?"

"Julie . . . do you know if Nadine got along with her stepfather?"

"Umm . . . I think they tolerated each other's existence. I don't remember her ever saying he was mean or anything, if that's what you're asking. But I don't know if they ever connected all that much."

"Did she ever call him 'dad'? Or refer to him as her father?"

"Um . . . not that I can remember. Maybe after we were friends. I doubt it though. She was close to her real dad, at least when she was little. I think it would've made her sad to do that. Her stepdad was a nice guy, but . . ."

"But?"

"But he was just kind of *there*, I think. I don't remember Nadine ever talking about him like he was a big part of her life."

I don't think of him as a dinosaur, like I usually do men his age. Maybe because he's married to my mother. So that makes him a different kind of mystery. A mystery I don't want to solve.

What did that *mean*?

And if Anthony was the fucked-up one, why would Nadine write *Perversion is in my blood*? Could she be referring to her mother?

"But she *lived* with him," I persisted. "Did they get along?"

"Well enough, I think. Where are you going with this, Henry?"

And what did she mean by a *dinosaur*? Yeah, I got that she drew dinosaurs in her little cartoons. But why was Anthony *not* a dinosaur?

"Nowhere," I mumbled.

"Oh, good," said Julie. "That's reassuring."

"Talk to you later," I said, and ended the call.

NADINE

ANTHONY STARES AT me when he sees me. I can see the surprise turn to calculation as he stands two feet from the car. I don't get out. I just sit and wait to see what he does.

I see his chest rise and fall. His moss green sweater is too big for him. He is shorter and wider here than he usually is in my memory.

He reaches for the door and gets in.

"You scared me, Nadine."

I don't say anything for a moment.

"I scare you, Anthony?"

His mouth tightens. One thin gray eyebrow blips upward.

"I said you *scared* me. I don't usually expect to find someone waiting for me in my car."

"But *do* I scare you?"

Anthony looks at me. I let him look—longer than I ever have. And I look back at him—longer than I've ever allowed myself. The roundness of his face and the baldness of his head have always made him look like a strangely aged toddler. But over the last few years he's become more jowly, lessening the effect. Now he just looks old.

"No," he says, still studying me. "What's up with your hair?"

I show him the Glenlivet bottle.

"This was going to be your Christmas present."

"Looks like Santa drank some."

His response is so calm and so perfect. I hate it.

I reach out the window, and slam the bottle against the side-view mirror. The plastic of the mirror shatters instead of the bottle. This isn't as satisfying as a broken bottle, but at least something is broken.

There is still a heavy bottle in my hand. Anthony's face is still calm—smugly so.

"No," he says. "You've never scared me, Nadine."

And then he starts the car.

HENRY

AMY MET ME at the door as I walked into the station.

"I found something you were looking for," she said, handing me a file. "Fabian didn't have much on this Greenblatt lady, but he had a couple of sessions recorded. I took the liberty of reading them. Not a pretty picture."

I opened the file as I walked to the interview room. "Is Greg still with Connor Osborne?"

"Yeah."

I stopped a few paces short of the interview room and read.

INITIAL SESSION PROGRESS NOTE

PATIENT NAME: Patricia Greenblatt
DATE OF SERVICE: 5/7/01

Medical personnel at the Brookhaven facility requested a consult with this patient because she is displaying signs of anxiety and possibly the first onset of dementia. According to one of the nurses on staff, this patient awoke on the night of 5/6/01 crying and reporting that an intruder had entered her room twice in preceding days. She could not identify which days, but said that both times he had exposed his genitalia to her and once he had forced her to touch them by threatening physical harm.

Brookhaven personnel report that the patient has shown no signs of dementia up to this point, and only suffers from occasional memory lapses.

During the session, the patient repeated the story reported by her nurse—of two visitations by an intruder with a knitted mask pulled over his face. She describes this intruder as tall with a "regular man's voice. Pretty deep."

When asked if she thought the incidents were dreams, the patient said. "No. They were during the day."

When asked why she did not report these incidents right away, she said, "I didn't want anyone to think I was crazy, and move me up to the Alzheimer's floor. But at night I got too scared to keep it to myself."

When asked if she had ever had similar experiences in the past, and if she wished to discuss that, she reported that once she had been in a crowded theater in the 1940s and the man next to her had run his fingers up and down her leg like a spider.

"So I got up and looked for another seat. I don't want to talk about that. That was more than fifty years ago. Why would you ask me about that? Is this going to be like the *Oprah* show?"

The patient was then tearful and asked if she could report this incident to the police without telling her children. She said she had made good friends here and didn't want them to move her to another place. She has resided at Brookhaven for five years.

"I'm happy when I keep busy, and there's at least things here to keep me busy."

This writer recommends honoring the patient's wish not to inform her children until she is more comfortable with their involvement. We will discuss this in our next session (tomorrow). Until then, the patient says she will "feel better" and "sleep better" if a female staff member routinely checks her room and surrounding hall area during the course of the night. The patient has asked to be moved from the ground floor to the second or third. This writer believes that will ease her anxiety level, but would likely involve a discussion with her children, for which the patient has repeatedly said she is not yet ready.

PROGRESS UPDATE

PATIENT NAME: Patricia Greenblatt
DATE OF SERVICE: 5/8/01

The patient was more tearful during this session, especially when the topic of her son came up. She says that she does not want to worry him and is embarrassed to have him hear her story.

She repeatedly asked, "Are you all deciding if you are going to move me somewhere? You think I have Alzheimer's?"

When this writer said that it sounded like she'd had a frightening few days recently, and that we all wished to help her get to the bottom of it, she expressed that she found it difficult to speak to a man about her current difficulties. She said that it was not the first time she'd had a violating experience and that, again, these were matters she did not want her children to know about.

For the remainder of the session, we talked about the patient's plan for the day—a shopping trip, a movie in the late afternoon. She felt both of these activities would help her take her mind off her recent difficulties.

This writer recommends that therapy continue with a female practitioner.

"Oh, fuck," I said.

"What?" Amy said. "What does it mean?"

"It means . . ." I wasn't sure. But whatever Nadine had told Johnny all those years ago, there was some truth to it here. In 2001. After Nadine had gone off to college. A decade after her father had died.

"Had ski masks been invented yet in the thirties and forties?" Amy asked.

"Why do you ask that?"

"Well, it seems like they were fixing to blame this thing on dementia and her mixing up her memories with the present. But did anyone use ski masks to be sexual deviants back then?"

"I don't know," I murmured. "Maybe they just put paper bags over their heads."

"Or hollowed out pumpkins," Amy offered.

"Who would *do* this?" I said.

Glancing over the file, I paused at the word *tall.* Anthony Gagliardi was short and squat. On the other hand, anyone might have looked menacing, and therefore tall, to an elderly woman presumably seated or in a bed.

Amy shook her head. "It's kind of interesting that you would still ask something like that at this stage. And I don't mean that in a bad way. But . . . anyway. This isn't the first encounter I've had with elder sexual abuse. It's a power thing. Someone who might be thought to have dementia is an easy target. I've never worked a case myself, but I've had colleagues who have."

Greg came out of the interview room. "Henry, what the hell? I've been waiting for almost an hour. Are you coming in here or not?"

NADINE

WHERE ARE YOU going, Anthony?"

Anthony ignores the question and turns onto Campion's main road. Soon we pass the library, and then the high school.

"Tell me what happened," Anthony says. "Tell me what happened with Mark Fabian."

Mark Fabian. Anthony was on first name terms with you. Maybe in the years since you were my Bouffant, you two even became friends?

"What happened this week . . . or what happened about twenty years ago?" I ask.

Anthony turns on his blinker. We're getting onto the highway ramp.

"Whichever you want to start with."

Anthony is gunning the engine now, to get ahead of a semi-truck in the right lane. The speed and the uncertainty of our destination take me out of myself even more than my hangover. I don't really care how the words sound as they leave me.

So I start with this week. I start with Monday afternoon.

MONDAY AFTERNOON, WHEN I sat so gingerly on your couch and you smiled so familiarly and said, "How have you been?"

I told you that lately I'd been living in Vermont—teaching phlebotomy half the year, and doing a variety of things the other half. You didn't ask if I had a husband or family, so I volunteered that information, just for your edification. No and no.

And then I tried, for once, to be straightforward with you. I said that I'd heard from my mother that you were retiring. I said that the news made me want to come talk to you once more. Just to see if we could put this all to bed, this thing I'd done. This thing I'd run from all these years. It seemed like a worthwhile exercise, right? As long as I didn't spend too much time on it, or take it too far? And you nodded uncertainly.

I told you that I'd been drawing pictures while I was here. Not pictures for anyone else but me. I know that no one would want to look at a picture I'd drawn of Gillette Castle or of my elementary school or the stump of my old climbing tree or the library steps where I'd read the J. D. Salinger stories my father said he loved. But I'd thought it was time to finally look at these places carefully. To sit down and draw them would require me to endure them for long enough to really remember things. In the end, I maybe thought that there dwelt in these spots the person who I fundamentally was—the person I might have been—had she not gone crazy, and then spent twenty years running from crazy. Maybe I thought she might come out and whisper in my ear some instruction as to how to live the second half of my life.

And even if she didn't, I at least had you, Bouffant. You to go back to and say, *I believe I've figured a few things out. I don't think I need to run anymore, from the girl with the X-Acto knife.* You who might even believe me, or at least know well how to pretend to.

You asked a bit more about the intervening years, so I told you a little more about phlebotomy, and travel nursing, and South Africa, and back to phlebotomy again. The occasional volunteer nursing—in Honduras and Liberia. And you looked like you wanted to interrupt me, and ask me details, because surely those things were actually more interesting than the girl with the X-Acto knife, and perhaps served to negate and silence her. But I talked fast and said that in all of those sessions, years ago, there was one thing I had left out.

I didn't ask if you'd ever looked at the gift I'd left you. Because that was like asking if you'd thought about me after I'd gone, which wasn't your job or maybe even your place.

"I should just tell you this one thing," I said. "This one thing I kept leaving out when I was a kid."

"Okay," you said. "If that's what you want, why don't you tell me?"

THE THING WAS that August evening when I was fourteen. It was 1994, and my dad had been gone for three years by then.

The thing was what happened when my mother and Anthony and I were outside on the patio eating pasta salad, thick with chunks of ham and cherry tomatoes, slippery with mayonnaise. I was trying to convince my mother to let me go to a music festival—Woodstock '94—with Julie and Amanda and Amanda's two older brothers. An overnight trip.

"Don't you think Dad would've let me do things like this?" I'd insisted, when every other argument failed.

"I honestly don't know, Nadine."

I hated the stiffness in her jaw, the irritation in her tone, the squishy sound of her spooning a second helping of pasta salad into her bowl.

"I mean, don't you think he was smart enough to know that a little independence is good for a kid my age?" I asked.

Anthony had sighed and glanced at my mother nervously.

"And I'm not smart enough to know that?" my mother said quietly.

"I don't know, *are* you?"

My mother stuck her fork in her bowl and sat back in her wicker chair.

"He wasn't perfect, Nadine."

"No shit, Sherlock. He died of an overdose. No one's deluding themselves that he was perfect. But he was smart. He wasn't smart about everything, but he was smart about this *kind* of thing."

My mother gripped her fork again, and stirred her pasta salad absently. *Squish squish squish.* I wanted to kill her. I wanted to puke. I couldn't believe I'd eaten a bowl of that stuff myself.

"You think so?"

"I *know.*"

"Nadine . . ." said Anthony. "Susan."

We ignored him, as we always did.

The look on my mother's face wasn't exactly skeptical, but distracted. She got that look when she would rather be watching *Oprah* or planting petunias or reading *Woman's Day.* One of the two dozen or so perplexingly boring activities that she found more relaxing and enjoyable than dealing with me. I knew she tried to hide it but I could *tell* when her brain had essentially shut off and her eyes were saying *Where's my Diet Coke? Where's the remote? Is there any microwave popcorn left?*

"I wish you were smart about some of those things," I said.

I watched my mother fling her fork on the table and breathe through her nostrils.

"You wish I was smart? Yeah. I wish that, too. I might not be smart, but at least I'm not sick."

"Sick? Come on, Mom."

I was tired of all the warnings of the dangers of addiction—the suggestion that what my dad had was an illness I could catch, too, if I wasn't careful.

"At least I'm not a pervert. At least I wouldn't show my thing to old ladies in an old folks home."

"What?"

"That's why he was fired, Nadine."

Anthony stood up and grabbed my mother's elbow.

"*Susan.*"

"Yeah?"

"What're you doing, Susan?"

"We needed to tell her sometime."

"Susan, let's come in the house."

"I think it's nice out here," my mother said primly.

"Well, not *anymore,* Susan. Jesus."

My mother turned to me with a stunned expression. She looked like she might cry. I knew then that it was true. She hadn't meant to say it. I'd backed her into it. I'd pushed her too far. She'd never meant to tell me.

She and Anthony were both watching me. I felt the pasta salad roiling in my stomach. I ran inside and slammed into the bathroom. I leaned over the toilet and gagged. Nothing happened. Nothing happened for a minute, and then five minutes, and then twenty. Horrified, I started to realize that nothing was ever going to happen. It wasn't coming up. It was going to stay inside me and burn a hole there, right in the middle.

HENRY

"LISTEN, YOU GUYS," Connor said as I sat down at the table with Greg. "I've come in here and I've waited this long out of respect for Dr. Fabian and his family."

I was silent. My head was still in Fabian's Greenblatt file. Obviously Fabian was well aware of what had happened to Mrs. Greenblatt in 2001. He was thinking about it when he'd also scribbled *TR 4/12/91.* He saw these two events as connected—at least, after talking to Nadine this week.

"Did you know anything about his family?" Greg asked.

Connor ignored the question. "I hope you've been calling back the dude who came in *after* me. Have you been asking *him* a few questions?"

I paused. It was entirely believable that someone came in during Connor's session. But one part of his question surprised me.

"How do you know it was a dude?" I asked.

"Because he went in the bathroom."

"Come again?"

"Dr. Fabian's office bathroom is right up against the wall

behind his desk. Really thin wall. I had no idea. A guy peeing sounds different from a lady peeing, you know what I mean?"

I could feel Greg looking at me, waiting for me to respond. But I was still puzzling over the Greenblatt file. There must have been a previous incident of some kind—or at least a previous rumor—if Nadine was somehow confessing it to Johnny Streeter roughly around 1996 or 1997. What did she know, and how did she know about it? And what did Eugene Morrison know, and when? Did he only know of the 2001 incident? Or did he know of something happening before then? If Morrison suspected—as anyone would—that there was a habitual exhibitionist and sex offender in the presence of the patients, why wouldn't he do a top-to-bottom investigation immediately? Because this was a problem that could bring all of Brookhaven—his baby—down completely, if the public heard that something like this had happened twice.

"Uh. Yeah. But you and Fabian were talking, right?" Greg asked. "You weren't focused on that. It probably could've been a man or a woman."

Connor stared at Greg.

"We weren't talking then. We were having what's called an awkward silence. The guy had come in and sat in the office for a minute, then went into the bathroom. We were both listening to it. It was kind of creepy, us both sitting there listening to this guy pee. I thought of all of the times I'd pissed in that office, when he was with the previous patient. They probably always stopped and listened. It's really kind of an unsettling thought, don't you think?"

"Yeah," I agreed.

And we all knew that Morrison would *die* for his baby Brookhaven. And he wouldn't let something so awful happen to its residents. He'd thrown himself at Johnny Streeter, for God's sake. I couldn't imagine he'd cover for anyone who'd victimized his patients. And yet it sounded like he *had.* Who on earth would he protect over *Brookhaven*? A doctor? A nurse? An orderly? Anthony Gagliardi?

"Look, Connor. I'm going to change direction here." Greg glanced at me as he spoke, then nudged my foot with his. "We were curious about something. Someone close to Dr. Fabian mentioned that he had an incident in which he unfortunately slipped and told a patient something he shouldn't have. Does that sound like a familiar or likely situation to you?"

Could *Eugene himself* have been the perp in Patricia Greenblatt's case? Could *he* be an extremely well-masked deviant?

"Umm . . . I don't know," Connor was saying. "Slipped, and, what . . . what's 'something he shouldn't have'? Like, he told someone they were sexy? Or he told someone they were batshit crazy?"

"Did Dr. Fabian ever mention other patients to you?" I asked.

"No. They're not supposed to do that."

"He never mentioned any previous patients, then?"

"No. If he did, I'd have had serious second thoughts. By *name,* you mean?"

"By name or . . . even not by name? Using other patients' situations to reflect on your own?"

"Not that I can think of. I don't think he had many patients whose situation was much like my own, but . . . maybe that's just me being egocentric. It's a small town and my family wasn't the only one that suffered."

"Look, Connor. I know this is a painful subject. But I know your sister died in the Brookhaven shooting."

Connor sighed. "Yeah. Uh. I figured you knew that. Yeah, that's why I started the therapy. Not right after the shooting. Like, a year after or so. I had no clue how to find a shrink. A guy at work gave me a recommendation."

"Someone who went to Dr. Fabian himself?" I asked. "Another patient of his?"

"No. I don't work with him anymore. His name is Scott Morrison. He used to be the financial officer at Carrick. I mean, back then. He left and now he works at Franklin Hospital. But his dad is a shrink, so he knows lots of shrinks and had a list of therapists he recommends."

His *kid*. Of course. Maybe five minutes out of this interview room and I'd have thought of it myself. Maybe not.

Greg seemed to notice my silence.

"So Scott was a friend?" he asked. "Someone you were comfortable chatting with about what happened to your sister?"

"Not exactly comfortable. But his dad was a victim, too, as you probably know. So I mentioned to him I was having trouble, yes. And he gave me the list of names."

"Were you aware of any other of Dr. Fabian's patients being involved in that shooting?" Greg asked.

"No." Connor's face stiffened as he folded his arms. "Why would I know that?"

"As I said, we'd heard that Dr. Fabian had been 'slipping' in his memory sometimes, and that had started to cause him some problems."

"Okay. Wow. I guess that's why he was retiring, huh? What, did he give one patient an earful about another patient?"

I was growing sick to my stomach, and Greg's teasing style of questioning wasn't helping.

"Connor," I said. "Were you aware that Dr. Fabian treated Johnny Streeter years ago?"

Connor's cheeks reddened so fast I thought they might burst into flames. It was exactly what I expected to happen.

"Are you fucking kidding me?" he said.

"Were you aware . . . ?"

"Are you trying to make me mad? What is this?"

"Were you aware of that before this moment?"

"No. Are you trying to get me to say something crazy? Dr. Fabian treated Johnny Streeter?"

"No to the first question. Yes to the second."

"That's nuts."

"It is," I murmured.

"Then there are probably *lots* of people who wanted to kill him."

"Yeah," Greg said. "That's what we thought."

"I don't know what you're getting at, fellas." Connor planted his hands on the table and pushed up out of his chair. "But I think this interview is over, because I'm not saying anything else to you guys without a lawyer."

"Great," I said. I stood up and went back to my desk.

NADINE

AND AS I told you the pasta salad story this Monday, I stared out the window at the bank parking lot. Except it wasn't a bank anymore. The drive-up window had been ripped out, and it was a coffee shop. As twilight fell, all that was visible was the string of Christmas lights crookedly festooning the storefront windows.

"How long was this before your incident with the teacher?" you asked.

"About a year," I said. "A little more."

You nodded. "You found out that your father had . . . exposed himself to some of the patients at Brookhaven?"

"Yes."

You looked concerned—unsettled, even. "Had it happened numerous times, or was there some misunderstanding or accident?"

"Accident?" I repeated. "Like a wardrobe malfunction?"

You smiled weakly. "I'm just trying to understand what happened."

"I don't know a lot of details. I just know that this one lady kept describing a person who was doing it to her. And no one believed her because she had dementia, and she wasn't able to give any kind of description. And then some other lady on a different floor started saying the same thing. But the description she gave sounded like my dad. So then they had to do something. And rather than have Brookhaven possibly get bad press right when they were starting to do so well, they fired him and I think even gave him a little money to go quietly, although I'm not sure about that part. This was all I could gather the one time my mom and Anthony were willing to talk about it. And I was afraid to ever bring it up again."

"Okay," you said slowly.

"I think they were ashamed of telling me . . . and after that, willing to pretend they never had."

You started shaking your head. "I'm trying to understand why you didn't tell me this. Then."

"Well, first of all, I always wondered if my mom had already told you, and you were waiting for me to bring it up."

"No, Nadine. I didn't know. My memory isn't great these days, but I'm pretty sure I'd remember if I knew this. With my connection to Brookhaven, and everything."

"Second of all, it was too painful." I hesitated. "And of course, not telling you gave me a little bit of power."

You paused and scratched your head. I noted how your hair was still basically the same style and fullness, even though it was shorter and less uproariously fluffy. And it was snow-white now. More comforting than distracting.

"There's always that," you said quietly.

"I mean that in a couple different ways. One, you could never fully judge me if I withheld one thing from you."

"And the other?"

"If I didn't tell you this one thing, then maybe I could tell myself it explained everything. It explained the awful thing that I'd done."

You nodded, and something about your gaze reminded me of the time you ate one of my cardamom crisps.

"Nadine . . . what was that year like for you?"

"What year?"

"Between finding that out and the incident with the teacher?"

My breath left me for a moment. I couldn't speak. The wetness bubbling up in my eyes embarrassed me. I wiped my eyes quickly.

"Lonely," I said.

"Of course. And what else?"

"I don't know how else to describe it except that it was even worse than the year *after* I stabbed the teacher."

You paused.

"Yeah," you said softly. "And how was it different, after?"

"Whatever else it was, it gave me something different to be ashamed of. Something else to run from."

After a silent minute or two, you said, "So how do you feel? Now that you've told me this?"

"Okay," I said. "It feels okay. I feel kind of detached from it now."

You nodded, and smiled sadly. "Then why tell now?"

I hesitated. "Because it's easier now."

"Why?"

"There's more to me now. Or—a little more, anyway. And I know this will sound as diabolical as I probably was then, but . . ."

"Yes?"

"It's easier now because I know you've got a secret, too."

You cocked your head slightly, like you used to do. And you almost asked what I meant. But then I saw a look of recognition take shape on your face. I didn't need to say it.

Johnny.

We were both silent for a couple of minutes. You stared out the window and I wondered if you were looking at the Christmas lights, too. There was a strain in your face that made me regret even referencing him, however obliquely. But maybe he was never far from your mind.

"In some cases," you said, "I think time is the only therapy that can work."

I recognized in your tone a resignation that was familiar from our old sessions. I was too young to understand it back then—to feel its weight. But I did now. I was old enough now.

"Do you say that to all of your clients?" I asked.

You grimaced. "No, Nadine. I don't think that would be a good idea."

I smiled. "Right."

And then, in almost an instant, I didn't feel much like a patient anymore. And you felt more like a person than you ever had in my memory. And now we were both tired, and the illusion didn't matter. The breakdown of the wall was less significant to me than I ever could have imagined it.

And anyway, we had only a few more minutes left. As I

understand the value of the dollar better now than I did at eighteen, I broke the silence.

"I haven't looked at a picture of my dad in about twenty years," I admitted.

"Would you like to now?"

"One time a few years ago I tried to draw him. And I couldn't remember enough to do it. Just that he had that long dark hair."

You were silent for a moment, and then a bewildered look crossed your face.

"Was it always long?" you asked.

"Yeah."

You took in a breath, bounced your knees, glanced out the window.

"Maybe . . ." You seemed hesitant—like you'd forgotten what you were about to say, or weren't sure you should say it. "Maybe it's time you tried to look at him again."

"Maybe."

"Nadine," you said, after a moment. "To that end . . ."

You didn't finish your thought.

"What?" I asked.

"When did your father die?" you wanted to know.

"When I was twelve."

"Yes, but what year was that?"

"Nineteen ninety-one," I said. "April 12, 1991."

You thought for a moment. "I'd like you to come in again. This week. Do you have time?"

"I wasn't planning on being your patient again. I just wanted to kind of . . . end things."

"I'm not asking you to be my patient. I just want to talk about this some more with you."

"My out-of-state insurance won't—"

"I don't want to charge you any money. For this session or for when we talk next."

"Now, I wasn't fishing for that."

"Nadine. *Please.* I think there might be more we both need to say about this. But I have another client coming in in ten minutes."

"Uh . . ." I was startled by the sudden change of tone in the conversation. This had felt like a sad but satisfying end. It didn't seem like we should see each other again. I should go draw some pictures and you should retire to Florida.

"Well . . . okay," I said reluctantly.

"I'll call you this evening or tomorrow morning to arrange a time."

"Can't we arrange one now?"

"I have to play with my schedule a little."

"Okay," I said, and tried not to think your behavior was a little weird. All things considered, I was still the weird one here.

WE'VE BEEN ON the highway for fifteen minutes. Anthony has settled into a sensible speed, following the middle-lane pace of the early evening traffic. It's dark now, so all I can see out the window are headlights and taillights.

"He asked to see you again?" Anthony asked.

"Yes. And then he called the next day and insisted I come on Wednesday morning. *Insisted.* That I come early, before his first scheduled patient."

"Now, why? Was he worried about you? Is there something you're not telling me? Some reason he'd have had to be worried?"

"About *me*? No. Not exactly. But he said something on the phone that shocked me."

"What?"

"He said, 'There's something you need to know. Your father. I don't think he did what they said he did.'"

"Jesus," Anthony muttered. "Jesus Jesus Jesus."

Anthony put his hand out in front of me. It took me a second to realize he was silently requesting the bottle of scotch. I took the cap off and handed it to him.

He struggled to grip it with one hand while keeping his other hand steady on the wheel. "Go on."

"And then he said he thought it was someone else."

Anthony took an audible swallow and winced.

"Anthony . . . someone will see you."

"I don't give a fuck."

I could tell by the way he enunciated the profanity that it wasn't true at all.

"Someone else?" he prompted.

"Yeah. And then he said, 'This is a really unusual situation. I just need to talk to you. Can you come in the morning?' And I said yes."

"And you went."

"Yes."

Anthony handed back the bottle. "And?"

"And when I showed up he was dead. In his office."

Anthony clenched his teeth and squeezed the steering

wheel with both hands. "Then why didn't you call the *police,* Nadine?"

"I don't know."

"And now things don't look good, since you ran," Anthony says.

"No," I admit.

"Now, why didn't you tell Dr. Fabian about that evening—that thing we told you—way back when you were his patient?"

"I don't know, Anthony. It seemed too gross to tell anyone."

"Jesus, Nadine." He smacks his bald head so hard it looks like it hurts. "*Jesus.*"

"What?" I say. "Say some other words besides *that* one."

"That's why I fucking *hired* the guy. What else could you have been talking about that you never talked about *that*?"

"Oh, I don't know . . . stabbing that teacher?"

Anthony puts on a blinker. He was taking the next exit.

"I could never convince myself those two things were unconnected," he said. "And I had hoped you could talk to *him* about it, since your mother and I weren't really . . . prepared. Do *you* think that was the reason you hurt that teacher?"

"Where are we going, Anthony?" I asked.

"I'll tell you after you answer my question."

The sign before the exit said UPTON HILL/BARNES MEMORIAL HOSPITAL. My heart is beating painfully fast, but I try to keep talking.

"I don't think that it could possibly be that simple. That the one thing explains the other. Because other girls wouldn't have done that, no matter what. I've come to accept that maybe there is something darker in me than there is in some other people. But it doesn't have control over me. I just have to live my life constantly wary of it, in such a way that it can never take over."

"Is that how you want to live your life, though?"

"I don't have a choice," I said. "But that's okay. Because what's the alternative?"

Anthony stops at a red light after the ramp. He faces me. "Exorcising it," he says.

The light turns green and I notice the signs he's following as he makes his next two turns.

"I wish that was possible, Anthony," I say. "Are we going to Barnes Memorial Hospital?"

"Yeah," Anthony says.

"For what? Are you going to check me in again?"

"What? Nadine, what do you take me for?"

"I don't know. Even if I don't scare you, you can still think I'm crazy."

Anthony shakes his head. It isn't until we're parked in the guest section of the hospital that he speaks again.

"The thing about your dad," he says, staring out the window to the front hospital entrance. "I believed it then. Your mother and I *both* believed it then. As did Eugene, who was the one who had to handle the actual firing."

"And was there a time you stopped believing it?"

Anthony was silent for almost a minute. I watched a couple hug by their car before they got in it. They looked very sad, and I wondered who they'd just come from seeing, and how bad of a shape this person was in. I wondered also about the nurse who had to tell them.

"Yes," Anthony admitted.

"And when was that?"

"Years later. After you'd gone to college. Years. I started to have my doubts, but . . ."

"Why? Why did you have doubts?"

"I think back then we all tended to have a simple-minded response to sexual violence, to the way we'd make accusations. Like, the guy drank and did drugs, so of *course* it was him. And in retrospect, that might not have been the fair or intelligent response. But also . . . well, I did hear some talk about another patient making a complaint years later, that also made me wonder, but . . ." Anthony ran his finger gently over the label of the scotch bottle.

"You didn't pursue it, I guess."

"No. It wasn't . . . my department. I kept out of it."

"What about Mom?" I asked. "Does she still believe it?"

"We haven't ever discussed it that way. Look, Nadine. We can talk about all of this later. We've got a bigger problem right now. The police detective that came looking for me was asking some very interesting questions that make me think he knows something about that time. About that . . . issue."

"Really?"

"Yes. It seems Mark wrote down some things before he died. About your session, or whatever."

"Oh, God, Anthony. Is that good or bad?"

"I'm not sure. The detective—he was asking me about someone. A nurse who worked at Brookhaven in 2001. I remembered her vaguely, but I couldn't remember her name. I had some suspicions about why she was relevant to this situation, but I'm not positive. I had someone in HR help me dig up her name. Her name was Bridget Lovell and I did a quick search and found out she works here. At Barnes. I called her a few times and finally, right before I left my office, she picked up. She wasn't willing to talk on the phone, or to meet me alone. But she said she'd talk to me in the lobby here after her shift."

"Oh." I look at the tinted windows of the front hospital entrance.

"Yeah. I think she wanted to talk to me in the presence of hospital security on the off chance that I'm nuts."

"Did she remember you?"

"Yes, vaguely, but still . . . it *is* all rather out of the blue."

"Are you going to give her name to the police?"

"Well, I wanted to see what she had to say first. I wanted to see if it would help you or hurt you."

"Do you want me to go in with you?"

"I thought I'd be going alone when I walked out of Brookhaven. But now that you're here, your presence might be useful in this conversation."

I look down at my coffee-stained coat. "I slept in my car last night and I'm hungover on top of that."

Anthony takes a small sip of Glenlivet. He misses his mouth slightly, and then wipes his face with the sleeve of his sweater. "You look fine. And I know you know how to fake it. Isn't that what you were just saying?"

We go into the hospital together.

HENRY

At my desk, I started typing Scott Morrison's name into some of our databases. No Connecticut convictions came up.

He worked at Franklin Hospital, just as Connor had said. He lived in Wallingford. In his license picture he looked just as dapper as he had the morning he'd brought his father to the station. Dark hair, speckled with gray. Well-proportioned face, except for slightly big ears. There was a 2013 black Kia registered in his name. It wasn't much, but it was something.

I found Greg in the break room, poking hard at the vending machine buttons.

"That neighbor of Fabian's you spoke to, who said someone was knocking on his door the night before he was found? Remember her?"

"Sure."

"I need you to do something for me. Can you go to her place? And show her this picture? Ask her if she's seen this guy around the neighborhood. Don't specifically ask her about the night of

Fabian's death. Don't feed it to her. Just show it to her and see what she says. Call me as soon as you get her answer, okay?"

"What about Connor?" Greg asked, after I'd explained to him what I'd found.

"Let him know he can go."

No sooner had Greg left than Wheeler was at my desk. "I just got a call from the shift commander at Eastern Correctional. Anything you want to tell me, Henry?"

"Yeah." I stood up. "I fucked up."

"If you needed something from Streeter, you know you were supposed to send Amy or Greg."

"It was a split-second decision." I bent my head down—a gesture of remorse that probably wasn't sincere. "I had some new information and I acted on it."

Wheeler was quiet for a moment.

"You used to be more predictable, Henry." He scratched the inside of his ear with his forefinger, digging deep. As if he might find the right next thing to say in there. "You used to be different."

"Yeah," I admitted. "I used to be."

"Guys?" Amy approached us. "Did you hear what dispatch just sent us? There was a disturbance in the Brookhaven parking lot. Greg's asking if he should go there first before talking to Fabian's neighbor."

"Brookhaven?" Wheeler said.

"Yeah. Something was broken. And a colleague thought he might have seen Anthony Gagliardi in distress before he drove away."

This information disturbed me, but I didn't know what to

make of it. Gagliardi was one of my main suspects until about fifteen minutes ago.

"Brookhaven," Wheeler said. "Amy, you go and bring Dan with you."

After they'd gone, I started piling files and notes in front of Wheeler.

"Look," I said. "I'm going to tell you what I've found today. And then I'm hoping we can talk about Eastern Correctional later."

I showed him the Greenblatt file. And Nadine's notes.

"Interesting," he said, when he was finished. "But this is all in the deep past. Like I was saying in my office. You need to work with *right now,* Henry."

"It *was* in the past," I said. I told him about Scott Morrison and handed him Fabian's article about the Westford assaults. As he was reading it, Greg called me.

"It was him, she says," Greg said. "She says that was who she saw Tuesday night."

"Okay, thanks," I said. "I'll call you right back."

"Did you hear that?" I asked Wheeler.

He nodded and raised his eyebrows. "And why do you think Scott Morrison went to see Dr. Fabian on Tuesday night? What was the motive, specifically?"

"I think Fabian called Eugene Morrison to talk to him about his son. I think maybe he was even going to report Scott to us. And I think Eugene must've told his son about it."

"Wouldn't that be against Fabian's confidentiality commitments?"

"Not necessarily. Because Scott wasn't his patient. And

after what happened with Streeter, and since he was about to retire, he was maybe like, *Fuck it*. He maybe thought it was more important to say something. Prevent someone else from having to get hurt."

"But why would he tell Eugene all of this?"

"Because they were friends. He didn't want to do it behind his back. Maybe he wanted to be transparent—or maybe he thought Eugene would have some kind of explanation. I don't know exactly. But he *called* Eugene Morrison, in any case. And I don't think he called him about what Eugene *says* he did. So now . . . now I'd like to go to talk to Eugene again. And have Greg get a head start and position himself near Scott's place in Wallingford."

"I don't know, Henry." Wheeler handed back the Westford article. "Are you going to hit someone?"

"No," I said.

"How do I know that?"

I stared at Wheeler—right at the bloody spot in his eye.

Because I think I get it, Fabian.

"Because this is different," I said. "This is something I can solve."

Wheeler blinked, maybe self-consciously. "Why not Scott Morrison first?"

"I know my way in better with Eugene. I know how to talk to him. I'll see what I can get out of Eugene first, then we'll go at Scott with it."

"Alright." Wheeler folded his arms. "Let's see what you can do."

NADINE

Bridget Lovell isn't much older than me. She has blue scrubs, a tight blond bun, and expertly applied mascara. That last thing makes me guess she isn't ICU.

"This is my stepdaughter, Nadine," Anthony says, once we're all sitting on the backless cushioned benches that line the lobby's glass. "She's a nurse, too."

Bridget looks at me briefly, then focuses on Anthony. "I didn't know you were coming with someone."

"It just happened that way. Now, I told you on the phone I needed to talk about 2001 at Brookhaven because it's come back to haunt us. And it's affecting someone close to me. Well, Nadine here is who I was referring to."

Bridget takes in a breath, and then nods. "Okay."

"Now, you said that Eugene Morrison seemed eager to get you a position elsewhere in 2001. He put in a good word for you at St. Joseph's, where he had lots of connections. And you were fairly eager to leave Brookhaven?"

"Yes. Well, it was a good first job. But what I'd really wanted was a position at a general hospital."

"Okay. And Dr. Morrison helped make that happen. Did it seem curious to you at the time that he was so helpful to you getting employment elsewhere? A new nurse who hadn't worked at his facility for even a year?"

Bridget touches the back of her hair and repositions her bobby pin. "At the time I wondered if I had mishandled a situation and he wanted to get rid of me."

"A situation?" Anthony repeated.

"It was with that patient named Greenblatt, like I said on the phone. I don't know how much you would've heard since only a few staff knew. But Mrs. Greenblatt claimed an intruder came into her room and flashed her . . . maybe even assaulted her, although I'm not clear on the details."

I stifle a gasp and wonder if my eyes are bulging with the effort. Anthony's face doesn't so much as twitch. I can't tell if he is unsurprised by this information or just skillfully poker-faced.

"Dr. Morrison was intent on protecting Mrs. Greenblatt's privacy," Bridget continues. "So I imagine someone in the administrative office—like you—might not have known the details."

"Okay," Anthony says. "So there was this highly sensitive situation with Mrs. Greenblatt and you feel that Dr. Morrison was not happy with how you handled it. So why wouldn't he put you on notice, or fire you? Why would he reward you by helping you get a better job elsewhere?"

"I was never positive about that . . ." Bridget hugs herself, crossing her arms and grasping her elbows. "But I suspected he just didn't want me to talk about what happened."

"Would you talk about what happened now . . . say, if the police asked you about it?"

"The police?" Bridget crosses her legs and squeezes herself tighter.

"They asked me for your name . . . for the name of this mysterious nurse who left Brookhaven in 2001. I thought I'd talk to you before I went ahead and gave them your name."

"I'll tell them about it if they ask," Bridget says. "But . . . I also have great respect for Eugene Morrison. I did then and I have even more since hearing about the tragedy, and what he did that day."

"We all do," Anthony says softly. "I imagine that's why you feel he must have had a reason to keep the circumstances of Mrs. Greenblatt's situation confidential."

"That's . . . *part* of it."

"Please," Anthony says. "Please, Ms. Lovell. This gravely affects Nadine. Would you *please* tell us the other part?"

Bridget finally lets go of her grip on herself, and lets out a breath. "Well, I didn't understand why. But I unsettled Dr. Morrison somehow. At *first* I thought it was because he thought I'd mishandled Mrs. Greenblatt's claim. But it wasn't until a little while later that I understood it was about something else. See, there was this cute intern, about my age, who I suggested Dr. Morrison ask about the night Mrs. Greenblatt was . . . victimized. I'd occasionally see him on my floor. He would joke that it was because my floor had the best snack machine. But I liked to think it was because he came to flirt with me."

"I believe he was *my* intern," Anthony says. "It was 2001? His name was Scott?"

"Yes," Bridget had replied. "But I didn't know his last name. Not then. I only realized it a year or two later. Chatting with a friend about my old job, about the Morrison family."

I hear myself make a squeaking noise. *Scott Morrison.*

He volunteered at Brookhaven when we were kids. He was older than me. So, roughly around when my dad worked there. When he—both of them—sported the badass long hair.

"And did all of that strike you as odd, when you put it all together?" Anthony asks.

"Yes, but by then . . ." she puts her palms out and then looks at me, as if for assistance. She has no idea what this means to me. She doesn't know that I can't speak.

"By then it was in the past," Anthony offers.

"Something like that," she says.

HENRY

I RANG EUGENE'S DOORBELL for a couple of minutes before he answered in plaid pajama bottoms and a loose red polo shirt.

"Henry," he said, letting me into the front hall. "What time is it?"

"I'm sorry to bother you, Eugene. But it's rather urgent."

"What?" Eugene seemed to be trying to catch his breath. I had startled him. "What is it?"

"I need you to answer a question for me." I closed the door behind me. "Which of your employees was exposing himself to patients? Was it Timothy Raines or was it Anthony Gagliardi?"

"What?" Eugene squinted at me as if I'd just shined a bright light in his eyes. "Henry?"

"We know that it happened. We read Fabian's old file about it."

Eugene staggered on his feet for a moment. I gently nudged him toward the padded black bench next to his coatrack, and helped him lower himself onto it—sitting right on top of a heap of scarves and gloves there.

"You all must be very mixed up. Anthony Gagliardi would never . . ."

"So it was Tim Raines, then?"

Eugene sighed. "Tim Raines. Oh, dear. That was a long time ago."

"Tim Raines died in 1991."

"Yes. Just a couple of weeks after we let him go."

"And you let him go for . . . exposing himself, or stealing drugs?"

"A little of each, Henry. We only suspected the drugs and couldn't prove it. The other thing was the final straw with him. We'd only ever employed him as a favor to Anthony. Anthony wanted to fix everything for that stepdaughter of his, but it all went to shit fast. Tim Raines wasn't really employable, even as a janitor. He just had so many problems."

"Why didn't you tell the police?"

"I was younger then." Eugene shook his head. "I was nervous about Brookhaven's success. We were starting to make headlines for our good work—about the indoor pool with the water therapy, and the Tai Chi, and all the special things we were doing for the residents. We were just starting to grow, and to fill most of the beds. We couldn't afford another kind of headline, not then."

Eugene pulled up a small red mitten from beneath his thigh—probably left on the bench by one of his visiting grandchildren.

"Okay," I said. "But in 2001 it happened again. What a terrible coincidence. How could that be? But lucky for you, nobody who knew about the first one also knew about the second one. Until Fabian. Fabian knew about the second, but didn't know about the first. Until last week. And he had some distinct ideas about who it was. He called you, right? That's why you two talked. Not because he wanted advice about an old patient. He needed to talk to you about something more personal, right?"

Eugene patted his pajamas absently with his free hand—looking for his phone, it seemed.

"We have your son already, Eugene. I've got another officer talking to him right now."

Eugene dropped the mitten.

"But you couldn't tell us what you actually talked about with Fabian. And putting us on the trail of a mystery 'old patient'—that could be just about anyone. We could be chasing that lead forever, into nowhere."

Eugene was silent.

"I don't know what my son has told you," he said. "If he has confessed to anything, he's protecting me."

"Protecting you from what?"

"He doesn't want me to go to prison. At my age. In my condition."

"You're saying you killed Mark Fabian?" I said.

Eugene stared at me. *At your age? In your condition?* I thought.

"Eugene," I said. "What did Mark say about your son when he called you?"

Eugene stared down at the mitten on the floor.

"Tim Raines was dead in 2001 when it happened again," I

said. "Who did you think it was, once you realized you had the wrong guy? Who was there in 1991 *and* 2001? I thought maybe Anthony Gagliardi, or maybe some other longtime employee. But there's someone who's been in and out of Brookhaven a lot over the years . . . first as a teenage volunteer, and then as an intern, and who else knows when, because his father was the director."

Eugene lifted his chin and let his gaze meet mine. "My son had a problem when he was young. That was more than a decade ago. That has nothing to do with Fabian."

Score one for the half-assed, Fabian. It wasn't everything, but it was motive.

"He called you after he did it, didn't he?" I whispered. "He needed your help. He knew we'd see the calls between you and Fabian and he knew there needed to be a reason for them."

Eugene shook his head. "I couldn't have Fabian telling those sorts of things to people. About my son, who had worked so hard to improve. And these things about Westford, too. *They* were ridiculous."

"I'm sure you didn't expect Scott to lose it when you told him about Fabian's call. You only expected to warn him, to strategize with him about what you'd do if Fabian told other people—or told the police. You knew he had a problem, as you say, when he was young. But you didn't know he was capable of this."

"So when I went into Mark's office to discuss it, I lost my temper."

I really admired this guy. Still, after he'd lied to me so many times. He would throw himself at the void for something or someone he loved. He was doing it right now. He was doing it so hard he didn't care that I wasn't listening.

"Still, when Scott called you after he'd done it, you needed to try and help him. How could you not? You knew that if you said something about a former patient, that would send us into a rabbit hole. He's been practicing for over thirty years, and wasn't necessarily a consistent record-keeper."

Eugene stared down at the red mitten again. "I have nothing else to say to you."

"Eugene?"

"I want to talk to a lawyer."

"I understand," I said.

I glanced at that mitten and thought of Olivia and Sophia, alone in the snow. Anything could happen to them and I would stumble after them—into the dark woods, into an icy river, into any cold oblivion. They had no guardian angel, but I would always try.

I said it again, because I couldn't think of anything else decent to say. "I understand."

NADINE

"ARE YOU READY to go to the police now?" Anthony wants to know, after he pulls out of the hospital parking lot.

"I don't know," I say.

"When do you *think* you'll be ready? Because we shouldn't go back to Campion till then. I think they've been doing drive-bys at our place. They're waiting for you. You need to *present* yourself, not let them find you."

"I think I need to find a way to brush my hair and brush my teeth. And just compose myself a little better."

"Okay. So we go to a Cumby's for a toothbrush and a splash of water, and then we drive back to Campion."

"I'll try," I say.

WHEN WE ARRIVE at the station, I'm surprised by how pretty it looks. The maple that stands between the police and fire buildings is bright with projected white lights that look like fairy sparkles. These lights are more delicate than the old-fashioned ones I'd seen outside your office window.

"I can't go in," I say. "I'm not breathing right yet."

"Take a couple of minutes, then."

"I don't know, Anthony."

"You keep running," he says, "and you'll never have a chance."

"A chance at what?" I whisper.

But I can't look at Anthony because I see his eyes are filling with tears.

We are still trying not to look at each other when a police car approaches the building and takes the space right near the front steps.

An officer gets out, circles to the back, opens the door, and starts to lead a very frail-looking elderly man up the front steps.

"Holy shit," Anthony says. "That's Eugene."

"Maybe we should come back," I say. "Obviously they're busy right now."

Anthony says nothing—just watches as the man hobbles up to the station door with the officer and disappears.

After a few minutes, two officers came out of the building—a male and a female. The guy officer is talking to the woman officer, leaning downward slightly because she is so short.

As they walk toward his car, his face comes into focus.

I feel my breath stop.

This is someone I've seen before. He'd told me he'd not done his homework. Just before I took out my box cutter knife. Just before everything went cold.

I want to feel some of that *before* again. Just for a moment. I open the car door and get out.

HENRY

SHE CAME OUT of nowhere and she was standing under Chief Wheeler's twinkly lights. As she stepped closer to me, the lights shifted on her pale face and she looked as white as ice. My fingertips tingled cold, but then she spoke.

"I know you," she said.

"Kind of," I said.

I saw Anthony Gagliardi approaching us.

"She just wants to talk," he said, and then repeated the statement. Like he thought I was about to shoot. He put his hand on her shoulder. She stepped sideways, out of his reach, and then the lights were no longer in her face. She looked human again.

"From a long time ago," Nadine added. Her voice was relaxed. Her hands were outstretched and empty. "If that counts."

I looked at Anthony's anxious posture next to her long, familiar frame. No, Anthony wasn't a dinosaur. Fabian was one. Her real dad was one. And so was that poor teacher.

Dinosaurs were fascinating in their inaccessibility. Anthony was simply, boringly, the closest thing she had to a father. Whether she wanted to admit it or not.

Am I getting close, Fabian? Am I any good at this?

"It counts," I managed to say.

NADINE

He reminds me that his name is Henry, and he asks me a thing or two about you, about Johnny, about Anthony and my father and the thing that happened at Brookhaven so long ago. He says he wants to talk to me more but he has something urgent to take care of first.

So he has his lady colleague bring me inside the station to wait. She lets Anthony come along but then separates us into different rooms.

A couple of hours later, Henry comes in to ask me a few last questions. First, about finding you. The position and the look of your body and face. About closing your eyes. The more we talk about you as a body and not as a person, the more you seem to die in my head. The pale and bloody man on the floor replaces the even-keeled listener who'd resided there for so long. I try not to cry. Not because I don't care, but because it feels selfish to mourn for an imagined listener when somewhere out there, strangers are mourning for an actual person. A person I don't know—and never knew.

Henry moves on to Brookhaven—to the things I was told about my father decades ago. About Dr. Fabian's final words to me over the phone. About Anthony, my mother, and Bridget Lovell.

When Henry seems satisfied with all of that, he says, "One last thing, though. The one thing I can't figure out is why you ran on Wednesday."

I look at Henry, his hair graying around the ears, his paunch straining his blue sweater. When I was sixteen, I'd have called him a dinosaur. But I'm not sixteen, and so I wonder instead what I look like to him. Probably not something good, but I know I can clean up nicely. I always have.

We are both almost old now. Almost. Not quite. There's still time left to be something besides what we once were.

"I've run from Campion for almost twenty years," I say. "I think I didn't know how to stop."

HENRY

IT WAS A long night at the station with the Morrisons.

Scott spent an hour railing against us for "forcing a confession" out of his embattled elderly father. He kept that up until we told him about Fabian's neighbor—who saw Scott pounding at the door of his house about twenty minutes before Connor Osborne heard a surprise "patient" come into the office. And about Bridget Lovell. And then about Nadine Raines's dad and the Carrick Center and what Fabian had apparently put together before he called his old colleague Eugene. So Scott stopped scolding us and eventually clammed up and said he needed a lawyer. Certainly he did.

Amanda was easier. At first, she sounded a lot like her brother. Our questionings had worn Eugene down. We ought to be ashamed of ourselves. He'd been fragile since the shooting. But when we brought up her brother's old hidden transgressions at Brookhaven, she didn't show much surprise.

"Whatever weird issue my brother had when we were kids," she said, "that doesn't prove he did anything to Dr. Fabian."

Whatever this "weird issue" was, exactly, I had a feeling Amanda had been familiar with it for a while. She maybe knew her father had tried desperately to make it go away.

"He's confessing to cover for your brother," I said. "You know that, right?"

Amanda was quiet for a long time.

"You know this will kill him either way, don't you?" she said softly.

"And so just let him take yet another bullet?" I said.

At this, Amanda glanced up at me with surprisingly little anger in her eyes.

"No," she said quietly. "I didn't mean it like that. I won't let that happen."

I sensed some relief in Amanda's demeanor. Someone else knew about her brother, and through no indiscretion of her own. Her father was the one who'd finally slipped—not her. Now her duty was going to be different—more transparent. It was three A.M. by then. There was a knowing exhaustion in her tone that made me think of Nadine's words in her notes to Fabian:

Just you wait, old friends. Just. You. Wait.

The words were prophetic but presumptuous. Yes, Nadine had experienced as a kid a darkness that I—and maybe Julie, and maybe some of our common friends—had escaped for a couple of decades. But there were others—like Amanda, perhaps—who were experiencing it quietly with her all along. With their heads down and their hands to themselves.

I let Amanda bring Eugene home for a rest.

And then, at the end of this long night, the fingerprint results came in in the morning, from the Apple Blossom evidence.

They told us what I already knew: Nadine's weren't a match with the bloody one from the scene. I had a feeling I knew who would be a match. I also had a feeling we would at least be able to bring Scott to trial.

WHILE WE WERE waiting for Scott's lawyer to show up, I had a couple hours to go home. When I went in to kiss the girls good morning, only Sophia was awake. Olivia was fast asleep on her fairy tale book, her elbow mashing down the last page of "Hansel and Gretel."

"She was up late asking me stupid questions," Sophia said.

"Like what?" I asked.

"Like why the witch needs to eat the kids if she has all that candy and cookies her house is made of."

"And you said?"

"Mommy said it was because that stuff's all sugar, and the witch probably needs protein."

"She did?"

"Yeah. But *I* said it was for the same reason that the witch in Rapunzel keeps her in a tower. Because witches are mean. They *like* to be mean. That's just how they are. At least the kind in the stories Olivia likes." Sophia sighed and tied her stuffed cocker spaniel's ears together. "Maybe if she understood the stories better, she wouldn't like them so much."

"I don't know, Sophia," I said.

Sophia untied the dog ears. "Do you think Santa is going to bring us a Saint Bernard?"

"Unfortunately, I think a Saint Bernard would be too big to fit in his sleigh," I pointed out.

"A puppy wouldn't be," Sophia replied. "And it would be good for my job I want to get."

"What job?"

"When I get older, I want to get a job throwing Frisbees at dogs."

"Is that a job?"

"Yeah. Remember we saw those people doing it at the fair? They had matching shirts and a matching van and tent?"

I did remember. Their van said PUPPY POWER, or something like that. I wasn't aware that when I brought my girls to the county fair they were actually scoping out career options.

"I guess they did, yeah," I said.

"So I need a dog to start training myself."

"It *does* seem like a good job," I admitted.

"I know. That's what I'm saying."

"But I don't know if Saint Bernards are that great at catching Frisbees."

"And I'm not that great at throwing a Frisbee yet. We'd work on it together."

She looked at me in a patient but pleading way. It was pretty clear to me the Santa Claus jig was already up for Sophia. She knew it was *me* she was asking for a giant dog. I wondered what else Sophia had quietly worked out while Olivia was asking me all of the questions. It might have been a con game between them all along.

"We'll just have to see what happens," I said.

I was buying time. I knew I wouldn't be able to keep up with the girls, but I had to pretend for a while longer. It would be nice, someday, to surrender to the knowledge that I've never fooled them. That maybe, in fact, I've never really fooled anyone.

DECEMBER 26, 2015

NADINE

I SPENT CHRISTMAS WITH Mom and Anthony, but I'm back here now. I've spent the afternoon walking around Breakneck Pond.

It's still clear and sunny, and still the mildest New England December I can remember. I sit by the pond and eat walnuts and an apple and feel vaguely wholesome. When I throw the core into the trees, I imagine for a moment that the rustle of it landing is the sound of his footfall.

I don't need to try to remember his face because my mother obliged my request yesterday and scrounged up an old photograph.

It's from the middle or late eighties, when I was still little and they were still together. He is sitting over a chocolate frosted cake, having just blown out its candles. His hair is pulled back and his face looks shiny.

He is younger, in this picture, than I am now. More startling than his youth is my age. I am all grown up now, or some equivalent. Like a tree that's grown around another tree, or some fixed human object—a fence or a lamppost. Grown bent and weird, but grown nonetheless.

I won't try to explain him. And he doesn't explain me. Even if there were times when I convinced myself he did. I brush my thumb over his hint of a smile. Ever the weirdo—just like me. *You were always so afraid of being disingenuous, you never smiled big, or for longer than a few seconds. You knew people could think the worst of you—and then they did. You didn't have the strength to defend yourself. I wish you had, but I understand. I do.*

I have to leave it there, for now. Even though I will always wish for his arms and his beer breath. I am still very much his. Our blood is still the same. I just have a little more endurance than he did. For the things people think of me, and for the things that are true.

I'VE MADE MY way back to my car and I'm on 84 now, heading toward the Mass Pike and then back to Brattleboro.

My phlebotomy class starts in less than two weeks. But after that, I have no plan for the summer. I'm not sure where I'll go. Somewhere out of the country, ideally, but I'm running out of funds and it might be better to get back into the U.S. travel nurse gigs for a while.

Do you think I should be responsible or should I be adventurous?

The question forms in my brain before I realize that I don't know who *you* is anymore. There isn't any *you* to whom to address the question. My mind scrambles for a new *you*—but comes up empty. There's no face to hang it onto anymore. I could probably find one in time. But I don't want to.

I open the window and let the winter air hit my face and joggle my cheeks. *You.* I mouth the word, letting the wind take it from my lips.

I leave the window open for a while. After about twenty minutes, my face feels raw and my head aches. I turn up the heat and the music and then reluctantly close the window. I drive and sing and feel better once the signs start to tell me that I'm not far from home.

ACKNOWLEDGMENTS

I have many people to thank here—

Lisa Walker, for early readings and encouragement. Sarah Hawker and Martin Eisner, for your time, patience, and professional expertise. Carrie Feron, for your insightful editing—and for letting me try new things. Laura Langlie, for all of your continued support. Carolyn Coons, Molly Waxman, Shailyn Tavella, and everyone else at William Morrow for your work on this book. My parents, for always cheerfully supporting my writing endeavors over the years. Jim MacFadyen, for kindly answering my first tentative e-mails about what would happen if a therapist was found dead in his office. Ilene Stahl, for answering questions about HIPAA and medical billing over appetizers. Cari Strand, for an especially good piece of advice at just the right time. Ross Grant, for making me laugh every day, no matter what.

ABOUT THE AUTHOR

Emily Arsenault is also the author of *The Evening Spider, The Broken Teaglass, In Search of the Rose Notes, Miss Me When I'm Gone, What Strange Creatures*, and the young adult novel *The Leaf Reader.* She lives in Shelburne Falls, Massachusetts, with her husband and daughter.

ALSO BY EMILY ARSENAULT

THE LAST THING I TOLD YOU

A Novel

"*The Last Thing I Told You* is an expertly woven tale of dark obsession and blood secrets. With her sharp eye and clear prose, Arsenault gives us a finely dissected portrait of a disturbed young woman as well as a tense thriller that defies categorization. Compulsively readable, and highly recommended."

—Francie Lin, Edgar Award-winning author of *The Foreigner*

THE EVENING SPIDER

A Novel

"A good old-fashioned gothic novel with a modern twist; a tale of dusty old journals, creaky houses, and ghostly whispers [...] Arsenault never strays from the task at hand, which is to keep you up all night with a light burning until you reach the surprising end."

—Melanie Benjamin, *New York Times* best-selling author of *The Aviator's Wife* and *The Swans of Fifth Avenue*

WHAT STRANGE CREATURES

A Novel

"*What Strange Creatures* is a smart, literary mystery that explores the depths of family bonds and loyalty."

—Jennifer McMahon, *New York Times* bestselling author

MISS ME WHEN I'M GONE

A Novel

"A very clever wordsmith." —*New York Times Book Review*

"Ms. Arsenault…reveals strange truths beneath everyday surfaces."

—*Wall Street Journal*

IN SEARCH OF THE ROSE NOTES

A Novel

"When Emily Arsenault was growing up, a teacher told the fifth-grader she was very good at writing. Give that teacher an A."

—*Hartford Courant*